NO GOOD DEED

A James Acton Thriller

Also by J. Robert Kennedy

James Acton Thrillers

The Protocol	*The Riddle*	*Atlantis Lost*
Brass Monkey	*Blood Relics*	*The Cylon Curse*
Broken Dove	*Sins of the Titanic*	*The Viking Deception*
The Templar's Relic	*Saint Peter's Soldiers*	*Keepers of the Lost Ark*
Flags of Sin	*The Thirteenth Legion*	*The Tomb of Genghis Khan*
The Arab Fall	*Raging Sun*	*The Manila Deception*
The Circle of Eight	*Wages of Sin*	*The Fourth Bible*
The Venice Code	*Wrath of the Gods*	*Embassy of the Empire*
Pompeii's Ghosts	*The Templar's Revenge*	*Armageddon*
Amazon Burning	*The Nazi's Engineer*	*No Good Deed*

Special Agent Dylan Kane Thrillers

Rogue Operator	*Death to America*	*State Sanctioned*
Containment Failure	*Black Widow*	*Extraordinary Rendition*
Cold Warriors	*The Agenda*	*Red Eagle*
	Retribution	

Templar Detective Thrillers

The Templar Detective	*The Sergeant's Secret*	*The Black Scourge*
The Parisian Adulteress	*The Unholy Exorcist*	*The Lost Children*
	The Code Breaker	

Kriminalinspektor Wolfgang Vogel Mysteries

The Colonel's Wife	*Sins of the Child*

Delta Force Unleashed Thrillers

Payback	*The Lazarus Moment*	*Forgotten*
Infidels	*Kill Chain*	*The Cuban Incident*

Detective Shakespeare Mysteries

Depraved Difference	*Tick Tock*	*The Redeemer*

Zander Varga, Vampire Detective

The Turned

NO GOOD DEED

A James Acton Thriller

J. ROBERT KENNEDY

UnderMill
PRESS

ISBN: 9781990418563

First Edition

10 9 8 7 6 5 4 3 2 1

For Brian Fraser.

The CFRA Nation will miss you.

NO GOOD DEED

A James Acton Thriller

"In the past, millions of German men shed their blood for this Reich. How merciful a fate to be allowed to create this Reich today without a suffering. Now, rise, German Volk, subscribe to it, hold it tightly in your hands! I wish to thank Him who allowed me to return to my homeland so that I could return it to my German Reich! May every German realize the importance of the hour tomorrow, assess it and then bow his head in reverence before the will of the Almighty who has wrought this miracle in all of us within these past few weeks."

Adolf Hitler, addressing the annexation of Austria.
Vienna, Austria, April 9, 1938

"The man who dies thus rich, dies disgraced."

Andrew Carnegie
1889

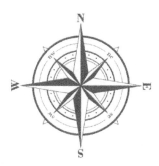

PREFACE

In June 2010, Bill Gates and Warren Buffett, two of the world's richest people, started a campaign called The Giving Pledge. It was meant to encourage the world's wealthiest to donate the bulk of their fortunes to charities and other philanthropic causes, either before or after their deaths.

As of this writing, there are 220 pledgers from 25 countries, who have committed to donating over $600 billion. It's a massive commitment, and if followed through, could change the lives of millions if not billions of people around the world.

It would also represent one of the greatest transfers of wealth in history.

Many laud the effort, though some oppose it. All have their reasons, but when billions are involved, the question begs to be asked.

How far would someone go to get their share?

Especially when they feel justified in taking it.

Grieshof Alley

Vienna, Austria

Present Day

Officer Heike Karner lazily guided the squad car toward the service yard. Her senior partner had noticed a wobble toward the end of their shift, and she had "volunteered" to take their unit to the garage. It meant an extra hour added to her shift, but what did that matter? Her husband was with the children at his parents' place for the weekend. She was supposed to have gone with them, but then everyone was called in because of the charity event and the added security required. She hadn't minded. Her in-laws weren't big fans of hers, not since she had become a police officer, and she could use the overtime to pay down some bills.

Everything seemed more expensive these days. If inflation were running at 2% a year, why did everything that mattered seem to be going up by ten? Her father was convinced it was a government conspiracy. If they admitted what the actual inflation rate was, then all the pensions and government programs indexed to it would go up by more than they could afford.

Her eyes were burning from fatigue when the calls started coming in about the detonations. She wasn't sure what to do. She was off duty, her car might have a problem, and she was well away from the action. She had radioed in and was ordered to return the vehicle then report back to her station in case she was needed.

A black SUV with tinted windows blasted through the intersection. She glanced up to see the traffic light was red, though so was hers, suggesting the light had just changed. She could forgive that at this time of night, but he had to be doing double the speed limit, and that was too damn dangerous.

She eased out into the intersection, checking to the left. Another SUV was heading toward her, but there was plenty of space and they had a red light. She gunned the engine and took off in pursuit. She reached over and threw on her lights and sirens, then radioed in the call. She received a quick acknowledgment and nothing more. They were obviously too busy dealing with whatever was happening in the city. From the bits and pieces on the radio, it would appear her family being away for the weekend was fortuitous timing.

Something caught her attention and she glanced in her rearview mirror. There was another vehicle behind her, closing in, its lights flashing. She rolled her window down slightly and the blaring of a horn could clearly be heard.

"What the hell is that all about?"

She stared ahead at the speeder, still driving dangerously, but now, so was the person behind her, and they appeared to be trying to get her attention. She cursed. She was chasing a reckless driver, though this person could urgently need help. She weighed her options and decided she had only one choice. She radioed in that she was breaking off the pursuit, then pulled her vehicle over to the side, putting it in Park and throwing open the door. She directed them to pull over and the SUV stopped behind her unit. The engine shut off and its tinted windows dropped.

Her heart rate picked up a few beats as she gripped her pistol, still in its holster. "What has you chasing down a police cruiser?"

A woman leaned out the window, speaking English. "I'm sorry, we had to get your attention."

"Why?"

"The vehicle you're pursuing is involved in the bombings, and there are armed men inside. They would have shot you if you stopped them."

Heike's eyes bulged and she paused for a moment. Tires squealed ahead and a man in the passenger seat pointed.

"Call for back-up!"

She spun and reached for her radio as the vehicle she had been pursuing returned then came to a halt, all the doors opening. Four men stepped out with weapons, and the passenger shouted, "Get down!"

Gunfire erupted and something slammed into Heike's shoulder, sending her to the ground in a heap of pain. As the bullets continued, she dragged herself behind her cruiser when the passenger grabbed her and pulled her the rest of the way. He reached for her gun and she

4

panicked, struggling to fight him off, but she was rapidly losing strength and couldn't resist when he pressed her back down with a hand to her chest.

"I'm here to help you."

The woman arrived a moment later and hauled her by her vest, pulling her farther from the gunfire as the man retreated along with them, now in possession of her weapon, but holding fire.

"Ammo," he whispered.

Heike had to trust them. She had no choice. She tapped one of her pockets and the woman retrieved her two spare magazines, handing them to the man.

"Do you have a backup weapon?" she asked.

"This isn't America."

"Three of them are coming. They're going to try to flank us," said the man.

Heike closed her eyes. This was it. She was going to die. She reached up and grabbed the woman's arm, opening her eyes and staring at her. "Leave me. Save yourselves."

The woman clasped her hand. "That's not who we are, dear." She pulled the baton off Heike's belt and extended it, crouching behind the rear bumper.

Then the unthinkable happened. The man engaged the gunmen, expertly, rapidly firing in bursts of two shots. "One's coming around the front," he warned, and the woman readied the baton.

"Just who are you people?" gasped Heike. "Are you law enforcement?"

"No, dear. We're archaeologists. I'm Laura Palmer, and this is my husband, James Acton."

Archaeologists? What the hell kind of archaeologists, dressed as if they were going to some fancy function, act like soldiers?

Her eyes bulged as she realized what was going on. They must have been at the charity gala that was attacked, and these assailants must be the terrorists responsible for the bombings across her city.

The man leaned out to fire when another torrent of gunfire erupted, unlike anything she had ever heard. He cried out and retreated, shaking his now empty hand. A man appeared with the most terrifying weapon she had ever seen, aiming it at them.

"Drop the weapon," the man ordered, and the woman dropped the baton. She indicated Heike.

"She needs medical attention."

The man with the gun raised it toward Heike and she opened her mouth to scream as the trigger squeezed, leaving a husband without a wife, two children without a mother, and a wounded city without one of its selfless defenders.

Vienna, Austria

March 9, 1938

"I'm scared."

Those two words out of all spoken finally gained Daniel's attention. The toy car he had been racing around the oval patterned rug froze as he listened to the conversation between his mother and father in the next room. Something was going on. What, he didn't know, but everyone was on edge. When his father had friends visiting, they would be in his office for hours, the conversations sometimes whispered, other times heated. His mother had cried more in the past several weeks than he had ever known her to, and it was disturbing, but the bits and pieces he could remember being said meant nothing to him, so he ignored it.

His mother and father would take care of it.

They always did.

He was nine years old. The world's troubles were nothing to him, but this was the first time he had heard either of them say they were scared. If his mother were, then something terrible was going on.

"I'm scared too," said his father.

Tears welled in Daniel's eyes. If his father were scared, something truly horrible must be happening, for his father wasn't afraid of anything. He was the strongest man he knew.

He crept closer to the door, his toy forgotten, the conversation more interesting than any handcrafted car.

His father continued. "We're all scared, but we have to keep calm in order to think straight."

"Maybe we're just panicking over nothing. Maybe it won't happen."

"The referendum has been announced. This is happening. It's inevitable, even if the government doesn't want it to happen. There's no stopping that man."

"Do we know when?"

Daniel crept a little farther ahead, peering around the corner of the door, just catching sight of his parents sitting in the drawing room, facing each other.

His father shook his head. "The referendum is in four days. How long after that, I don't know, but it will be soon. Days, maybe weeks, but definitely not months. Peter says shipments of flags have already arrived for the occasion and are being distributed throughout the country."

His mother's chin dropped to her chest and she closed her eyes. "I can't believe this is happening." She sniffed. "What are we going to do?

You know how they feel about us here. In Germany, it's even worse. If they bring their hatred with them, how will we survive?"

"I've already put all my business affairs in order, and I've handed all my cases to other partners in the firm. I've begun liquidating as many of our assets as I can without raising suspicions. If they think we're going to run, we'll be the first they come after. We can't trust anyone anymore."

His mother's eyes widened in shock. "Do you really think someone at the firm would betray us?"

His father grunted. "We're Jewish. They've barely tolerated me this long. I'm there just to get the Jewish clientele. Once the Nazis arrive, I fear that clientele will be rounded up and they'll no longer need my services. Most of my coworkers will be happy to hand me over."

His mother wailed, falling into his father's arms. "But these people are supposed to be our friends!"

He hugged her, patting her head. "You're old enough to know by now that the only real friend a Jew ever has is another Jew." He released his embrace and handed her his handkerchief. She dabbed her eyes dry as she sniffled.

"What are we going to do?" she finally asked.

He shook his head slowly. "I don't know. There's really nowhere for us to go. It's too late. The border is already closed, probably to stop people like us from fleeing. You know they've rejected our application to leave the country every time I've applied. I don't know why, but I must be on a list for some reason."

"Could we hide somewhere?"

"And just where would you propose we hide? Our Jewish friends are just as much a target as we are, and none of our Austrian friends have offered to help, nor can we risk asking them."

"We could rent a room somewhere. An apartment under different names."

"And when the money runs out, or they ask us for our identification papers?"

"Well, we can't just do nothing. We have to at least try."

"I know, my dear, but I just don't know what we can do. Once the Nazis are here…"

His mother looked away. "I've heard stories about how they treat Jews. They're horrible. They're destroying Jewish businesses, beating Jews in the street, blaming us for everything from the Depression to the common cold. If you can't work, then we'll starve, we'll lose our home, and we'll need to live off the charity of others in a country where there is no charity for people like us. And the prospects of being beaten, raped, or murdered by some Nazi in a black SS uniform is not a future I want to be a part of."

"What are you saying?" asked his father, his voice barely a whisper.

His mother stared into his father's eyes, tears flowing freely. "I'm saying there's another way."

"You don't mean…"

"Can you think of a better way, a way that protects us all from the horrors to come?"

His father's shoulders slumped. "No."

"Will you take care of it?"

"I'll talk to Peter." He held up a finger. "But we use it only as a last resort. Only if it looks like the worst is going to happen. Agreed?"

His mother responded with a trembling nod, her eyes closed, her shoulders shaking. They held each other tight, and Daniel retreated back into the dining room where he had been playing, wondering what his parents had just agreed to do.

And what a Nazi was.

Acton/Palmer Residence

St. Paul, Maryland

Present Day, Four Weeks Earlier

Archaeology Professor Laura Palmer sat curled up in her favorite chair as her husband, James Acton, prepared the ingredients for taco night with Tommy Granger. Tommy's girlfriend, Mai Trinh, sat in the corner of the couch, stretching, wincing each time.

"What's with you today?" asked Laura.

Mai rolled her neck. "I started Vovinam classes last night."

James' knife paused. "Vovinam? What's that?"

"It's a Vietnamese martial art. I didn't know there was a school in the area, but I found one a couple of weeks ago, so I signed up and started last night. I used to do it when I was a kid, but I haven't even thought of it in years. I figured it might be a good idea to learn some self-defense techniques, considering what you two are always getting us into." She flashed a smile.

Laura regarded the young woman who had helped save their lives in Vietnam, paying a very high price, now exiled to the United States. But she had embraced her new life, obtained her citizenship, and now lived with Tommy, a young man who absolutely adored her.

James returned to slicing a green pepper, glancing over at Tommy. "Are you taking the lessons as well?"

Tommy shook his head. "No. If I did, I wouldn't have an excuse for when she kicked my ass."

James laughed. "Your choice. But I will say that some of the best times Laura and I have had together have been during training, and when you're all done and sore all over, nothing beats rubbing each other down." His eyebrows bobbed suggestively.

Laura gave him a look. "Behave, James."

"Who? Me?"

Tommy smiled then looked at Mai. "Maybe I should join you."

She perked up at this development. "That would be wonderful! I think you'd really enjoy it. It's tough, especially at first, but once you get in shape, it's a lot of fun."

Tommy groaned. "In shape? This is starting to sound more and more like exercise."

James stared at him. "What did you think it was, a video game?"

Tommy blushed then offered a weak rebuttal. "Who? Me?"

James shook his head. "Dude, you gotta get your head out from behind a screen every once in a while."

Laura's phone vibrated with a message. She brought up the email and gasped at who it was from.

James, concerned, put down his knife, rounding the kitchen island. "What is it?"

"It's an email from Mr. Meitner."

"Who?"

"You know, the founder of Meitner Telecom, the company that bought out my brother's."

"Oh. Does he want his money back?"

Tommy snickered and fist bumps were exchanged between him and her husband. She finished reading the message then filled in her wisecracking partner. "He's inviting us to a charity event in Vienna. Apparently, he's giving away the bulk of his fortune before he dies."

"Just how much is that fortune?"

Laura Googled the man's name. "Over twenty billion, according to this."

Tommy whistled. "Do you think he'd donate to the Granger-Trinh House Down Payment Fund?"

Laura put her phone down. "You two are saving for a house?"

Mai nodded. "We don't want to pay rent forever, so we've started setting a little bit aside each month. It's not much, obviously, but it's a start. Maybe in five or ten years, we'll have enough."

Laura glanced at James, who gave her a surreptitious wink. She leaned toward Mai. "If you two want to buy a house, then we'll give you the down payment."

Tommy's jaw dropped. "Oh my God, thank you!"

Mai's eyes shot wide. "Hell no!"

Laura almost laughed at the reactions, the vernacular she would normally expect from each of them swapped. "Why not?"

"You two have done too much for us already. That's just too much."

Laura pointed at the phone. "You do know how much that man paid for my brother's company, don't you? And that I inherited everything when he died?"

Mai shook her head. "No, I don't know, though I imagine it was a lot."

"It was. It's enough that few can understand what it's like to have the fortune we do, and nothing gives us greater pleasure than to help others, especially our friends. Now, if we thought for a moment you two were irresponsible and couldn't afford your own home merely because you're squandering your money, then we wouldn't make the offer. But we know you. You are two young, hard-working adults who have brought so much joy to our lives, that we would love to do this for you."

Mai looked over at Tommy, his mouth still agape. He shrugged at her as James reached over and pushed Tommy's jaw up, the teeth clicking in the silence. Mai's shoulders slumped, her voice dropping to barely a whisper. "I don't know what to say."

"You say, 'thank you!'" cried Tommy. "You say, 'thank you so much!'"

Tears rolled down Mai's cheeks. "You have no idea what this means to us, what it means to me. I never thought I'd own my own home. I always figured I'd just be living with my father until he died, and then whatever family I had would continue in the same space we had for generations." She sighed. "I just wish my family could be here with us. I know my mother is looking down upon us, thanking God that I found you. Not only have you two become two of the best friends I've ever had, you've taken care of me like…" She hesitated, her chin dropping to her chest and her voice cracking. "Like you were my parents."

Laura burst into tears and held out her arms. Mai bolted from her seat, rushing into them. They hugged each other hard, both sobbing. "You know we think of you as our daughter, and we'd do anything for you. We love you." She glanced over at Tommy, whose eyes glistened. "We love both of you."

James punched Tommy on the shoulder. "I'd say like a son, but it would come off as incestuous, since you'd be boinking your sister."

Tommy's eyes shot wide. "Huh, I never thought of that."

James squeezed the back of Tommy's neck, giving him a shake.

Laura let go of Mai and grabbed a tissue from the end table, handing it to the young woman, then pulling one for herself. Noses were blown, eyes were wiped, and the moment of bonding continued in silence until the timer rang on the oven, signaling the chicken breasts were ready. Awkward giggles and smiles were exchanged as the moment was ended without anyone having to be the first to do so. James pulled the steaming tray out of the oven, then set the meat on the stovetop to allow it to rest.

"So, are we going to this charity event?" he asked.

Laura looked at him. "What?"

"Meitner's charity event. Are we going?"

"I think we absolutely should. After all, it's thanks to him that we live such a posh lifestyle."

James stared down at his Hawaiian shirt and Bermuda shorts, then back at his wife. "I think you and Victoria Beckham have two entirely different definitions of posh."

Vienna, Austria

March 15, 1938

Daniel peered out from between the curtains at the street below. It was exciting. Exhilarating. He always loved a good parade, and red was his favorite color. Red flags with a curiously shaped symbol in the center were everywhere. He had seen it before but had no idea what it meant. All he knew was that the people down below, lining the streets on either side, were jubilant as soldiers in crisp uniforms marched down the road, followed by cars and trucks and tanks. It was the tanks that excited him the most. He had never seen one in person. He had only heard of them. They were so loud, the entire apartment shook. He covered his ears with his hands, but there was no removing the smile from his face.

His parents were in the next room with one of their friends. They had sent him to his room, but he had listened at the door as he always did.

"The Nazis are here," declared his parents' friend, a man Daniel called Uncle Peter, though he wasn't his actual uncle. He was an apothecary.

What that was, Daniel had no idea. Daniel's father was successful, and from the visits he had at other houses, they lived far better than most. Peter had a son and daughter that he played with sometimes, and his home was just as nice if not nicer.

He wasn't sure why one family lived better than another, though on the playground at school, some children with homes far more modest than his would make snide remarks behind his back, loud enough that he could hear them suggesting it was because his father was a lying cheating Jew or some other variation of the insult.

And again, he didn't understand it. What did being Jewish have to do with anything? It had hurt his feelings the first time he heard the insults, enough to send him home crying. His mother had consoled him and explained that it wasn't his fault, that his father was a success because he had worked hard at school, attended university, and become a lawyer. He had put the work in, and now was enjoying the rewards. He hadn't lied, he hadn't cheated, he hadn't done anything wrong, but those with less were often jealous, and he should pay them no mind. He should simply walk away.

But it was difficult, especially when his friends would snicker at some of the insults made by others. He had other Jewish friends that attended a different school where it was all Jews, and had asked why he wasn't going there instead of the regular Austrian school. His father's explanation had made no sense to him, but his father would never lie, and would always do what was best. The reason had something to do with wanting him to receive the best education available to anyone, so that in the future, no one would judge him negatively by the name of the school he attended. What the name of a school could have to do with anything he didn't know, but he hadn't asked again. It was all too confusing.

The last tank rumbled past, the last soldier disappeared from sight, and the crowd quickly dispersed. Within minutes, it was as if the parade had never happened, though the flags hanging from windows remained. He was disappointed it was over. He stepped back from the window and his stomach growled. He opened the door and walked down the hallway, the conversation between the adults whispered. He entered the drawing room and stopped, waiting, as taught, for a break in the conversation. Peter was handing out pieces of folded brown paper. Daniel had seen them before when someone in the household was sick, and knew them to contain medicine.

"It's very simple," said Peter. "If you have time, just mix the powder with a glass of water and drink the entire thing. You can make a tea of it if you wish. If you take it before you go to sleep, you won't wake up. If you can't wait for that, you'll just get tired and eventually pass out. There will be no pain, and there's nothing they can do to counteract it."

"What if there's no time for water?" asked his mother.

"Just pour the powder into your mouth and swallow as much of it as you can. There's enough in each pouch to do the job several times over."

His father reached out to shake Peter's hand. "Thank you for this, my friend. You have no idea how much this means to us."

Peter took the hand. "You know I'd do anything for you and your family. With the Nazis here now, things will become extremely difficult for all of us who don't believe in their cause."

"What are you and your family going to do?" asked his mother.

"I've already prepared doses for all of us should it become necessary."

"But you're not Jewish."

"No, but I vocally opposed allowing the Nazis to come here, and protested the treatment of our Jewish population. They might not be coming for me at first, but they'll eventually reach me. I have no intention of allowing the Nazis to take me and my family prisoner to torture until they're done with us. Our country died today, and any hopes of a future I would want to raise my children in along with it."

His mother collapsed back in her chair, the folded paper pressed to her chest. "I can't believe it's come to this. We should have gone to America when we had the chance."

His father frowned at her. "Things aren't that great there for people like us either."

"That may be, but at least we would be alive."

"It's too late for that, so there's no point thinking about it. Nobody could have predicted that things would have progressed so swiftly. We all thought we had more time. I just wish I knew why they keep refusing our application to leave. If they don't want us here, why keep us?"

Peter frowned. "I'm hearing a lot of stories like yours. They're letting those they think they can't use leave, and holding on to those they think they can exploit. They might think you could be useful to them at some point."

His father grunted. "Who knew a good education and a successful career could doom one's family."

His mother sat up, placing the folded paper on the table. "How long do you think we have?"

Peter shrugged. "Not very long before they start restricting your movements. Then from what I've heard, they'll conduct a census to identify all the Jews, then they'll come in and determine everything you own that they want, and they'll seize your assets at some point. From there, who knows? The Nazis are very methodical. I have no doubt they have a stringent plan already in place. In Germany, they already have hundreds of laws dictating how the Jewish can live."

"Or not live."

"What do you think their ultimate goal is?" asked his father.

Peter sighed. "As I've said before in our conversations, throughout history, what has always been the ultimate goal of a fanatical leader? The British and French are fools if they think they can make peace with a man such as this. The more time they give him through their appeasement policies, the more time he has to rearm Germany. Nobody wants war right now, nobody is capable of war right now, yet he rearms. It's clearly not for defensive reasons, for there are no enemies out there strong enough to engage anyone. He's taken back the Saar, the Rhineland, and now Austria, all without firing a shot. This man wants Europe, and once he has it, the world. Once someone finally says no to him, that's when war will be declared, and that's when we truly need to worry, for while the population is distracted, things will be done in the name of national security. And when things go wrong, when food becomes scarce, when battles are lost, scapegoats will be needed. Just like during the Depression, it was the Jews who were blamed, it was those who supported the Jews. I fear intimidation and beatings will be just the beginning. Neighbor will turn on neighbor, and anyone different, anyone who doesn't support the cause, will be in prison. And when the prisons are full, they'll be forced to…make room."

His mother stared at Peter for a moment, saying nothing, then she gasped. "Daniel! How long have you been standing there?"

He shrugged. "I'm hungry."

"Then why didn't you ask for a snack?"

He shrugged again. "I was waiting for a chance to, but you all kept talking for so long."

His father looked at his mother and tilted his head toward the kitchen. She rose. "Come, I'll get you something." She extended a hand and he took it, following her into the kitchen. He stared up at her.

"Mother, when we go to sleep for the last time, can I sleep in your bed?"

She cried out and collapsed against the wall, sliding down the floor.

"Father!"

Footfalls rushed toward them and his mother reached out, grabbing him and holding him tight, repeating over and over, "We can't do this!"

Hotel Sacher Wien

Vienna, Austria

Present Day

Archaeology Professor James Acton stared at himself in the mirror, adjusting the stupid bow tie for the umpteenth time. He hated dressing up, though tolerated it, especially for events like this where so much good was about to be done. The final number that Meitner was donating hadn't yet been made public, though speculation was running rampant in the press. Most were suspecting at least ten billion would be donated, more likely twenty. From what he had read about Meitner, he was expecting at least that.

Laura stepped into the room in a stunning evening gown, slit high up the side. He growled at her and she wagged a finger. "Don't you dare get any ideas, mister. You realize how much time I spent getting my hair and makeup done?"

He gave her a look. "You sat in a chair and gossiped for two hours with Mai. Don't act as if there was any effort on your part."

She held up three fingers.

"Am I supposed to read between the lines, or was it three hours?"

Two fingers dropped.

He laughed and walked over to her, leaning in for a kiss. Her palm blocked his advance, her fingers splayed out, gripping his entire face as she pushed him back.

"When we're back here after the gala, I'm all yours, but until then, this"—she waved a hand indicating her entire body—"is off-limits."

Acton gave his best pout. "Did you buy that dress or is it a rental?"

"I bought it. It's from a local designer from back home. I thought it'd help give her some exposure."

He grinned. "So, I can rip it off you tonight?"

She looked at him askance. "You'll do no such thing."

He chewed his cheek, tilting his head. "So, I can patiently stand in the corner and watch you undress, fold it, and put it away?"

She patted his cheek. "Now you're getting it."

He grunted. "Then you better brace yourself. The moment that dress leaves your hands, this coiled snake is springing at you."

She eyed his crotch. "Which coiled snake?"

Another grin. "I like the way you think."

She gave the little guy a squeeze.

"That didn't help. You're killing me, woman."

There was a knock at the door and Acton stepped into the suite's living area, peering through the peephole. "It's Hugh and Spencer." He opened the door and smiled broadly at his friend and his son in their tuxedos, delighting in the fact Interpol Agent Hugh Reading appeared as uncomfortable as he felt. "Don't you two look handsome."

Reading growled. "Don't you start. Whoever invented the bow tie should be drawn and quartered."

Acton stepped aside, inviting them into the room. "Agreed. How about you, Spencer? What do you think of the penguin suit?"

The young man shrugged, standing in front of a mirror near the door, checking himself out. "I think if there are any single ladies there tonight, they better watch out."

Reading beamed a smile at his son, but still admonished him. "You be on your best behavior tonight."

"I always am."

"If your Instagram page is any indication, you certainly aren't if there's a pub involved."

Spencer's eyes widened slightly. "Are you cyberstalking me?"

Reading shook his head. "You'd think a generation that has grown up with social media would understand privacy settings and how stupid it is to publish every moronic thing you do on the Internet for future employers to see."

"And fathers," added Acton.

Reading nodded sharply. "And fathers. Just look what's happening these days. People's careers are being destroyed for things they did ten, twenty, thirty years ago. Do you think there's nothing you've posted on there that somebody in ten years from now won't find offensive and decide you shouldn't be a police officer anymore? I've said it before and

I'll say it again, clean up your social media and stop posting your entire life on it. Nobody gives a shite what you had for breakfast or how many bicep curls you did today."

Spencer shrugged. "My fifteen-thousand followers on Insta would suggest somebody cares."

Reading growled. "If I ever get a time machine, I'm going back and making sure Zuckerberg never learns how to turn on a computer."

Acton laughed and called over his shoulder toward the bedroom. "Hon, you better get out here. Hugh's already in a mood, and you always seem to put him in a better one."

Laura entered the room and both Reading-family jaws hit the floor. Senior reached over and pushed his son's up, and Acton did the same for the father. Laura smiled, sending Acton's heart racing.

"I take it that means I look good."

Three heads bobbed, then Reading finally stepped forward to give her their customary hug. Acton raised a finger to stop him but was shocked when Laura embraced him.

Acton raised both hands in the air. "Hey, hey, hey, flag on the play here! Why does he get a hug and I don't?"

"Because he's a gentleman and won't slobber all over me. You're liable to try and mount me."

He tilted his head toward Spencer. "She's got me there."

Spencer snickered and shook Laura's hand. "You look amazing, ma'am."

"Thank you, dear. But call me ma'am again, and I'll turn you into a soprano."

Spencer gulped and Acton and Reading exchanged grins. Another knock at the door had Reading in his customary role of protector waving Acton off. He checked the peephole then opened the door, Tommy Granger and Mai Trinh entering.

Acton beamed at Mai as any proud father would, and Laura rushed forward, gushing. "Oh my God, Mai, you look so beautiful!"

Mai's shoulders rolled inward and her head dropped. "Oh, I don't know."

Tommy patted her on the back. "See, I told you. You're stunning!"

"He's right," agreed Acton. "You look beautiful."

Mai's head rose slightly and she smiled awkwardly. "You really think so?"

Reading agreed. "Stunning."

He swatted his son on the arm, and all Spencer could manage was, "Uh, yeah," and Acton could swear there was a little bit of drool in the corner of the young man's cheek.

Acton laughed. "Well, if that doesn't confirm it, I don't know what would."

Reading backhanded his son on the shoulder again as he continued to ogle the Asian beauty. "Manners, young man."

Spencer continued to stare then finally tore his eyes away. "Huh?"

Reading just shook his head at his son.

Acton glanced at Tommy to see whether he would be jealous, but instead found pride on the young man's face. Acton pretended to hold a microphone to his mouth. "So, Miss Trinh, who are you wearing tonight?"

Mai giggled and struck a fifties pin-up pose. "Chantal L'Heureux, a local designer with a promising future from Baltimore."

Laura walked up beside her, mimicking the pose. "A *very* promising future, I would say." Acton gave two thumbs up and Laura turned to Mai. "Did you give Tommy his instructions?"

"Yup, no jiggy-jiggy until the dress is back in the box."

Tommy flushed and Acton punched him in the arm. "What, you don't think we know you two bump uglies?" The young man's cheeks turned a deeper red and Acton laughed. "Don't worry, I got the same instructions."

Reading groaned. "I do *not* want to hear about all the sex I'm not having." He tapped his watch. "Shouldn't we be heading out now?"

Laura nodded. "Our limo is waiting downstairs. Once we're through the red carpet, one of Mr. Meitner's people will meet us and take us backstage to meet our host."

"Have you ever met him before?" asked Reading.

"Only once at my brother's funeral. A very sweet old man with a kind heart. This final gesture of his is exactly what you'd expect from the life he's led. He's a very generous man."

"He is that," agreed Reading. "But why the spectacle?"

"I suspect he's doing it to pressure other billionaires to do something similar. He's certainly not the first to indicate they would be donating the bulk of their wealth before they died, but I do believe he's the first to actually do it, certainly in this amount."

"Do you really think the newspapers are right?" asked Spencer. "That he's going to donate ten or twenty billion?"

Laura shrugged. "No idea. That's part of the excitement of the night. People around the world will be glued to their TV sets wondering if their favorite charity is going to win the lottery. Hundreds of charities are going to receive money tonight. His donations could improve millions of lives, could save millions of lives. We should all be honored to be a part of it." She held out her hand and Acton stepped over, taking it. "You should all know that we're going to be making a donation tonight as well, in all our names."

"How much?" asked Spencer.

Reading swatted him. "Manners, boy!"

Laura laughed. "Take it easy on the poor boy. He won't be able to raise his champagne glass."

Reading rolled his eyes. "If you saw the photos I did of last weekend, you'd be thanking me."

Laura smiled at Spencer. "How much is unimportant. However, it'll be enough to make a difference, though obviously nothing compared to what Mr. Meitner is doing."

"Though maybe when you die…" Spencer ducked the blow this time.

Laura exchanged a glance with Acton, who answered. "We've already had our wills updated. Our friends and family will be taken care of, of course, but the bulk of what we have will go to a charitable foundation that we're setting up. But"—he smacked his hands together—"that's a discussion for another time, because I don't plan on being dead anytime soon, despite the best efforts of whoever I pissed off at some point in a previous life. Now, my understanding is there's a fully stocked limousine sitting downstairs waiting for us. I say we get inside, test Spencer's drinking arm, and let the festivities begin."

"Hear! Hear!" cried Spencer. Alone. There was a brief silence then everyone erupted in laughter.

Acton headed for the door. "Let's go get Spencer's drink on!"

Vienna, Austria

August 3, 1940

Brakes squealed and tires screeched, then the shouts of dozens of men broke his happy humming as Daniel played with his toy car. There was little left in the house. He wasn't sure how long it had been since the Nazis arrived, as he had lost track of the days locked inside, unable to go out, unable to see his friends or attend school. Even his parents' friends didn't come by anymore, except for Uncle Peter. He would come and take something from the house, some small piece of furniture, some piece of art, something sitting on the mantle for years, and when he'd return, he'd have either money or food.

From what Daniel understood, his father wasn't allowed to work, so they had no money coming in to buy the things they needed. He always had enough to eat, though he noticed both his mother and father, especially his father, were much thinner. At mealtime, his plate was always full, while those of his parents were mostly empty.

And he hadn't seen either of them genuinely smile since the day of the parade.

He would spend his days mostly in his bedroom, playing with his toys or reading one of his books. Sometimes he'd be in the dining room, which used to be his favorite place, but now the oval rug with its pattern that he could race his car on was gone, and so was the table that he had played under for so many years. It was an empty room now that echoed every sound made. His bedroom was the only one left mostly untouched.

The only thing they ever did as a family was listen to the radio in the evening, huddled in his father's office, the volume so low it was hard to hear. He didn't understand most of what was being said, not because it was in English, which was a language his parents had taught him from birth, but because it was about places he had never heard about. All he knew was there was a war, and it wasn't going well for the good guys.

He enjoyed spending the time with his parents as they all sat on the couch, one of the few pieces of furniture left in his father's office. His favorite part was racing around the office, finding all the hidden pieces to the radio, then helping his father assemble it. His father had always been a tinkerer. Taking apart and putting back together radios, gramophones, small motors—it was his hobby that he always devoted a couple of hours a week toward. Daniel would always be at his side, handing him the tools, handing him the pieces, sometimes allowed to reassemble the simpler things.

He loved it. The time spent with his father, always so busy, was precious. Just the two of them, the silence only broken by his father explaining what the various pieces did and quizzing him on everything taught. It was like school, but a fun school. There were no textbooks or chalkboards. Just him and his father, using their hands to make something work that hadn't before. He always did well in school, and he did enjoy it, but nothing compared to those few hours spent with his father every week.

And now, with the added aspect of finding the pieces and assembling them, then disassembling and hiding things yet again after what they were listening to was finished, it was the most fun he had.

Yet while he enjoyed it, he hated the effect it had on his parents, for nothing they heard ever made them happy. When they were sad, he was sad, and sometimes he found he had to leave whatever room they were in, especially when it was just his mother. She cried more now than she didn't, and she'd cling to him if he were in the room, saying she was sorry over and over, but never answering his question when he would ask her what she was sorry for. His father rarely smiled. He hadn't seen him cry yet, though he was quite certain he had heard him on several occasions behind his closed office door sobbing and praying.

So, he had taken to praying as well. Though they didn't go to Temple anymore, his father would guide them in prayer, and he would study for his Bar Mitzvah. He stopped pushing his car and wondered if he would even have a Bar Mitzvah. He hadn't seen any of his friends or family in a long time. He frowned. Could the biggest day of his life, when he would finally become a man, be spent with just his mother and father? He couldn't remember the last time he had had a sweet. Would there even be anything special to eat?

He growled and headed to the window to peer outside and see what these horrible Nazis were up to now. He didn't know who they were or what they wanted, but they had ruined everything. They had taken away the life he had known, the life he had taken for granted. His friends were gone, his family was gone, everything he had grown up with was gone. All that was left was a bare apartment and his parents, who weren't the same people anymore.

His parents had been happy, but now they were miserable all the time. When his mother had shown him his jacket with the Star of David sewn onto the arm, he had thought it was wonderful. He had always been taught to keep his faith to himself unless he was only with other Jewish people. Yet now, he could proudly display who he was and what he believed in. But his parents weren't happy about it, yet they refused to tell him why, and it was frustrating. If he would soon be a man, then shouldn't he know what was going on? They kept shielding him from the truth. He was old enough to know they were protecting him, but he had always heard from his father that strength came through knowledge, and if he needed to be protected, then didn't he need to be strong?

He peered out the window and gasped. Dozens of soldiers, if not more, were streaming in and out of a building across the street. Windows were thrown open and clothes and other things were dumped out onto the cobblestone as men, women, and children, many of whom he recognized, were led out and loaded into the back of a truck. His jaw dropped as he realized every single person led outside had the Star of David on their arm or chest.

He recognized Jacob, his best friend from school that he hadn't seen in ages. He reached to open the window and shout down to him, so excited to see him, when Jacob's father grabbed him, running away from the soldiers. Jacob's mother chased after them and a soldier yelled, "Halt!" But before any of them could stop, gunfire stripped away Daniel's innocence as he witnessed the murder of Jacob and his family on the streets below. A man in black, who appeared to be in charge, walked over and drew a handgun. He stood over Jacob's father, aiming the gun at his head, then fired a single shot. Jacob's father's body shook once, then was still. The man used his boot to kick the body off Jacob. Jacob's head turned slightly and another bullet was fired.

Daniel cried out, recoiling from the window. Heavy footfalls rushed toward his bedroom and his mother burst into the room. Her eyes darted toward the window and she gasped at the swaying curtains.

"I told you to stay away from the windows!"

But he didn't hear her words. His best friend was dead, shot by one of these Nazis, and for the first time since this entire ordeal had begun, he understood why his parents were so scared. Everything he had heard up to this point, the hushed conversations, the radio broadcasts, they all referred to battles, to fights between the two sides, but never was there any mention of children being shot in cold blood just because they had a Star of David sewn to the arm of their jacket. He stared up at his mother as tears flowed down his cheeks.

"Are they going to kill me like they killed Jacob?"

Vienna City Hall, Ground Floor VIP Suites

Vienna, Austria

Present Day

Meitner smiled broadly as they were shown into the room backstage of the impressive Vienna City Hall. "Professor Palmer, it's so good to see you again."

Laura Palmer stepped forward and shook the man's hand. "I was so pleased to receive your invitation. It's such an honor."

"You deserve to be here. I've kept my eye on you over the years, especially after your brother passed so tragically and I found out you inherited his entire fortune. I've been impressed with what you've done with it."

"We try."

Meitner smiled from his wheelchair and turned his head toward Acton. "I could play dumb and pretend I didn't know exactly who you were, Professor Acton, but I've followed your career as well since you came into Professor Palmer's life. Archaeology has always been a fascination of mine, as well as history. In fact, I've spent many years attempting to track down a family heirloom that I just reacquired. Perhaps you would like to see it?"

Acton's interest was already piqued. "I'd love to."

Meitner gestured toward the others. "Very good, but first, I think introductions are in order?"

Laura stepped aside. "Mr. Meitner, may I present Agent Hugh Reading of Interpol. His son, Constable Spencer Reading of the London Metropolitan Police. Thomas Granger, University of St. Paul, and his partner, Mai Trinh, also of the University of St. Paul."

Meitner bowed his head. "It's a pleasure to meet you all, and I'm pleased you could be here on such an important occasion. As you may know, I intend…" Meitner suddenly stopped, a coughing fit taking over.

A man Acton hadn't noticed emerged from a corner with a glass. He pressed a straw into Meitner's mouth, and several drags of what wasn't water, though Acton was certain wasn't alcohol either, were drawn, and the coughing subsided. The man reached for an oxygen mask dangling by the side of the chair when Meitner waved his hand, dismissing the need.

"I'm okay now, Bernie, thank you." Meitner smiled at them sheepishly. "I'm sorry you had to see that, but it's one of the curses you face when you're over ninety years old. It's why I've decided to do this today rather than risk waiting any longer."

Laura kneeled beside him, taking his hand. "Are you going to be all right?"

Meitner patted her hand. "No, but as long as I am for tonight, that's all that matters."

"Is there anything we can do?"

Meitner shook his head. "The best doctors in the world have assured me my time has finally come, and I'm okay with that. I've led a long, fulfilling life, honored my family, I hope, and tonight will establish a legacy that will hopefully last long after my name is but a footnote in history."

Laura wiped a tear away then laughed. "And here I was worried my husband would mess up my makeup."

He reached up and patted her cheek. "Not to worry, my dear. I have two granddaughters here tonight who I suspect are close enough to your age to be helpful. They have everything you could possibly need in a room just down the hall."

"Thank you," said Laura, rising and adjusting her dress.

There was a knock at the door and Bernie opened it. A woman entered and bowed slightly.

"It's time, sir."

"Of course, of course." Meitner reached into his breast pocket and retrieved a memory stick. He passed it over to the new arrival, who extended a shaking hand to take it.

"Don't be so nervous, my friend. It's only twenty-five billion dollars you hold in your hand."

Acton's eyebrows shot up with the number to be donated confirmed at the high end of the speculation building for weeks. It was humbling.

"Y-yes, sir."

"Bloody Nora! Did you hear that?" hissed Spencer.

Reading elbowed his son and Acton suppressed a smile as Meitner delighted at the display.

"Yes, son, it *is* a lot of money, and it'll do a lot of people a lot of good."

Reading cleared his throat, gesturing toward the new arrival as she left. "Does she have security protecting her?"

Meitner batted a hand. "This entire place is swarming with security. She's only going fifty feet down the hallway. I can't go anywhere these days without a team of at least a dozen. One of the curses of the world I helped create, despite having stepped back from running the day-to-day operations." He sighed. "I founded Meitner Telecom, but I suppose some would say I stuck around a little too long to still be useful. So much is changing and so rapidly, that I found not only did I have no interest in trying to keep up with the latest developments, my bliss was found in my workshop, tinkering with the old toys."

"Sometimes happiness is the simpler things."

Meitner agreed. "That's exactly how I feel these days, young man." He waved a hand at the closed door. "But nothing is simple about tonight. My security people have set things up so that none of the security protocols can be seen during the broadcast. That memory stick contains my private key. My people will have the account balance displayed on a screen for the public to see, and then in what I've been assured will be a quite dramatic display, a series of rapid transfers will take place into accounts set up by the various charities, and while my twenty-five billion number will rapidly dwindle, their empty accounts will fill as rapidly. Hopefully, by the end of the night, others like myself will be inspired."

Laura squeezed Acton's hand. "We won't be making any announcement, as that's not who we are, but when we return home, we'll be donating ten million dollars, spread out among the charities you chose tonight. It's a token amount compared to what you're doing, but we've already set up our wills so that when we pass, the bulk of our fortune will fund causes that are dear to our hearts."

Meitner smiled broadly, extending a hand to each of them. They both took his hand and Acton was surprised at the strength of the squeeze he received. "Thank you both. I know, Laura, that your brother would be proud that the legacy he left behind is in such good hands. I pray more will feel like you two."

"Hopefully, more like us who have been fortunate will follow our example."

"Hopefully," agreed Acton.

"Oh, I almost forgot!" Meitner glanced over his shoulder. "Bring it to me, would you, Bernie?"

"Yes, sir."

Bernie lifted a briefcase from the floor and placed it on a table. He entered a combination and opened it, removing what appeared to be a jewelry box. He handed it to Meitner, who then opened the box and turned it around. Everyone leaned in and gasped at a beautiful necklace, littered with diamonds and other precious stones, all set in a substantial gold chain.

"It's stunning," whispered Mai.

"It was in my family for a very long time. I was forced to sell it at one point to get my start, but I vowed if I ever could, I would buy it back. It took me a while to find it, and the owner didn't want to part with it, but I made him an offer he couldn't refuse."

Acton chuckled at the Godfather impression.

Meitner stared up at Mai. "Perhaps the young lady would like to wear it tonight?"

Mai's eyes shot wide as she took a step back. "Oh, no, I couldn't!"

"I insist. I think it will look lovely on you. And it would warm my heart to see someone enjoy it in my presence one final time."

Mai glanced at Laura, as if seeking permission. Laura nodded encouragingly and Mai finally acquiesced. "Well, I suppose."

Meitner handed the box to Tommy. "Why don't you do the honors, son."

Tommy gulped and took the box. He lifted the necklace out gingerly, handing the empty box to Acton. Mai lifted her hair and the inexperienced Tommy fumbled putting it around her neck as his hands trembled.

"Umm, just how much is that worth?" asked Spencer.

Another swat from his father was dodged.

"In dollars, you don't want to know, but to the family, it's priceless."

Mai trembled. "Are you sure you want me wearing this?"

"Absolutely." The old man stared up at her, his eyes glistening. "The last time I saw that worn was over eighty years ago by my mother." A tear rolled down his cheek, unnoticed.

There was a quick rap at the door, answered by Bernie. A woman stepped inside. "Everything's been confirmed, sir. We're ready to go."

Meitner smiled. "Everybody, this is Azar Vida. She's in charge of making sure this show runs smoothly." The woman flashed a smile at everyone. Meitner gestured toward her. "I have to get ready now. Agent Reading, I have no doubt you would be interested in the security we've put together for this project."

Reading agreed. "I would, as would my son, I have no doubt."

Spencer's head bobbed. "Absolutely."

Tommy raised a hand. "If we're talking the cyber side of it, I'd be interested too."

Meitner regarded the woman. "Miss Vida, do you mind?"

"Not at all, sir."

Acton suppressed a smile. It was evident she did mind, and he didn't blame her. This was probably the biggest night of her life, and the last thing she likely had time for was playing tour guide. Handshakes were exchanged with the old man, and as they were about to leave the room, he cleared his throat. "Don't forget, Miss Trinh, to return that necklace. We wouldn't want this night to be remembered because of a theft, now, would we?" Her cheeks paled slightly and he laughed. "Don't worry, dear, I have no doubt the moment you put that necklace on, Bernie arranged a member of my security detail to watch you."

Bernie stepped forward. "As protection, of course, not distrust."

"Of course."

Vida opened the door impatiently. "Sir, if I'm going to give them a tour and make sure this goes off without a hitch, we better leave now."

Meitner waved his hand at the door. "Go. And, Miss Vida, if you don't have time, just say it."

Vida's shoulders slumped and she smiled sheepishly. "I'm sorry, sir. It's just that I've been brought in last minute, as you know, and I just want to make sure everything goes off smoothly."

"I know, I know. Get one of your subordinates that you can spare to give the tour." Meitner turned to Laura. "I'm sure you understand."

"Of course. If it's too much of a bother, we'll happily forgo the tour. We don't want to cause any difficulties."

Meitner batted his hand. "Nonsense. You're my honored guests and I'm one of the richest men in the world. If I can't cause headaches for my staff, then what's the point of having all this money?"

Laura chuckled, as did the others. "What you're doing is a great thing, and I'm sure it'll go off smoothly and inspire many others. Good luck tonight."

Meitner bowed his head. "Thank you, Professor."

They followed Vida out of the room, Bernie shutting the door behind them. The guards stationed there earlier remained, but a new one trailed them, undoubtedly the necklace's assigned escort. Acton glanced over at Mai, who kept touching the necklace, her fingers still trembling, though the smile suggested it was a combination of fear and excitement, and he couldn't help but choke up as he witnessed what would become a story she would tell for the rest of her life. And as he followed Vida, Laura's hand held in his, he adjusted his bow tie, excited to be part of history in the making.

Despite the penguin suit.

Vienna, Austria

February 19, 1941

"Are you sure you want to do this?"

"Yes," replied Daniel's mother. It was a rare day. Uncle Peter, the apothecary, was here while his father was out on some sort of business. They were venturing outside more out of desperation, the food deliveries from Peter and a few others now scarce. Even his own plate was mostly bare now. "Just make sure my husband doesn't know."

"I'm very uncomfortable lying to him."

"Just don't mention it then, and you won't have to lie. But we're going to do it tonight."

"You're sure?"

"Yes. It's too dangerous now. Every night another building is searched and the Jews are taken away. I want to do this peacefully, on our own terms."

"But you're willing to let your son potentially suffer?"

Daniel peered around the corner to see his mother shaking her head, her eyes red as tears flowed. "If you could arrange for all three of us, it would be a different matter, but like you said, one child is much easier and far cheaper."

Peter sighed heavily. "I wish there were something more I could do, but the arrangements I've been able to make were only for my family. Adding your son almost scuttled everything."

His mother reached out and took Peter's hands, squeezing them. "Thank you, thank you for saving our son. All I ask is that you tell him of us, of how much we loved him, and how sorry we were that it came to this."

Peter held her hands to his chest. "I assure you that his life will be filled with stories of his family, and when it's safe to do so, I will make certain he is raised in the Jewish tradition." His mother collapsed into Peter's arms, sobbing as he held her in silence. After a few moments, he gently pushed her away. "I'll be back tonight as discussed to collect Daniel. Is there anything you want me to do to your..." He sighed heavily and she shook her head.

"No, unless during our death we suffered some indignity, leave us as you find us. Just save our son. That's all that matters."

Peter closed his eyes for a moment before opening them and staring at her. "Then this is it?"

She nodded. "I suppose it is. I know if my husband knew what was happening, he would thank you."

"And you're still not going to tell him?"

She shook her head. "No. We discussed it before, and he said it was too dangerous. Daniel could be captured and unspeakable things done to him. I believe he deserves a chance. Just make sure he has his powder with him so that if anything does go wrong, he doesn't suffer." She stepped over to one of the few remaining tables in their home, and Daniel noticed for the first time a small bundle wrapped in brown paper, tied with a string. She picked it up and handed it to Peter. "Payment for your people, plus hopefully enough to ease your journey, and perhaps even give our son a start in his new life. They've been in our family for generations and are worth far more than their weight in gold."

Peter clasped the small package to his chest. "I was surprised you were able to hold on to them for so long."

"I refused to let Joseph sell them. They're too precious to me, but when the decision was made to end this, they lost all meaning. If by leaving the family that has held them for so long, they can save our son's life, then I believe my ancestors will forgive me." She inhaled sharply and closed her eyes. "Now go. Joseph is due home any moment."

Peter stepped back. "Your son will never forget you or his father. This, I swear to you."

Vienna City Hall, Ground Floor VIP Suites

Vienna, Austria

Present Day

Laura knocked gently on the door then stepped back. She and Mai had decided to let the boys have their fun in the control room, and instead take advantage of the opportunity to touch up their makeup. The door opened a moment later and a woman scowled at her.

"What do you want?"

Laura put on her best smile. "I'm Laura, this is Mai. Mr. Meitner said we might be able to touch up our makeup here."

The woman frowned. "Well, he says a lot of things that are inconvenient for others."

Laura resisted the urge to snap back. "If it's too much trouble, that's fine."

Another voice from the inside called, "Oh, don't mind her. Come on in, there's plenty of room."

The woman exhaled loudly and stepped back inside, leaving the door open. Laura shrugged at Mai and entered. The woman who invited them in was sitting at a makeup table applying eyeliner. She glanced at them then gasped when she spotted the necklace on Mai's chest.

"My God, would you look at that? I can't remember the last time I saw it."

"What?" asked the other woman, her head turning toward the door. The scowl deepened. "Well, that just takes the cake, doesn't it?"

She clearly wasn't pleased, and Mai paled slightly. Laura bristled. "Mr. Meitner insisted she wear it."

"Of course he would," snapped the woman Laura was rapidly taking a dislike to.

The other woman rose and stepped over to Mai, staring at the necklace. "It looks lovely on you, dear. And don't pay my sister any mind. She's just in a mood because Grandpa is giving away all her money."

"*Our* money."

The nice one glanced over her shoulder at her sister. "None of it's *our* money. It's his."

"If Mom and Dad were still alive, he would have left the money to them and then they would have left it to us."

"You know that's not true. And what do you care? We're rich. It's not like he's leaving us penniless. I couldn't even begin to spend all the money I have. You just can't stand that it's going to people you turn your nose up at. You really should be more charitable. You'd be a happier person."

"My share would make me plenty happy."

Laura watched the uncomfortable exchange. "Perhaps we should leave."

The good sister batted a hand, dismissing the suggestion. "Nonsense." She examined Laura's face. "Let me guess. My grandfather made you cry."

Laura chuckled. "He did that."

"Well then, you definitely need a touch-up." She directed her toward her seat and glanced over her shoulder at Mai. "You, my dear, don't need a stitch of makeup. All eyes will be on that necklace."

Mai stared at the floor, a hand running over the precious piece of jewelry.

The woman sighed. "I don't know if I've seen that more than half a dozen times in my life. I'm Michelle, by the way. The rude one is my sister, Holly. What did you say your names were again?"

Laura finished reapplying some eyeliner. "I'm Laura Palmer."

"I'm Mai Trinh," murmured Mai.

"And how do you know our grandfather?"

"He bought my late brother's company some time ago."

Michelle eyed her in the mirror. "Late brother? You seem rather young to have already lost a brother."

"He died in an accident."

Holly, standing against the back wall with her arms folded as Mai occupied the second chair, grunted. "And when he died, did he give all of his money to charity?"

Laura finished her makeup, relinquishing the chair to Michelle. "No, he left everything to me."

"See! That's what a responsible adult does. Keeps the money in the family."

Michelle rolled her eyes. "Nonsense. We come from money—"

"That's not true. Grandpa came from nothing."

"Argh!" Michelle jerked a thumb toward Mai. "How many generations has that necklace been in our family?"

Holly glared at her. "You know full well that nobody knows."

"Exactly, because it goes back beyond Grandpa."

"What *is* the story behind the necklace?" asked Laura. "Your grandfather mentioned that he had recently reacquired it."

Michelle beamed. "It's an amazing story. Are you invited to the after-party?"

"Yes, we are."

"Then that's perfect. I'll make sure he tells you the story, but I guarantee you, when it's finished, you'll need to fix your makeup again."

Vienna, Austria

February 19, 1941

Daniel sat on the couch between his mother and father, the evening broadcast finished. Nothing they had heard put his parents in a good mood. If anything, they were sadder than ever. Little had been said all evening, though the meal's size was exciting. It was a feast unlike any they had enjoyed in ages. Not since these Nazis had arrived. He had shoveled more food into his mouth in one sitting than in the previous week. It had crossed his mind that perhaps the war he heard about on the radio, but never saw on the streets, might be ending, though judging by what he had just heard and his parents' reactions to it, that wasn't the case.

"I think it's time," said his father.

His mother agreed. "I'll go make the tea."

Daniel rose with his mother and followed her into the kitchen. He clung to her hip, saying nothing as she boiled the water and poured it into three teacups, chipped and cracked, all that was left of what was once an impressive service. She picked up one of the folded papers that Peter had provided so long ago. It had his father's name on it. His mother opened it and shook the powder it contained into the cup, then stirred it with an old spoon, any luster it might have once had long gone. She handed the cup to him. "Go give this to your father, but make sure you don't drink any of it. It'll make you sick."

"Won't it make Father sick?"

She shook her head. "No, it only makes children sick."

Daniel shrugged and headed into his father's office, disappointed to find the radio had already been broken down and hidden away. He handed him the cup.

"Thank you, son." His father tousled his hair and smiled at him. "Now, you go get yours and we'll all enjoy it together. Then tonight we sleep as a family."

Daniel's eyes shot wide and his face brightened. "You mean I can sleep in your bed tonight?"

"Yes."

Daniel bounced then ran back to the kitchen. His mother handed him a cup and pointed at him. "Slow down. I don't want you spilling any."

"Yes, Mother." He carefully walked back to the office and took a seat beside his father, his mother joining them a few moments later. They all sipped their tea and Daniel winced. "This doesn't taste like tea."

"It's a different kind," explained his mother. "It's good for you. Just make sure you drink it all."

He didn't want to. The taste was bitter. From the conversations he had overheard since the powder had arrived in their home long ago, he knew there was something bad about what they were drinking, but what that was, he wasn't sure. It couldn't be that bad since Peter was coming to get him this evening, though no mention of it had been made by either of his parents.

There was more going on here than he was aware, than he could understand. His father reached out, draping an arm over the back of the couch, then shuffled closer to him, his mother doing the same on the other side, and the three of them finished their tea, his parents holding him and each other, nothing being said.

With their teas finished, his father rose. "Let's get ready for bed."

His mother cleared the dishes and Daniel scurried to his room, changing into his pajamas before heading happily to his parents' bedroom. He found his father in the bed, patting the empty space in the middle. He grinned at the rare treat and sprinted toward the bed then dove through the air, landing far short of his goal. He scrambled up toward the headboard then tucked up his legs and shoved them under the bedding. He squirmed around, finding a comfortable position, then smiled broadly as his mother entered the room, closing the door. She climbed in the bed beside him, then, after settling in, nodded at his father. His father reached over and turned out the light, plunging them into darkness. Heavy curtains on every window in the house, apparently the law for some reason, meant no light could be seen from the outside. It made him wonder if this were more punishment because they were Jewish, or if everybody had to follow the same rule.

But he wasn't troubling himself with such thoughts now. He was enjoying the moment. The bed shook as his parents turned onto their sides, facing each other. Their arms stretched over him and they moved closer to each other, pressing against him.

He loved it.

Whenever he slept in their bed, usually during a lightning storm, he never felt safer. And right here, right now, was the only time he had felt safe since the day the Nazis had arrived, parading past their home.

"I'm sorry," said his father. "I should have tried harder."

"What more could you have done? You kept us safe this long," replied his mother.

"I should have acted sooner. I should have had less faith in my countrymen than I did. I should have known the Nazis would win. I should have taken us from here long before they arrived."

His mother shuffled closer. "What's done is done. And now it's over. Let's just go to sleep and end this nightmare once and for all." She kissed his forehead and Daniel felt a large warm hand on the side of his face as his father leaned in and kissed the top of his head.

"God forgive me for what I've done," whispered his father.

Daniel said nothing, briefly wondering what his father meant, what he could possibly need forgiveness for from God.

He yawned and his mother whispered beside him, "That's it. Go to sleep. This will soon be over."

Daniel yawned again and twisted to face her, his eyes heavy. He struggled to stay awake as his parents drifted off on either side of him, their breathing heavy and steady. He wanted to enjoy this moment for as long as he could, for he didn't know when the next storm might strike or the next special occasion might occur that would have him invited into his parents' bed.

He just wanted this moment to last forever.

And as he lay there, battling sleep, a thought occurred to him. Wasn't Uncle Peter coming tonight? He yawned again and lost the battle.

Vienna City Hall, Ballroom

Vienna, Austria

Present Day

The crowd finally sat as Meitner waved them down after yet another standing ovation. The ballroom was filled with society's elite from around the world. Billionaires and mega-millionaires mixed throughout the crowd, along with hundreds of representatives from the charities about to benefit. Though the front rows were filled not with the privileged, but with scores of Vienna's orphaned as honored guests.

Acton and the others had box seats with a stunning view of the proceedings. He glanced over at Laura, who sat dignified in her chair, though her smile revealed how excited she was to be here. He reached over and took her hand as Meitner thanked the crowd for being there. He rolled his chair closer to the edge of the stage and leaned forward, staring down at the children.

"You children are the ones I am most excited to see here today." He waved his hand at the rest of the crowd. "Most, if not all of these people, have no idea what it's like to be orphaned, to have lost their families and to be alone in this world, terrified of what the future might bring. But I'll let you in on a little secret. I, too, was an orphan. I lost my family during the war. Back then, there were no charities to help me, but I survived. And thanks to the forethought of my mother, I was able to thrive. And my pledge to you is that whatever remains of my fortune when I die, will be used to set up scholarships for children just like you, all around the world, so that you never have to fear whether you'll have a future."

Laura squeezed Acton's hand then let go as the crowd leaped to its feet, applauding the additional generosity. It continued, and Meitner pointed at the children. "That's for you, not for me. They're applauding your future, not my past." He raised a hand and the crowd settled down, returning to their seats as he wheeled back to centerstage. A large screen stretched across the stage, showing the Meitner Telecom corporate logo of a defiant child holding a radio up to the world, sans the company name. Acton wondered if it held some significance, or was the invention of a team of marketers. The screen faded to black, then flared back to life. The left showed Meitner's account balance of $25,000,000,000, and a series of at least 100 boxes on the right each showed the number zero underneath the name of the charity they represented.

During their security tour, it had been explained by the young man Vida had handed them off to, Roy Wagner, that all the account numbers for the charities had been pre-loaded with the amounts they were getting, and once Meitner pressed the ceremonial button, which had no function other than to trigger a light display, someone in the back room would initiate the transfers. Meitner's account would actively drop as the transfers were made, then the charities would phone in live as they confirmed their balance had increased, and the numbers on the screens would be updated. There was a small army of people in the bowels of the building coordinating everything, with scores of cameras scattered throughout to broadcast the event to the world, and document it for future productions and posterity's sake.

"And now, ladies and gentlemen, the moment you have all been waiting for." The crowd hushed as Meitner placed a hand over the ceremonial red button in the center of the stage, the middle of the display showing a shot of his impossibly wrinkled hand, shaking over the trigger. "I now dedicate my life's work to the children of our future, and pray that it proves an inspiration to those with more than they require to dedicate their wealth to those in desperate need."

And with that, the hand dropped onto the bright red button and a series of explosive pots fired confetti into the air as strobe lights and lasers flashed throughout the hall. The audience erupted in cheers, leaping to their feet, the children in the front rows ecstatic.

But Acton was focused on the displays, staring as the $25 billion number rapidly ticked down. His heart pounded with excitement, and he had to tear his eyes from the massive number and instead focus on the scores of smaller displays, all still stubbornly at zero. He exchanged a glance with Laura, and Tommy leaned forward.

"Do you think something's wrong?"

Acton pulled out his phone to text Reading, who had asked if he could remain in the control room with his son, as he found the inner workings more interesting than the event itself. Vida had granted him permission, and they had remained there. A cheer erupted from the crowd as Acton's thumb hovered over his phone. He looked up and saw one of the accounts now showed $50 million deposited. A second appeared showing $75 million, and the crowd roared again.

Meitner smiled broadly. "And now, ladies and gentlemen, that we know it's working, this is where it gets truly exciting."

The decrease in his account balance kicked into overdrive, and in less than a minute, another five billion had been drained, the climax of an evening of presentations drawing to a close.

"Something's wrong," said Laura.

Acton once again tore his eyes away from Meitner's account balance and glanced at his wife. "What?"

She pointed. "Look at the other balances. Nothing's happening."

Forgotten in all the excitement of $25 billion being distributed, he had neglected to watch the beneficiaries' accounts. Everything was a wall of zeros except for those first two successful transactions. He sent a text to Reading.

Is something wrong?

The phone vibrated in his hand a moment later.

Not sure. I'll get back to you.

Acton showed Laura the message as Bernie rushed out on the stage and whispered something in Meitner's ear. The old man's eyes bulged and he grabbed his chest before slumping in his chair. A collective gasp rolled through the crowd as they sprang to their feet, and somebody shouted what Acton already feared.

"Somebody's stealing the money!"

Vienna City Hall, Control Center

Vienna, Austria

Reading stood with Spencer against the rear wall of the Control Center. What had begun as a fascinating piece of history unfolding live in front of their eyes, had soon turned into confusion, then panic. Dozens of people manning the phones were taking calls from charities around the world as they questioned where their money was. Vida was in a state, and she rushed to the front of the room, holding both hands up in the air.

"Quiet!" she ordered, and the room fell silent, the only sounds from the phones and the machines. "Has anybody confirmed any of the transfers successfully arrived after the first two?" Nobody replied, and she paled further than she already was. "Is there any chance our lines are just jammed?"

Somebody rose. "They are, ma'am. Everybody's calling in now and we're being overwhelmed. We were set up for maybe ten or twenty calling in to confirm their balances and then hanging up, but we've got over one-hundred charities trying to get through at once, repeatedly."

"Shut down all incoming calls," directed Vida. "Start calling the charities in the order that the deposits were supposed to have been made, one by one. I want it confirmed whether the money is in their account or not, from somebody who's actually sitting in front of a computer looking at their balance. I don't want anything second or third hand. I want actual eyeballs on the balances." She smacked her hands together. "Go!"

The room sprang into action and everyone with a phone was on it. Vida turned and stared at the displays and Reading shook his head as everything remained stubbornly at zero, yet Meitner's account balance continued to drop like a rock. He stepped forward.

"Excuse me, but don't you think you should halt the transfers?"

Vida spun toward him, squinting in the low lighting. "Who's that?"

"Agent Reading from Interpol. If the money isn't arriving, don't you think you should stop sending billions of dollars out the door?"

She stared at him for a moment then her jaw dropped. She pointed at Wagner, snapping her fingers rapidly. "Stop the money! Stop the money!" Wagner hit several keys on their keyboard and everyone turned to see the balance of Meitner's account continue to fall. "Is that just a lag, or did the withdrawals not stop?"

"It's not a lag, ma'am," said Wagner, manning the computer running the show. "Something's wrong. I can't stop the transfers."

Vida rushed over and reaching across the workstation, yanking something from the computer as Reading strode forward, Spencer on his heels. She gripped a memory stick in her hand that Reading presumed was the one Meitner had handed over earlier in the evening. She turned to him, her eyes wide. "What do I do? It's twenty-five billion dollars!"

"Call Mr. Meitner's bank. Have them halt any transfers that are still coming out."

She pointed at a woman sitting nearby. "Do it." The woman grabbed her phone, rapidly dialing.

Reading pointed at the computer that he assumed was controlling the transfers. "Is that machine doing all the transfers to the accounts?"

She nodded.

He turned to Wagner, not sure what to ask.

Spencer stepped in. "Is the software running on that computer, or is it remote?"

"No, for security reasons, it's running on this terminal."

Spencer stepped over and hauled the computer out, tearing the power cord from the back. Everyone turned to face the displays at the front of the room, and the account balance continued to drop, then finally froze.

And the room gasped.

Less than $3 billion was left, and at this moment, all indications were that over $22 billion had just been stolen.

Vienna City Hall, Ballroom

Vienna, Austria

People were on their feet now, concern slowly replaced with anger from some. Bernie had wheeled Meitner off the stage the moment the elderly man had collapsed, and no explanation had been given for the accounts remaining empty.

It was a disaster, broadcast around the world.

A rumble in the distance followed almost immediately by the entire complex vibrating, momentarily silenced the crowd. The power flickered out then a moment later emergency lighting kicked in.

A slow, loud beeping noise sounded, and staff rushed out into the aisles as a recorded voice blared through the PA system in German, then repeated the orders to evacuate in English and several other languages. Someone screamed, triggering a mass rush for the exits.

"What do we do?" asked Tommy.

"We remain calm," replied Laura. "There's no need to panic."

"But wasn't that a bomb?"

"We don't know if it was a bomb, though it did feel like an explosion."

"Well, if there was an explosion, doesn't that mean there was a bomb?"

Acton shook his head. "Not necessarily. It could have been a natural gas explosion, industrial accident, any number of things. Let's not speculate."

Mai frowned, her hand pressed against the necklace on her chest. "But it has to be an emergency, right? They wouldn't order an evacuation so quickly just because of an accident. They would come over the PA system and tell people what was going on, then ask people to leave in an orderly fashion."

Acton pulled at his bow tie. "You're right. Whatever happened, it must have happened nearby, and is obviously enough of a concern to the security team that evacuation is necessary."

"Then shouldn't we get the hell out of here?" asked Tommy.

Acton pointed down to the panicking crowd below. "You'll just be stepping into that. Let's just wait a minute for things to clear out a bit." He moved the curtain aside and peered into the corridor behind their booth. There were plenty of the well-heeled rushing past, but that didn't concern him.

It was the fact the guard assigned to Mai's neck was nowhere to be seen.

He stepped back inside. "The guard's gone."

Laura eyed him. "Guard?"

"For the necklace."

Her eyebrows shot up. "You're kidding me. Did he run away?"

Acton shrugged. "He didn't look like the type to run from a fire alarm."

"Maybe he went to check on things?" suggested Mai, both hands covering the necklace.

"He's got a phone." Acton pulled his out to confirm it was still working when a second rumble shook them.

"Secondary explosion?" suggested Laura.

"Could be, but I still don't think it's hitting the building. It doesn't feel close enough."

Tommy stared at him. "You can tell?"

Acton chuckled. "Son, I've had so many damn explosions go off around me in the past few years, I can guarantee you this one didn't hit the building we're standing in."

"So then maybe we're safer in here."

The curtain was flung aside before Acton could agree, and a staff member entered saying something in German.

Laura replied in English. "Do you know what's going on?"

The man shook his head. "No, we've just been ordered to evacuate the building, that's all I know. Now, I need you to leave immediately."

"Very well."

They left their booth and the man directed them down the corridor. Acton turned to Laura as he pulled out his phone again. "I'm going to let Hugh know where we're going." He was about to send a text message when he cursed. "I don't have a signal."

"Really?" Laura retrieved her own cellphone from her clutch. "Neither do I."

Acton turned to Tommy, their tech wizard, who already had his own phone out, his thumbs working it furiously. "I'm picking up other signals, so it's not the corridor we're in blocking it. It's the cellular service itself that's out."

"Are we all with the same company?" asked Mai. "Could it just be that they're down?"

Tommy shook his head. "No. We'd just be switched over to another carrier. This is different. It looks like the entire cellular network is down."

They rushed through a set of doors held open by two staff members who directed them toward the stairs. Acton was tempted to rush down them but forced himself to maintain a reasonable pace after noticing Mai struggling to keep up, her dress not designed for running, though Laura wasn't having any issues with hers slit up the side.

"Everybody remain calm. It could still just be an accident."

Another rumble swayed the chandeliers overhead, and he exchanged a concerned look with Laura. They both remained silent, not wanting to worry the others. It could still be an accident, but he doubted it. A series of explosions took out the power and communications, only moments after it appeared over $20 billion had disappeared?

That was too much of a coincidence.

It had to be related, and it meant once again, they might be in the thick of it.

Vienna City Hall, Control Center

Vienna, Austria

Reading cursed as the faint emergency lighting cast a dull glow over the Control Center. All the equipment appeared to be on battery back-up as the displays were still active.

"Just remain calm, people. The generator will kick in within a few seconds," said someone behind them, and within moments, she was proven correct.

Reading pulled out his phone to check on the others, firing off a quick text message, but received an error. He showed the phone to his son. "What the bloody hell does that mean?"

Spencer leaned in then pulled out his own phone. "Cellular service is down."

"This is bullshit." Reading strode over to Vida, huddled in the corner with several of the armed security detail, her back to him. One of the men made eye contact then whispered something. Vida turned and

Reading didn't give her a chance to say anything. "What the devil's going on? We have explosions, power failures, and now communications failures, only moments after twenty-two billion dollars goes missing? There's no way this isn't all connected."

She shook her head. "I have no idea. The building is being evacuated. Perhaps you should go and be with your friends."

Reading dismissed the idea. "This is now a law enforcement matter, and I'm Interpol. I'm going to be staying right here until the local authorities arrive to take over."

"Take over what?"

He stared at her dumbfounded. "The investigation, of course! Don't you get what's happening here? If twenty-two billion has indeed just been stolen, this is the biggest theft in history, and it happened right under all our noses. Everyone in this room is a suspect, because the way your assistant described the security to me, this should be impossible. Someone in here did this, or someone who had access to this room did this."

Vida sighed heavily. "You're right, of course." She glanced at the three men she had been talking to. "Let's go find Mr. Meitner and let him know what's going on." She turned on her heel and headed for the exit as another rumble rippled through the room.

Spencer joined his father, his face flushed with the excitement of the situation. "What are we going to do?"

"We're going to do what we were trained to do. Figure out who's behind this, and help bring them to justice. But first, we need to make sure the others are all right."

Vienna City Hall, East Emergency Exit
Vienna, Austria

Acton's grip on Laura's hand tightened as they emerged into the night. Fires flickered in all directions, thick black smoke billowing upward, merging with the heavily overcast skies threatening rain. He guided them to the side, away from the throngs, now in more of a panic as they witnessed the evidence of what was clearly a major coordinated attack on the city.

"This can't be good." Tommy held his phone up high as he slowly turned. "There are no cellphone signals anywhere in the area."

"No power either," said Acton, just noticing why the fires were so visible.

Laura scanned the crowd. "We need to find Hugh and Spencer."

Acton glanced back at the doors. "Well, they're not going to let us back inside."

"If he couldn't find us here, where would he look for us?"

Acton thought for a moment. "Ultimately, the hotel, I guess."

Laura surveyed the chaos. "Maybe that's where we should go. If this is all about stealing the money, then it might be wise to get away from ground zero. For all we know, they might decide to blow up the building to hide the evidence."

Acton tensed at the idea and glanced at Tommy and Mai, who, despite being adults, he still felt responsible for. "The hotel is quite the distance from here, and there's no way we're going to get a taxi. The police will cordon off the area any minute now."

"What about our limo?" asked Tommy. "It should be nearby."

Laura glanced back at the entrance. "The driver said to just text him when we were ready and he'd be at the VIP entrance within a few minutes. That means he has to be parked nearby." She flagged an employee. "Where is the VIP entrance?"

"You have to get out of here now!" replied the flustered woman.

Laura remained calm. "That's what we're trying to do. Where is the VIP entrance?"

The woman pointed to their left, then resumed ushering the thinning crowd away from the building.

"Let's get moving," urged Acton. "I don't want to be around this place any longer than I have to."

Laura placed a hand on his shoulder, steadying herself. "Just a second." She raised her right foot and twisted the heel off, then did the same with the other.

Mai's eyes shot wide. "Oh, I forgot!" She quickly removed her own heels as Acton and Tommy both stared in amazement.

"I didn't know you could do that."

Laura rolled her eyes at Mai. "Men."

Mai giggled.

Acton gave them both looks. "What? You think you know every secret about men?"

"Yes," they both echoed.

"Your sex is an open book," added Laura.

Acton shook his head. "Okay, you know the opening on the front of men's underwear?"

Mai nodded.

"You know what it's there for?"

She blushed. "Well, it's so that…"

"Oh God, James, don't make her say it," admonished Laura. "It's so that you can stick your little guy through it and pee standing up."

Acton glanced at Tommy. "Tell them."

Tommy grinned. "We don't use it."

Both women stared at them. "Then why the hell's it there?" asked Laura.

Acton shrugged. "No idea. But I think I've made my point."

"Fine." Laura held up her detached heels. "It's a new invention. You need to watch more Shark Tank." She pointed in the direction the staff member had indicated for the VIP entrance. "Now, let's get moving. And as soon as we get back to the hotel, I'm Googling why the hell men's underwear have an opening that they don't use." She gave him the eye. "I hope I don't find out it's just because my husband and the company he keeps"—she cast the eye over at Tommy—"are merely uncouth."

"Hon, you already know that." He gave her a toothy smile then gently jabbed Tommy on the shoulder. "Better uncouth than all that fumbling, heh?"

They proceeded across the front of the building as the conversation continued, the distraction keeping them all calm. They rounded the side and Laura pointed at an entrance. "That looks more familiar, doesn't it?"

Acton agreed then glanced at Tommy. "Any signal?"

"Nope."

Acton cursed. "Then we can't text our driver."

Another explosion, this one the closest yet, erupted on the street running in front of City Hall. Acton grabbed Laura and swung her so his body shielded her, as Tommy did the same with Mai.

The blast quickly subsided, leaving behind the screams, which were far more disturbing. Acton urged them all forward. "Okay, we're definitely getting the hell out of here. That was closer for a reason." They jogged toward the entrance and Acton flagged a staff member who had a small hand-held radio. "Where are the VIP cars?"

"What's your name?"

"Professor James Acton."

The man held the radio to his mouth. "Bring the car for Professor James Acton around."

"It'll probably be under my wife's name, Professor Laura Palmer."

The man relayed the additional information, then turned to them. "We're doing the best we can. We pulled these old radios out of storage when all of our communications went down. We've got all the drivers in a group. I radio my partner, he calls out the name, and the driver gets his car then brings it here. It's slow, but it's working. You hopefully won't have too long to wait."

"Where are the drivers?"

"Just around the corner."

Acton stared at the line of cars and the panicked VIPs waiting to get in them. He turned to the man. "Call him off. We'll go to him."

"Are you sure?"

"Yes, I don't want to get stuck in this mess. Not when they're detonating bombs a few hundred feet away."

The man relayed the cancelation and Acton took Laura's hand. "Let's go."

They continued along the side of the building and rounded the corner where they found a large group of chauffeurs in a huddle, everyone appearing nervous as screams and sirens from the front of the building echoed.

Acton raised his hand. "I'm looking for Kristoph, the driver of Professors James Acton and Laura Palmer!"

A hand shot up in the middle of the crowd. "Right here, sir!"

The crowd parted and their driver, Kristoph, emerged. "I'm glad to see you're safe, sir." His eyes narrowed. "Weren't there six of you?"

"The other two were in the control room when this started. They're both law enforcement, so we'll just have to trust that they're all right. Can you get us to the hotel?"

"Absolutely. I'll get the car." He pointed to a cleared area. "Wait for me there."

"Okay."

Kristoph rushed off and Acton led them to the indicated section of the parking lot when he noticed activity to his left. "What the hell?"

Vienna City Hall, Ground Floor

Vienna, Austria

Reading headed down a long corridor, Spencer at his side. The last explosion was close. Too close. The Control Center had been ordered evacuated and the alarm, now blaring over the speakers, was rapid, an all-personnel evacuation order now broadcasting. His concern for his friends was growing. He wasn't sure what was going on yet, but he had little doubt everything was to sow confusion after the massive theft.

He turned to Wagner, who had briefed them on the security. "Your thoughts on this being an inside job?"

Wagner shook his head. "Absolutely not. Everybody was vetted. The security team crawled up everyone's ass for months. I had friends from ten years ago getting phone calls about me. There's no way it was an inside job."

"So then, it was outside. Hackers?"

Again, Wagner shook his head as they continued down the corridor. "Impossible. Closed system. We only had one open connection, and that was directly to Mr. Meitner's bank. Everything else was being phoned in. This was as secure as it can get, which means…" The man paused.

"Which means?" prompted Reading.

"Which means it had to be an inside job," finished Spencer.

Wagner sighed. "You're right. It has to be an inside job, but I have no clue who it could possibly be. We've all been working together for months on this, and like I said, we've all been vetted. And besides, this isn't just somebody hacking from the inside. You heard those explosions. That's terrorism. Doesn't that mean there have to be people outside that are involved?"

Reading agreed. "And more than one person means a conspiracy."

"Or hired hands," suggested Spencer.

Wagner shook his head. "But what about the bombs? It's one thing to hire some thugs, but how do you get explosives?"

"You can get them," said Reading. "If you know the right people."

"But how would anybody working for Mr. Meitner know people like that?"

"They shouldn't, however, your security people might. And a lot of them could be ex-military, ex-Special Forces. They might have contacts."

"Would former soldiers do that?"

"Most mercenaries are former soldiers. Just because you're a soldier doesn't mean you're automatically a good person. There are always bad seeds in every population, but it also doesn't mean you can't fall on hard times and take desperate action. And your share of twenty-two billion could be a lot of temptation. The real tell will be what we find outside."

"What do you mean?"

"I mean, what are those explosions targeting? If it's mass casualties, then I'm guessing terrorism. If they're limited to electrical and communications infrastructure, then that's more likely private guns for hire. A good man who's fallen on hard times might commit a crime, but he's not going to intentionally target the innocent. It would go against all of his training."

They emerged into the cool crisp air, police, fire, and ambulance arriving, the crowds directed away from the building and down the streets by staff and emergency personnel. Reading stopped at the bottom of the steps, scanning the crowd for Acton and the others. His eyes came to rest on a chilling scene on the roadway in front of the complex just as Spencer pointed at the same area.

"Look!"

Dozens were down, the smoldering wreck of a car proof of the cause. A car bomb had been detonated, likely the last large explosion they had felt, which changed the equation. This was a mass casualty event. This was either terrorism, or a theft so brazen that those behind it didn't care who was hurt. All they cared about was getting away with the money.

Wagner was beside himself. "Why do this?"

"Because they're little shites who don't give a damn about innocent lives," spat Spencer.

Reading shook his head. "No, think about it. The money had already been stolen when they shut down the power and communications. Right now, nobody is after the money. They don't even know it's missing unless they were in that control room. By now, whoever took it has transferred it to hundreds if not thousands of different accounts around the world, and the mules are already being used to withdraw the cash. Targeting those people wasn't necessary."

"Like I said, they're pieces of shit."

"I won't disagree with you there, son, but there's something else going on. We said this is an inside job, which means someone in that control room was involved." He jabbed a finger toward the slaughter. "That's the distraction. As soon as that went off, all the emergency services focused their attention there, so that whoever is behind this could make their escape." He turned to Wagner. "There are no cars here, and they're not going to escape on foot. Where would they go?"

Wagner shrugged. "I have no idea. Beyond the control room and the main stage, I haven't really seen much."

"What about where we were dropped off?" suggested Spencer.

Reading shook his head. "No, but you might be onto something. The limo driver said to text him and he'd be there in a couple of minutes. That means there's a staging area for all the vehicles."

Wagner's eye shot wide. "I know where that is. It's in the back." He glanced back at the doors, now blocked by several police officers. "I guess we're not going that way. We'll have to go around the outside."

Reading held out a hand. "Lead the way."

Vienna City Hall, West Side Parking Lot

Vienna, Austria

Acton pointed toward what had caught his attention. "Isn't that Azar Vida?"

"Who?" asked Tommy.

"The woman in charge of the entire show."

Laura's eyes shot wide. "I think it is!"

They all stared as Vida strode swiftly toward a vehicle, surrounded by several men in suits, all with chiseled features that suggested ex-military. An SUV sat idling by the curb and they all climbed in, the doors slamming shut. The vehicle surged away, toward the rear gate leading to the street that ran across the back of the complex.

Acton shook his head. "That doesn't look right."

Laura agreed. "That's like the captain abandoning his ship before his crew."

"And why would that many security personnel be with her when they only assigned one for the necklace?" asked Mai.

"Something's wrong here." Acton jabbed a finger toward the SUV. "I think somebody stole the money, and she's in on it."

Laura stared at him. "That's a bold accusation."

"You disagree?"

"Oh, I agree, but we can't accuse her of that without any evidence."

"We need to follow her to see where she goes. It could be completely innocent, but if she is behind this, she could be the only one who can get the twenty billion back. The futures of millions of lives depend on it."

Their chauffeur arrived in an SUV with the window rolled down. "I hope you don't mind, but since there were only four of you and the limo was boxed in, I switched vehicles with another one from my company."

Acton smiled. "This is perfect. Now, get out."

Kristoph's eyebrows shot up. "Pardon me?"

"Get out. We need the vehicle to follow somebody who might be behind what's going on. No time to explain. Get another vehicle and bring them back to the hotel." He jerked a thumb over his shoulder at Tommy and Mai.

Kristoph climbed out. "Are you sure you want to be chasing after these people, sir? The radio says there have been at least a dozen explosions all across the city."

Acton turned to Laura, the better driver of the two of them. "Are you able to drive in that?"

Laura reached down and tore the bottom half of her dress off, wincing at the sound. "I'm so sorry, Chantal, but your dress, as beautiful as it was, never fit my lifestyle."

Acton grinned and turned to Tommy and Mai. "Get back to the hotel, and as long as it's safe to remain, stay there. Hugh and Spencer will probably try to contact us there. Tell them what happened."

"Yes, sir," said Tommy. "Be careful. These people are dangerous."

Acton grunted. "They always are." He jumped in the passenger seat and Laura gunned them across the parking lot toward the rear entrance, where half a dozen vehicles were lined up to go through the security checkpoint. He pointed. "That's them! They're about to go through!"

Laura kept barreling toward the line-up. "If we wait our turn, we'll lose them."

Acton searched for an alternative as Vida's SUV pulled onto the street. Accelerating swiftly, Laura jerked the wheel to the left, taking them directly toward the guardhouse. "You're not planning on doing what I think you're doing?"

She hammered on the gas. "And just what is it that you think I'm doing, darling?"

"Assuming that every guardhouse is actually just a flimsy shed like in Hollywood movies?"

She jerked the wheel to the left again, putting them into what normally would be on-coming traffic, and blasted through the entrance gate, left open for emergency vehicles. She hammered on the brakes, cranking the wheel hard to the left as they careened onto the city street, then floored it again, sending them barreling after Vida and her accomplices, captors, or innocent men escorting their charge to safety. He was of mixed feelings as to who he hoped they were chasing. If Vida were innocent in all this, then they weren't placing themselves in danger, but it meant the guilty party was still out there, and $20 billion meant to help the less fortunate in the world was permanently gone.

But if Vida were involved, there might still be a chance to recover what was stolen.

Vienna City Hall, West Side Parking Lot

Vienna, Austria

Reading rushed around the corner, his chest burning from the effort. His desk job at Interpol was not keeping him in shape. At least with Scotland Yard, he was usually on his feet all day, visiting crime scenes, interviewing witnesses. He got his 10,000 steps in a day back then, though, as Spencer had explained to him, that was a bullshit number made up by a Japanese marketing company decades ago to advertise their fancy new pedometer. Regardless of the number's relevance, he'd be surprised if he did a thousand steps a day now. Every time his friends got him into a situation like this, he swore he'd get in better shape, but inevitably found himself exhausted at the end of the day, sitting in front of the TV on the couch, eating some takeout or munching on a bag of crisps.

He rounded the corner and stopped, bending over and grabbing his knees as he gasped for breath.

Spencer skidded to a halt. "Are you all right?"

"Just give me a minute," gasped Reading, pointing toward a group of chauffeurs. "See if you can find our chauffeur, and if anybody knows if the others came through here. I'll be with you in a minute."

Spencer sprinted toward the gathered drivers with Wagner. Reading stood straight, shoving his chest forward, expanding his lungs as much as he could as he inhaled deeply through his nose and exhaled through his mouth, his breathing slowly coming under control, the burning in his chest easing. He forced himself forward, though walked this time.

"Mr. Reading!" shouted someone.

He turned to see Tommy and Mai waving, and breathed a sigh of relief that at least two of those he felt responsible for were safe. He hurried over to them, his head on a swivel as he searched for his friends. "Are you two all right?"

Tommy nodded. "A little shook up, but we're fine."

"Where are Jim and Laura?"

Tommy pointed at the road and an SUV accelerating loudly. "That's them there."

Reading watched the SUV race out of sight. "Where the hell are they going?"

"We saw that woman, umm, Azar Vida, I think her name was, leave with some of the security team. The professors thought that was suspicious, so they decided to follow her."

Reading cursed as he scratched his chin. "That *is* suspicious. Why the hell would she be leaving in the middle of a crisis when twenty-two billion was stolen under her watch?"

Wagner's jaw dropped. "Could she be the inside man?"

Reading turned to him. "The head of the entire show was actually the thief?" Something clicked, a memory from earlier in the evening. "How long has she been with the team?"

Wagner's eyes shot wide. "That's right! She was a last-minute replacement. She's only been here a couple of weeks."

"What happened to her predecessor?"

"She was killed in a car accident."

"That sounds like quite the coincidence."

Spencer's eyes narrowed and he nodded toward Mai. "Where's the security guard for that thing?"

"He disappeared when the alarm sounded," explained Mai.

Reading frowned. "It almost sounds as if the entire security team, or a good portion of it, might be involved. I highly recommend you take that off and put it somewhere out of sight."

Mai's face slackened. "I hadn't thought of that." She turned her back to Tommy, who fumbled once again before finally succeeding in removing the necklace. She opened her clutch and Tommy deposited the priceless piece inside as a limo pulled up and the driver stepped out. Reading recognized him as their chauffeur from the beginning of the evening.

"Ah. There you are. I was beginning to worry," said Kristoph. "Shall I get you back to your hotel?"

Reading pointed to his three companions. "Get them to the hotel. I'll be remaining here."

Spencer gave him a look. "Bollocks to that! I'm staying with you. A crime has been committed, and we're the only two witnesses that aren't civilians."

Reading's chest swelled with pride and he patted his son on the back. "All right then. Take them to the hotel." Reading turned to Tommy and Mai. "Go to your room and stay there as long as it's safe to. This is Vienna, not Cairo. If the authorities say to leave, then leave, and follow their instructions. Keep your cellphones with you. Make sure they're charged if you've got power to do so. Eventually, they'll get service restored, but if we don't hear from each other within twelve hours, we meet outside the American Embassy."

Mai stared at him, her eyes saucers. "Do you really think it's that bad?"

Reading shook his head. "Not at all. I think the danger is probably over, and this was all a distraction. If Vida is behind it, she's gone. My only concern is that power and communications might take some time to restore, depending on how bad the damage was and how extensive it was. I have no doubt they'll have it rerouted long before tomorrow morning. It's just a precaution." He pointed a finger at Tommy. "But you, you are my research department. As soon as you've got access, I need you to pull everything you can find on Meitner, his family, his company, the charities he was giving money to, anything you can think of. We need to find out who's behind this and why."

"I thought you said Vida was behind it?"

Reading shook his head. "No, she's involved, but I don't believe she's in charge. I think our best lead is the security team. If we find out who chose them and who vetted them, we might get a better sense of who's actually behind this and why." He turned to Kristoph. "Get them to the hotel safely."

"You can count on me, sir. As soon as I've dropped them off, I'll come back for you."

"That won't be necessary."

"Just the same. I'll be here if you need a driver."

Reading smiled. "I appreciate that." He turned to Mai. "When you get back to the hotel, lock the necklace in the room safe."

"Doesn't the hotel have a safe? Maybe it'd be safer there," suggested Tommy.

Reading shook his head. "The moment you hand that over, people in the hotel will know, and it could become a temptation. Things that expensive usually come with a guard for a reason. Right now, the safest bet is to just put it in the room safe and don't let anybody know you have it."

Mai held her clutch tight to her chest. "What if someone comes for it?"

"If someone comes to steal it, then give it to them. The necklace isn't worth dying over. And if it's one of Meitner's people, ask for proof. If you're not satisfied, demand to speak to Meitner himself."

"I think he might be dead," said Tommy.

"What are you talking about?"

"Well, he collapsed on the stage. His butler, or whatever you call him, came out, whispered something in his ear and he collapsed. He was probably telling him about the money." Tommy paused. "What did happen to the money? Was it actually stolen, like the professors think?"

"It looks that way. Twenty-two billion dollars seems to have vanished." Reading noticed Mai's knuckles were white as she gripped her handbag, and he put an arm over her shoulders. "Don't worry, my dear, nobody's coming after the necklace. Hardly anybody knows you have it. This has nothing to do with that piece of jewelry. Even if it's worth twenty-five million dollars, they were after twenty-five billion."

Mai's eyes shot wide. "Oh my God! Do you think it's worth twenty-five million dollars?"

Reading chuckled, regretting giving a number and having made things worse. "No, I don't believe it is. But with the rich, who the hell knows. Just keep it in your handbag, get to the hotel, put it in the safe, and forget about it. You two have more important things to do than worry about that piece of jewelry. Remember, it's not your job to protect it. It's the guard who was assigned to it."

"And he buggered off," muttered Spencer.

Reading turned to Kristoph. "Get them to the hotel. Now."

"Yes, sir." Kristoph opened the rear door and Tommy helped Mai inside then followed. They both gave Reading weak smiles and waved as the limo pulled away.

Reading turned his attention to more pressing matters. "We need to find out who's in charge here, and tell them what we know. I'm worried Jim and Laura don't realize how serious the situation is. These people have already killed, and they won't hesitate to kill again to get away with twenty-two billion dollars."

Vienna, Austria

February 19, 1941

Daniel sat up with a start, listening to the still of the night for what had woken him, but heard nothing. He lay back down, closing his eyes, and drifted off again, sandwiched between his parents. This was his favorite part, waking up in the middle of the night, his parents sound asleep on either side of him, their breathing so heavy, so comforting.

His heart hammered as he realized it wasn't something he had heard that woke him. It was something that he hadn't.

His parents weren't breathing.

He pushed up on one elbow, listening to his mother, but heard nothing. He reached out and touched her. His hand recoiled. She felt cold. He leaped up on his knees and shook her. "Mother, wake up!" But there was no reply, not even a groan of protest. He spun around. "Father, wake up, there's something wrong with Mother!"

But there was no response from him either.

"Daniel?"

His heart nearly stopped and he sprang to his feet, pressing his back against the headboard as he put as much distance between him and the voice as he could manage.

"Daniel, it's me, Uncle Peter."

Daniel raced across the bed and leaped into the air toward the black mass standing in the doorway. His uncle caught him and held him tight. "There's something wrong with Mother and Father!"

"I know, Daniel. It's all going…it's going to be all right." Peter put him down in the hallway. "You stay here." Peter entered the bedroom and the light flickered on. Daniel peered around the doorframe and watched as Peter placed two fingers on his mother's neck then did the same with his father before straightening the bedding. He made the sign of the cross, and Daniel's eyebrows shot up his forehead at the Catholic gesture.

Is Uncle Peter not Jewish?

Peter turned off the light and stepped into the hallway. "Let's go to your bedroom and get dressed."

"What about Mother and Father?"

"They are in a better place now, and they've arranged for you to go to a better place."

"Where?"

"America, if all goes well. We must leave now. You must do everything I say. No hesitation. No questions. Understood?"

Daniel nodded.

"Good, then let's get to your bedroom and get dressed. We're going outside, so dress warm."

Daniel hurried toward his bedroom. He flicked his light on and his jaw dropped. All of his clothes were laid out on the bed. A small suitcase sat open beside them with a little package sitting atop, wrapped in brown paper and tied with a string. He stepped over and saw something written on it.

For Daniel, when he is safe.

It was his mother's handwriting.

"Quickly now, get dressed," said Peter from behind him. Daniel scrambled out of his pajamas then put on the clothes his mother had laid out as Peter took the small package and sniffed. Daniel glanced up at him and saw the man wipe a tear from his eye before returning it to the suitcase and snapping it shut. Daniel was soon dressed, and Peter turned off the light. "Now we're going to go to my house. You remember where that is?"

"Yes, Uncle."

"Good. If something should happen and we get separated, you go to my house, understood?"

"Yes, Uncle."

They stepped out the front door and into the hallway, Daniel gripping his little suitcase tightly. The door clicked shut then Peter led him by the hand to the stairwell, their footfalls echoing loudly. Peter stopped then bent down and slipped his shoes off. He picked them up in one hand then lifted Daniel up with his other arm. They headed swiftly and silently down the stairs to the ground floor. Peter put him down then slipped his shoes back on. He bent over and whispered in his ear.

"Now, I need you to stay completely silent. Do exactly what I say. No questions, no hesitation. Understood?"

Daniel nodded, his lips pressed together tightly, and Peter smiled at him in the pale moonlight. "You're a good boy." Peter took him by the hand and they stepped out onto the street, the street he hadn't been on in ages.

Peter took the suitcase, and as he led them toward his home, Daniel glanced over his shoulder toward where his best friend had died, shot along with his parents by the Nazis simply for being Jewish. He couldn't fathom why anybody would hate people just because they were a member of a religion.

They walked quickly for five or ten minutes, how long, Daniel wasn't certain. At each intersection, Peter would have them stop and listen, peering around every corner before proceeding. His uncle stepped out into the street, checking both ways, and extended his hand toward Daniel when somebody shouted, "Halt!"

Peter's eyes bulged. "Hide!" he hissed.

Daniel stood frozen in fear as footfalls rushed toward them, echoing down the empty street. Then he remembered what he had been told.

Do everything I say. No questions. No hesitation.

He turned and darted into a doorway as Peter raised his hands, facing the oncoming soldiers. Two men rushed up, their rifles aimed at Peter.

"What are you doing out after curfew?"

"I'm an apothecary. I had to deliver medicine to one of my customers. It was an emergency."

"Identification!"

Peter reached into his pocket and produced his papers, handing them over to one of the guards who slung his rifle.

"You know the penalty for being out after curfew?"

"Yes, sir. Of course, but it was a matter of life and death. A friend of mine who's a doctor had a patient that was having heart problems. He called my home and begged me to deliver the medicine, otherwise his patient would die."

"And just who was this patient?"

Peter hesitated. "I really shouldn't say."

A gun barrel was shoved against his chest.

"You dare refuse to answer?"

Peter vehemently shook his head. "No, no, I'm not refusing. I'm just saying the patient might not want it known he has heart problems."

"I don't care what the patient wants! You'll give me a name and you'll give it to me now, or I'm going to shoot you where you stand."

Peter's shoulders slumped. "Very well, but I highly recommend you don't repeat this to anyone."

The rifle was pressed harder.

"It was Reichsstatthalter von Schirach."

Both men stepped back at once.

"Now you see why I didn't want to say the name."

The soldier doing the questioning lowered his weapon slightly. "Why wouldn't he use a German doctor and apothecary?"

Peter leaned in slightly, lowering his voice. "Do you think he wants High Command to know he has heart troubles? His staff arranged an outside doctor so that nothing would go on the official record. If you report me being out after curfew, then there might be an investigation, and his secret might be revealed."

"Stay right where you are." The two soldiers stepped away and a huddled, whispered conversation was held for a few moments before the second rifle was slung and Peter's papers were handed over. "Get home now, and don't let us see you out again."

"Yes, sir. Thank you, sir." Peter turned and hurried away, and Daniel's heart pounded as the man disappeared from sight. The soldiers stood there for a moment, talking among themselves about what they had just heard, then finally turned around and headed in the opposite direction. Daniel remained hidden in the doorway until their footfalls could no longer be heard, then wondered what he should do before remembering he had already been told.

If something should happen and we get separated, you go to my house.

He stepped tentatively back onto the road and peered in both directions. The soldiers were nowhere to be seen. He scurried off after Peter, struggling to remember where the man lived. He had been there many times with his family, but not since the Nazis had arrived, and then it was always in the light of day when they went. If it were dark on the way home, he was usually asleep in his father's arms. It wasn't far, because they always walked, even in the winter, so he had to be close, as they had already come some distance before the soldiers interfered.

He sprinted in what he hoped was the right direction, then skidded to a halt as he noticed how loud his steps were echoing. He remembered what Peter had done in the stairwell. He slipped off his shoes and picked them up, running silently in his socks, pausing at each intersection as he had seen Peter do. He darted across yet another street, and as he passed an alleyway, a figure emerged from the shadows, grabbing him.

Vienna City Hall, East Side Courtyard

Vienna, Austria

Present Day

Inspector Felix Winter stood back, surveying the scene, his hands on his hips as he shook his head. He had never seen carnage like this before. Not in Vienna. Things like this weren't supposed to happen here. It was like a war zone. The car that had detonated was torn apart, shrapnel spread in every direction, the pavement scorched, the dead and wounded strewn about. Ambulance crews were just arriving, the power outage in the area causing traffic gridlock. By the last count, there had been thirteen detonations throughout the city, and initial reports were that they all targeted communications and electrical infrastructure. Cellphone service was out, power was out, and even their police radios were overwhelmed.

There were some reported injuries and a couple of deaths at the other sites, but this was the only one that intentionally targeted civilians. The briefing he had received on the way here indicated a charity event had been underway when the first detonations went off. He had heard about the event, of course, but had paid it little mind. It was just rich people being rich, showing off to their friends. He was quite certain there were so many strings attached to the ceremonially transferred money that, in the end, most of it would line pockets rather than help people.

He had seen it before. His family had struggled. Growing up, life hadn't been easy, the institutions that were supposed to be there to help families like his so underfunded that he had lost any faith he had in the charity of others. When people in BMWs are pulling up to food banks, you know there's a problem with the system.

It was why he had become a police officer. Police could actually help people. They made a difference. They and other frontline workers like fire and paramedics, doctors and nurses, were in the heat of a daily battle, holding back that line of chaos with little help from the system meant to support them all. But the system was a mess, overpaid bureaucrats with their paperwork stymying everyone at every turn.

He had grown up with the European Union, so he knew no different, though his father and his grandfather hadn't, and spoke wistfully of the days when things ran far more efficiently. But those days were long gone. Brussels had a firm grip on the entire continent, and Brussels loved its forms. The American Constitution was under 5000 words. The European Union's was over 60,000.

And it got worse from there.

He sighed, imagining the amount of paperwork he'd have to file when this was over. He pointed at one of the uniformed officers he recognized. "Gunther!"

Gunther waved then jogged over. "Inspector, quite the mess, isn't it?"

Winter frowned. "That's one way of putting it. What can you tell me?"

"We were assigned to perimeter security. We heard something, wasn't sure what it was, then the power went out and almost immediately the evacuation alarm sounded for the building."

Winter regarded him. "How soon after?"

Gunther shrugged. "I don't even think it was a minute."

"Now, that's odd, isn't it?"

"What do you mean?"

"I mean, you don't evacuate a building immediately, just because the power goes out after an explosion in the distance."

"No, I suppose not. Do you think they knew something we didn't know out here? Maybe there was a bomb threat phoned in."

"Could be. We'll have to check that out. Have you found anyone in charge yet?"

Gunther shook his head. "Nobody. Everybody just came streaming out of all the exits, and we were directing them away from the building, then this thing went off and everything turned to shit. Seven dead, dozens wounded."

"All right, tell everyone to fan out and start questioning the crowd. We need to find somebody who was actually involved in organizing this thing, not just attending it."

"Yes, sir." Gunther stepped away, calling the other officers over and giving them their instructions.

"Sir!"

Winter turned to see his partner, Hans Strobl, running up. "I was beginning to wonder if you would make it."

Strobl rolled his eyes. "It's a nightmare out there." His eyes bulged as he finally noticed the carnage around him. "What the hell happened here?"

"Car bomb." Winter pointed toward the building. "We need to find somebody in charge."

Strobl hesitated. "Do you think it's wise to go inside? There could be another bomb."

Winter shook his head. "No. If they had a bomb inside, they would have detonated it. They blew up a car out front instead, and they did that after people were evacuating. That tells me they wanted casualties, so if they could have gotten a bomb inside, they would have. They would have killed a lot more."

"Maybe it was just terrorists sending a message to the rich and famous."

"Then why all the other detonations? Why this power outage? Why are communications out? Something else is going on here, and we need to find someone in charge to see what the hell happened. The building has been evacuated, so we're not going to find them inside. Start going through the crowds and see if you can find someone."

"You got it." Strobl headed back in the direction he had come where a crowd was gathered. Winter surveyed the area, his trained eye going over everything, first focusing on any other vehicles in sight, his fear that a second might be rigged to target first responders. This would be a nightmare to work, and right now, he didn't even have a suspect or witness to interview.

He spotted a notorious British sportscar parked nearby, its lights flashing, its hood up. He spotted Gunther. "Gunther! What's the story?" He pointed at the car.

Gunther dismissed it with a wave. "That's nothing. I saw the guy limp up earlier. Engine's blown. What did he expect?"

Winter laughed, happy he couldn't afford such nonsense. His Volkswagen kept him happy. He resumed his survey, and as he slowly turned, taking in the scene, he spotted three people swiftly crossing the square in front of the building. One was late-fifties, early-sixties, another in his thirties, and the third in his twenties, whose gait matched the older man.

Father and son?

Whoever they were, the older man had a bearing that suggested he was accustomed to being in charge.

Another rich, entitled person I now need to deal with.

The man raised his hand. "Does anybody here speak English?"

Everyone turned their head. He produced an ID. "I'm Agent Hugh Reading from Interpol. I need to speak to whoever's in charge."

Winter's eyebrows rose.

Well, that changes things.

Winter halted his survey and headed toward the man. "I'm Inspector Winter. What's Interpol doing here so soon? I just got here myself."

Reading extended a hand and he shook it. "I'm not here officially. I was attending the gala with my son and some friends."

Winter's eyebrows rose. "Interpol must pay far better than the Austrian Federal Police."

Reading chuckled. "Don't let the tuxedo fool you. I'm just a poor working man like you. My friends, however, are ridiculously wealthy."

"So, you were here when it happened?"

"We were the proverbial flies on the wall."

"Good. Most witnesses aren't trained observers. I always prefer when there's a professional I can talk to. What can you tell me?"

"My son, who's a London Police Officer, and I, decided to observe what was going on in the control room rather than watch the gala itself. Are you aware of what was happening here tonight?"

"Peripherally. Publicity stunts don't really interest me."

Reading grunted. "Me neither, which is why we were in the control room rather than witnessing the spectacle. Mr. Meitner was donating twenty-five billion of his wealth to over one-hundred charities tonight, and during the transfer of the funds, something went wrong."

Winter's eyes narrowed. "The transfer of the funds? You mean, he actually was giving away the money, not just creating some sort of fund that he directed, or his descendants directed?"

Reading shook his head. "No, no, no, this was completely legit. He was transferring the money directly into the charity accounts, and then it would be up to them to do with it as they saw fit. While this was a publicity stunt, it was meant to encourage other well-heeled people to donate in a similar fashion. But when the money started to transfer, it didn't arrive in the charity accounts, but it did leave his account. According to Wagner here, who was one of the staff in the room, hacking the system should have been impossible unless it was done from the inside. Two of my friends, the ones who are stupidly wealthy and run toward danger far too often, spotted the woman in charge leaving the building with several of her security team just after everything fell apart."

"Did they see where this woman went?"

"No, but they followed her."

Winter's eyebrows shot up. "Your friends followed her? What would possess them to do that?"

"They're rather unique individuals." Reading pointed toward the back of the building. "They went onto the street that goes across the back then went left. They're in a black SUV. So were Azar Vida and her security detail. I need you to put out a call to have your people watch for them and intercept. My friends aren't armed, and if they catch up to them..."

Winter's head bobbed as Reading's voice trailed off, obviously concerned for his friends. Something tweaked. "You say they aren't armed as if they normally are."

Reading's son snorted, his father explaining. "My friends have a security detail for when they're in dangerous countries. It's led by an ex-Special Air Service colonel. They've been trained in hand-to-hand combat, weapons, tactics, and have been in more combat situations than most soldiers. Like I said, they're unique individuals."

Winter shook his head. "I can't wait to meet them." He beckoned his partner over. "Hans, contact dispatch and have everyone on the lookout for two black SUVs heading south from City Hall. Lead vehicle might have armed suspects. If they're spotted, wait for backup before engaging."

"Copy that." Strobl stepped away, using one of the patrol officers' radio to call in the information.

Winter returned his attention to the Interpol agent. "What else can you tell me?"

Reading shook his head. "You're not going to believe this, but right now, it appears twenty-two billion dollars has been stolen, and unless we can catch who's behind it, could be gone permanently."

Margareten Street

Vienna, Austria

"Don't get too close."

Laura eased off the gas a little at Acton's warning. She had a lead foot but was an expert driver, having raced her brother's Porsche on tracks for years before it was torn to shreds by an Apache helicopter piloted by one of their good friends. She had never replaced it, considering it a frivolous indulgence, though with the lives they led, there were no shortage of opportunities for her to put her skills to the test.

"They've slowed down," she said. "They don't seem to be trying to escape anymore."

Acton had to agree. "Looks like they're trying to blend in and not bring attention to themselves." He looked back as they went through a green light. "How many is that?"

Laura glanced at him. "What do you mean?"

"I mean, after we got out of the power outage area, have we hit a single red light?"

Laura stared ahead then jutted her chin forward. "Lots of reds ahead." As soon as the words were out of her mouth, the next light turned green and the SUV they were tailing sailed through and she followed a few seconds later as the light turned yellow.

"That was rather short. Don't get too far behind, or we might lose them."

"Don't get too close, don't get too far behind, make up your mind."

He chuckled. "Yeah, yeah, okay, you're driving." The next light turned green then red a few seconds later. "Now, there's no way that's right. Somebody's controlling these lights."

"Multiple detonations, twenty-plus billion possibly stolen, traffic lights under control. Just who the hell is behind this? This is Dylan-level stuff."

"Careful," warned Acton, pointing ahead at a car about to cut them off, but Laura had already spotted the offender and gunned her engine as she switched lanes, surging through another yellow light. She was right. This was a large operation, timed literally to the second. It was exactly the type of operation he had seen being run by his former student, CIA Special Agent Dylan Kane. The question was whether this was a private operation with large amounts of money, or government.

"I can't see it being government," said Laura, and he smiled slightly. Sometimes he thought they shared one brain. And with their propensity to do things exactly like what they were doing right now, some might agree for the wrong reasons.

"No, I don't think so either. Twenty billion's a lot of money, but any country that's poor enough to need it, probably couldn't pull off an operation like this. It has to be an inside job."

"If it's an inside job, then who?"

"No idea. How much of the company does Meitner still own?"

Laura shrugged. "No clue, but I do remember reading an article a few years ago that he was slowly divesting himself of most of his interests. I guess we know why."

"So that donating all his money wouldn't require a massive sell-off that might hurt the company."

Laura gunned the engine again, barreling through another yellow light. "I think they might be on to us."

Acton stared ahead at Vida's vehicle. It appeared to be traveling at the same speed as it had been all along. "What makes you say that?"

"The timing is getting shorter. Whoever is controlling the lights might have access to the traffic cameras as well, and spotted us."

"Maybe we should back off and let them go. This could be getting too risky."

She shook her head. "No, they haven't reacted yet in the vehicle. Whoever's controlling things might just think we're taking advantage of the lights."

Acton pursed his lips. "Okay, let's keep going, but the moment we see them react, we get the hell out of here and leave it to the authorities. We've proven our point."

"What do you mean?"

"We were following her to see if she was involved, and now we know she is."

"Do we?"

"Somebody is controlling the lights. There's no way that happens for innocent people."

Laura cursed at herself. "You're right. I can't believe I didn't pick up on that. I was so excited about the chase, I forgot what we were actually doing here. We still should try to see where they're going though, agreed?"

Acton pulled out his phone and launched the maps app, then noticed the bars at the top of the screen. "Hey, I've got a signal again."

"Text Hugh and the others. Let them know where we are and what we're doing."

Acton's thumbs flew over the keyboard, first sending a message to Reading, then another one to Tommy and Mai. "Done." He returned to the maps. "If we keep going straight on this road, it looks like we'll come to a highway that rings the city. That could take us anywhere in Europe eventually."

"So, that means the only way we'll know where they're going is if we keep following them. This is where I wish we had someone like Leroux with his eyes in the sky."

Acton's eyebrow shot up. "Why the hell don't we try and see if we can get him to help?" He launched the secure app on his phone Kane had installed for emergencies just like this. He wrote as succinct a message as he could, explaining what was happening, then sent it. "Hopefully, Dylan isn't incommunicado, otherwise we might not hear from him for days." He leaned back, resting his head and frowning as he noticed the last couple of lights Laura had surged through were red, the green merely lasting a split second. There was no doubt now that whoever was the puppet master here was aware they had picked up a tail. Yet the vehicle in front still didn't react, as their handlers attempted to lose them with the traffic lights.

Laura blasted through another red and they both cursed as the vehicle ahead of them accelerated rapidly, quickly leaving them behind. She hammered on the gas but Acton waved her off. "No, it's too dangerous. You're going through red lights. We've been lucky so far, but somebody could get killed."

She sighed heavily and eased off the gas, then a smile spread as she pointed ahead. "Look!"

Phuket, Thailand

CIA Special Agent Dylan Kane groaned in pleasure as Chantana, a masseuse he had known for years, worked her magic. Things were a little different since he had seen her last, however. He was in a committed relationship, and though he might have to stray while on the job, decompression time between missions didn't count. She had been disappointed when she had stepped into the room and dropped her robe, revealing a ridonculous body that she was about to cover in oil and rub all over him. The little guy had threatened to salute, and he didn't blame him, but he waved her off. "Not today, my dear. Just a normal massage." The pout would have made lesser men give in. After all, what happened in Phuket, stayed in Phuket.

But not today.

And not him.

Lee Fang meant the world to him, and every time he had to do something for the job, he was racked with guilt, despite the fact she was fully aware that these things were still happening. She had been Chinese Special Forces, working in intelligence, which certainly helped. She knew what the job entailed, and what you sometimes had to do for the mission. Once he had confessed to her, and she had forgiven him and told him it was all right, it had helped ease his pain, but to indulge today would be wrong. His old ways were done with. He loved his new life, and he would never do anything to jeopardize it.

Next time I should order a masseur.

He shuddered at the thought. A man's hands rubbing all over his body held no appeal to him. He wasn't a homophobe by any stretch, even some of his undercover jobs requiring him to pretend he was gay or bisexual. None of that bothered him, but he knew what he liked, and he liked women.

Chantana's hands kneaded his ass cheeks, and he flexed them a number of times in an alternating pattern. She giggled. "You want I should…"

"No, just the massage, thank you."

"This girl must be really special."

"You have no idea."

"I'm jealous."

He laughed and glanced behind him at the gorgeous woman who hadn't put her robe back on. "You know you're my number one girl in Thailand. But this man jiggy-jiggies with only one girl now."

She smacked his butt, sending a surge of pleasure through his entire body, and she knew it, raising her hand to do it again, hoping to change his mind. He was about to object when a series of electrical pulses surged through his wrist, his CIA-modified TAG Heuer watch indicating he had a secure message. He groaned.

"You like?" Another smack. "I know you like."

He rolled onto his side, raising a hand. "Okay, that's enough. You better be careful. If my girlfriend finds out that you're trying to sleep with her man, she could get very upset, and she knows martial arts."

Chantana struck a fighting pose, her breasts bouncing. "I know martial arts too."

Kane grinned as his eyes indulged in the old adage, "You can look but you can't touch." He tapped his watch. "I forgot I have to be somewhere, so we'll have to cut this short." She frowned and he grabbed his wallet off the table, fishing out equivalent to a month's pay and handing it to her. Her eyes bulged. In the past, the massage had always led to an evening on the town, and then another night together in one of the finest hotels. He pressed the money into her palm. "Find yourself a nice man who treats you right. Marry him, have some babies, be happy. Stop chasing dirty men like me."

She hopped up on her toes and planted a kiss on him that threatened to knock down the walls he had constructed between her and his libido. He grabbed her shoulders and gently pushed her away. "Nice try."

She grinned then shrugged. "Will I see you again?"

"Probably, but next time at least wear a bathing suit."

She smacked his ass again then sashayed out of the room, his eyes finally breaking their lock on her ass as the door closed. He entered a coded sequence by pressing buttons on the watch's sides, and a message appeared, indicating he had a secure private communiqué from his old archaeology professor.

He groaned again.

It was never good news when he heard from the professor like this. Something was wrong, and Acton and his wife were apparently once again magnets for trouble. He grabbed his cellphone and logged into his secure app, pulling up the full message, his eyebrows inching up his forehead as he read the brief summary. There wasn't much he could do from Thailand to help, but if $20 billion had just been stolen from an American citizen live on international television, he had little doubt the American government would be getting involved. And because it had happened on foreign soil, that could include the CIA.

He forwarded the message to his best friend, Chris Leroux, asking him to see what he could do. He fired back a quick reply to Acton informing him, then headed to take a shower.

A very *cold* shower.

Vienna, Austria

February 19, 1941

Daniel opened his mouth to scream when a hand was clamped over it. "Daniel, it's me." He collapsed in Peter's arms and his shoulders shook as he sobbed in relief. "Quiet now. We don't want them hearing us. Everything's all right. We're almost there."

Daniel sniffed heavily then took Peter's hand. A couple of minutes had them at Peter's building. They climbed several flights of stairs then Peter tapped gently on his door in an odd fashion. It opened, revealing a pitch-black home. Peter stepped inside, pulling him along with him. The door was closed then a light snapped on. He smiled in relief at the sight of Peter's family, a family he knew well but hadn't seen in so long.

"Any trouble?" asked Peter's wife, Renata.

"Nothing I couldn't handle."

"And Joseph and—" Her eyes darted toward Daniel and she didn't finish her sentence.

"Peacefully."

She squeezed her eyes shut and he could see the glistening of tears threatening to erupt. She breathed deeply through her nose then nodded before opening her eyes and smiling at him. "And how are you doing, Daniel?"

He shrugged. "I'm all right, I guess. How are you, Aunt Renata?"

She dropped to a knee and hugged him. "I'm fine, dear. We're all going to be fine, soon enough." She squeezed him hard one more time then stood.

Peter turned to his children. "Is everyone ready?"

"Yes, Father," echoed his son and daughter, Hermann and Erica.

"Good." He checked his watch. "They should be here any minute now. If anyone needs to use the washroom, now is the time."

Daniel shoved his hand in the air. "I do."

"You know where it is. Hurry up."

"Yes, Uncle."

Daniel darted down the hallway, his eyes looking about the well-furnished home, his aunt and uncle obviously not suffering like his family. He spotted the bundle his mother had given his uncle earlier in the day, sitting on a table. He ignored it, continuing his sprint to the washroom. He began to pee when he heard the front door open. It must be the people they were waiting for. He pushed as hard as he could, finishing his business. He flushed the toilet and washed his hands, sniffing his fingers, not having smelled soap in so long. He opened the bathroom door and stepped out into the hall. At the far end, near the entrance where everyone was gathered, stood a man he had never seen before, a whispered conversation between him and Peter underway.

The man noticed him and jerked his chin toward him. "And this is the fifth that's caused us so much trouble?"

"Yes."

"And who is he to you?"

"Let's say he's my nephew."

"And he doesn't have parents of his own who can save him?"

"No, he doesn't." Peter's voice cracked. "Not anymore."

A lump formed in Daniel's throat and his shoulders shook as his mind finally acknowledged what it had always known. The whispered conversations, the powders, the uncharacteristic sharing of the bed. It had been planned all along. All this time, his parents and Peter had protected him from the truth.

His parents had killed themselves.

They were dead.

Tears welled in his eyes and he was about to give in to the overwhelming sadness when Peter called his name.

"Daniel, my boy, it's time to go."

He wiped his eyes dry with the back of his hands as the bits and pieces of the conversation he had overheard melded together in his brain. This was what his parents had wanted, and he was determined to not ruin the plan they had sacrificed their lives for. He sniffed deeply and scurried down the hallway to join the others.

"Daniel, this man's name is Karl."

"He's going to help us get away from the Nazis?"

Peter smiled. "Exactly. When this is all over, we'll all be safe from them."

"Are they why my parents are dead?"

Renata inhaled sharply behind him and Peter frowned, his head bobbing slowly. "Yes, Daniel."

Daniel squared his shoulders but said nothing.

"Are you going to be all right?"

Daniel nodded, not certain if he were telling a lie, but determined to be brave as his parents would want.

"Good. Now, it's important you do everything Karl says."

Karl stared at him. "The most important thing is to remain quiet. No matter what you hear, remain quiet. Understood?"

"Yes, sir," said Daniel.

Karl turned to the other two children. "Understood?"

Both Hermann and Erica echoed, "Yes, sir."

"Good." The man checked his watch and tapped it with his finger. "The truck will be outside in two minutes."

Peter's eyes narrowed. "Won't a truck on the road after curfew raise suspicions?"

Karl shook his head. "No, it's a delivery truck, fully licensed with all its papers. It has a hidden compartment behind the cab. We're going to go down to the main lobby. Peter, you'll go first and climb inside so that you can help the others. The children will go next, then you, Renata. Nobody says a word, no matter what." He tapped his watch again. "Let's go." He pointed at their feet. "Shoes off until the lobby." Everyone took their shoes off when Karl paused. "Where's the payment for the boy?"

"Oh! I almost forgot!" Renata headed back into the living room and returned with the bundle that his mother had given Peter earlier.

Karl untied the string and unwrapped the package. Daniel gasped at the sight of his mother's prized gold spoons. He hadn't seen them in ages. They used to be proudly on display, never used but always admired, and now here they were tied together in a tiny bundle, stacked one against the other as if common cutlery. Karl tested their weight with his hand then nodded, apparently satisfied. "This is more than you owe. We'll settle up when we get out of the city." He wrapped them back up, tied the string, then stuffed the package into one of his coat pockets.

He turned off the light and they headed out into the hallway, tiptoeing in silence to the stairwell. They rushed down to the lobby then everyone put their shoes back on as a truck pulled up outside. Karl stepped out onto the street and slid aside a panel just behind the cab. He beckoned for Peter who turned and smiled at the others. Holding a finger to his lips, he rushed out and climbed inside. Hermann and Erica went next, then it was his turn. He stepped out, his heart hammering, all thoughts of the recently realized tragedy forgotten. He headed for the gaping hole in the truck's side, terrified, and as Karl reached out to pick him up and put him inside, shouts erupted from down the street.

"Halt!"

Footfalls reverberated off the buildings and the cobblestone. Karl put him down then dropped to a knee, reaching behind his back. A pistol appeared and he fired several shots. Renata screamed and rushed out of the building to grab Daniel as gunfire from the soldiers erupted. Karl cried out, dropping to the ground. Renata gasped and spun before collapsing beside him. Peter shouted from inside the truck as its engine roared to life. The gunfire continued and Daniel squeezed his eyes shut, pressing his hands against his ears, trying to drown out the horror around him. He had heard gunfire once before, when his best friend Jacob and his family were killed, and he never wanted to hear it again.

He was going to die.

But that wasn't what his parents would want. They had sacrificed everything saving him, and he wasn't about to let the Nazis ruin their plans. He forced his eyes open and scampered toward Karl's body. He reached into the man's coat pocket and gripped the bundle of spoons so precious to his mother, then scurried back inside the building as the truck roared away, Peter shouting the entire time for God to help his family. As Daniel pushed through the doors, the gunfire continued. The truck careened around the corner and he prayed they would get away.

But none of that mattered now.

The soldiers were closing in.

He sprinted through the lobby toward the rear entrance to the building. Peter's family often used it as a shortcut to the stores, taking him with them if he were visiting. He burst into the alleyway then rushed into the night, fear and uncertainty gripping him as he wondered how he could possibly survive on his own with Nazis around every corner.

And he prayed to the souls of his mother and father to guide him.

Arndt Street

Vienna, Austria

Present Day

Laura hammered on the gas the moment the light turned green and surged after the police car giving chase to the SUV. "Call Emergency. We need to warn the cops that this isn't a normal traffic stop. There are armed men in that SUV."

Acton dialed 112, always making it a point to know what the emergency number was for whatever country he would be in. Instead of help, he got a tone indicating his call couldn't be made. He cursed. "The circuits must be jammed. I can't get through. Everybody and their dog are probably calling family and friends to make sure they're okay, what with all the detonations."

"Did your texts to Hugh or Tommy get through?"

Acton checked his phone. "Hugh, no. Tommy, yes."

"Text Tommy the situation. Text messages are always more reliable than phone calls. See if he can get through to the police."

"Good thinking."

Acton fired off a message, sending their current map location along with it. He cursed at the police car racing after the speeding SUV, its lights and sirens now on. "I wish I had my Glock," he muttered.

Laura grunted. "I wish I had an M4."

Acton punched the dash. "I just wish I had a working cellphone! We need to somehow warn them!"

Laura reached over and threw her flashers on then hammered on the gas. She flashed the headlights and pulsed the horn. "Hopefully, he'll figure whatever we're trying to get his attention for is more important than stopping a speeder."

"Let's hope you're right, but you do realize it means they get away for the moment?"

"Yes, but if we can stop that officer, he can radio it in, and hopefully other units can pick up the vehicle knowing what they're getting themselves into. Either way, we could be saving this guy's life."

As the three cars raced through the light evening traffic, Acton's phone vibrated with a message from Tommy.

Can't get through. Still trying.

He held up his phone, flashing the message at Laura. "Tommy says he still can't get through."

A smile spread on Laura's face as she pointed ahead, their vehicle immediately slowing. Acton turned to see the police car pulling over to the side, the SUV they had been chasing continuing down the road. The door to the cop car was thrown open and a female officer stepped out, pointing at them then directing them to the side of the road. Laura hammered on the brakes, bringing them to a rapid halt behind the squad car. She cut the engine and pressed the buttons to lower all the windows so the woman had a clear view inside, everything but the windshield heavily tinted.

The officer strode toward them, her hand on her pistol grip, saying something in German.

Laura leaned out the window. "I'm sorry, we had to get your attention."

The officer eyed her. "Why?"

"The vehicle you're pursuing is involved in the bombings, and there were armed men inside. They would have shot you if you stopped them."

The woman's eyes bulged and she paused for a moment. Tires squealed ahead and Acton cursed as he pointed toward Vida's SUV, its reverse lights blaring as it raced toward them. "Call for backup!" he shouted.

The officer spun. She reached for her radio as the vehicle shuddered to a halt, all four doors opening, four men stepping out with weapons drawn.

"Get down!"

Gunfire erupted and the officer dropped with a scream. Acton and Laura ducked below the console as bullets tore into the engine block and windshield. Laura pressed the button to restart the SUV, but it was dead, the shots having done their work.

"We have to get out of here!"

"Not from this side," said Laura.

Acton threw open his door and stepped out. Laura followed him. He hit the ground and peered under the vehicle. He could see four sets of feet, still standing by the SUV. The police officer was still alive and had dragged herself between her vehicle and theirs. He scrambled over to her and pulled her the rest of the way, then turned her over and grabbed her gun from its holster. She struggled to stop him, but he pushed her down.

"I'm here to help you."

She stopped resisting and he turned to cover them as Laura dragged her by the vest. There was a lull in the gunfire and he popped his head up. Three of the men were now walking toward them.

"Ammo," he whispered over his shoulder. A moment later two mags were pressed into his extended hand. "Three of them are coming. They're going to try to flank us." He adjusted his position as Laura and the officer exchanged words. He spotted his opportunity and leaned out, putting two in the left-most target's chest, then redirected his aim at the next target, squeezing the trigger twice, dropping him as well. He fired on the third but he had already reacted. Bullets sprayed the air from the remaining gunman and Acton ducked back down.

"One's coming around the front," he warned as he again adjusted his position. He leaned out to shoot when another burst of gunfire, unlike anything he had ever heard, erupted. An impossible shower of bullets shredded the area, one slamming into his weapon as he took aim, stinging his hand and forearm. The gun clattered to the ground and within moments, the shooter had a Glock 18 with a ridiculous 100-round Beta-C magazine trained on them.

"Drop the weapon," the man ordered Laura, and a baton she was gripping clattered to the ground. She slowly stood as she raised her hands, then nodded toward the officer.

"She needs medical attention."

The man glanced at the downed officer, then aimed his weapon directly at her head and squeezed the trigger.

"Bastard!" cried Acton. He charged the man but was pistol-whipped from behind, and as his world faded, he heard Laura cry out for him, then another gunshot, her scream silenced.

Hotel Sacher Wien

Vienna, Austria

Tommy slammed the receiver back in its cradle, having resorted to trying the landline, the cellular system jammed. "I can't get through."

Mai stepped out of the bathroom, now in street clothes, as he sent off another message to Acton, letting him know of his continued failure. He rolled from the bed and quickly stripped out of his tuxedo.

"There's only one thing I can think to do."

Mai regarded him. "What's that?"

"Go outside, find a cop, grab him, and force him to listen to us so he can radio it in."

Mai's eyes bulged. "You're not actually going to grab one, are you?"

He flashed a grin. "If I have to."

She gave him a look. "Is it wrong that that turns me on?"

Something tweaked in his underwear and he wagged a finger at her. "Don't you dare start anything."

She laughed. "Even I wouldn't do something like that with the professors out there chasing criminals." She tossed him clothes from his suitcase, and he quickly donned them. Within minutes, they were headed out the door. They rode the elevator in silence, though the tourists that accompanied them were babbling in various languages, all clearly terrified at what was happening in the city they had decided to visit. They emerged into the lobby, finding long line ups at every desk in sight.

Tommy jogged over to one of the bellhops. "Do you speak English?"

"Yes, sir. How can I help you?"

"I need to find a police officer. It's urgent."

"Has something happened?"

"Yes. Nothing at the hotel, but I need to get a message through to police headquarters, and none of the phones are working."

"Yes, the lines have been swamped with all the bombings and our Internet is down."

"Right, so, any idea where I can find a police officer?"

The man shook his head. "Not really. But if you go out the doors and head right, it'll take you to one of the main streets. Maybe you'll be able to flag one down there. Unfortunately, sir, it's not something I really pay attention to."

"Okay, thank you." Tommy took Mai by the hand and they headed out the doors, then went right as instructed.

Mai pointed. "Look!"

Tommy's head spun toward where she was pointing and he gasped at their luck. He raised his hands in the air and began waving. "Hey, over here! Police! Over here!"

The squad car that had just swung around the corner turned its lights on and continued past them. Tommy cursed then breathed a sigh of relief as it pulled a U-turn, coming back and stopping at the curb in front of them. A window rolled down and something was said in German.

Tommy bent over. "Do you speak English?"

"Yes, sir. What's the emergency?"

"Are your radios working?"

The officer frowned. "What's the emergency, sir?"

"We were at the gala. We were witnesses to what happened. The people we were with are in pursuit of those responsible for the bombings and the theft."

"Theft?"

"Over twenty-billion dollars was stolen. Hasn't anybody told you?"

Words were exchanged between the officer and his partner.

"Where are your friends?"

Tommy brought up the map that Acton had sent him with their location. "This is the last report I have for them from a few minutes ago."

The officer grabbed his radio and Tommy stepped back, his shoulders shaking as help was finally on its way for two of the most important people in his life.

Vienna City Hall, Courtyard

Vienna, Austria

Reading stood with Spencer as Winter interviewed a group they found that had been working in the control room during the theft. He remained silent as the inspector did his job and did it well, only occasionally prompting the witnesses when they needed help remembering the sequence of events. Unfortunately, they had learned nothing beyond what they already knew.

Winter summed it up. "So, this should have been impossible, and the only way for it to have happened was for someone on the inside to change the destination accounts, and those accounts were on the memory key that Mr. Meitner provided."

Heads bobbed and Wagner, who had become the spokesman for the group, vocalized their agreement. "Yes, sir."

"So then, either the list of account numbers was tampered with before he handed it over, or it was done after."

Reading's eyebrows climbed slightly. It hadn't occurred to him that the account numbers might have been changed before Meitner had handed the memory key over. If that were the case, then the inside man might not have even been in the room, might not have even been on the same continent.

He dismissed the idea. If that were the case, then why all the detonations, especially the one in front of the building? Knocking out communications and power made sense. It gave those behind this time to transfer the money to so many different accounts, it wouldn't be traceable before it was already gone. But killing people in front of the building just for the sake of killing them? That didn't fit. It had to be a distraction so those involved could get away, though it could also have been a message.

We took the money from the rich and bloodied their noses as well.

But then there was Vida. Why had she left the building with an armed escort? Where did the guard watching the necklace go? If a guard abandoning his post out of fear were the only thing out of place, he'd be willing to dismiss it. But when other members of the detail leave under suspicious circumstances, he had to think something more was going on. Yet it could still be as simple as Vida being evacuated by several of the security team, a team much larger than just those that apparently went with her. It could all be innocent, and they were merely a protective detail helping Vida escape not the scene of the crime, but a possible target for a terrorist attack. For all he knew, with communications still down, she might be at her hotel trying to reach the authorities. She could be innocent in all this, and when Acton and Laura caught up to her, everyone could share a good laugh.

Something came in over the radios that had the police in the area agitated. Winter's partner, Hans Strobl, joined them, saying something in German. A quick conversation was held, Winter growing more tense by the moment. An order was snapped and Strobl rushed off. Winter turned to Reading who had held his tongue for about as long as he could.

"There's been an officer-involved shooting. Apparently, she was in pursuit of a black SUV when another one became involved. The details are sketchy, but at least three people are dead."

Reading's stomach churned and he took an involuntary step back as if distancing himself from the source of the news might lessen the blow. It had to be his friends. The question was, were they among the dead, or had they done the killing? He couldn't count the number of times he thought they had paid the ultimate price for their meddling, but they had always proven him wrong. Yet both had been shot in the past, and eventually, their luck would run out. He looked at a hand on his shoulder, Spencer standing beside him.

"Are you all right?"

Reading inhaled deeply and closed his eyes, saying nothing, fearing his voice might betray him.

Spencer took over for his father. "Do we know any further details? Male, female, which SUV they came from?"

"No. Officers are responding now. All we have is a phoned-in witness report."

"You need to take us there."

"My partner is already getting us the car. We'll head to the scene and find out for ourselves. Don't give up hope, Agent Reading. Right now, we don't know if your friends were even involved."

Reading grunted. "You don't know my friends."

Vienna General Hospital

Vienna, Austria

Meitner frowned as his blood pressure was checked yet again. "I just fainted, that's all. You would too if you were just told twenty-two billion of your money had been stolen."

The nurse's eyes bulged then she turned her head. "Is he delusional?"

His granddaughter, Michelle, stepped into view, shaking her head. "No, he's not. We don't know the details yet of whether it was actually stolen or if it was just a technical error, but my grandfather is the founder of Meitner Telecom."

The nurse shrugged. "Sorry, I don't keep up on those types of things. I assume it's big?"

"One of the biggest," said Meitner. "And the sooner I can get out of here, the sooner I can start searching for my money."

The doctor walked into the room. "So, how is our patient doing?"

"Perfectly fine as far as the numbers go, Dr. Rainer," replied the nurse. "His blood pressure is back to normal and his body is lapping up that IV drip we've got him on. He says he fainted because of shocking news."

Rainer reviewed the charts then examined the monitors for a moment. "And what news was that?"

"That some bastard stole twenty-two billion from the less fortunate of this world."

Her eyes narrowed and she checked the chart again. "Oh, you're *that* Meitner? That would explain all the guns in my hospital. I take it the charity event didn't go well."

Meitner grunted. "That's one way of putting it. Now, can I get the hell out of here or not?"

Rainer shook her head. "Sir, you're over ninety years old, and you're suffering from dehydration and shock. We need to keep you overnight for observation."

"Nonsense."

Michelle came closer. "Listen to her, Grandpa, you're going to do no one any good if you're dead."

He glared at her, but the concern in her eyes melted his heart instantly and he slumped back in his bed. "Fine," he said, waving at the doctor. "However, there's twenty-two billion dollars to be found, and I'll be conducting the investigation from this room."

Rainer opened her mouth to object when he held up a bony finger.

"That's my condition, or I leave."

The woman frowned. "Fine, but it's contained to this room. I don't want your people disrupting my hospital."

"Agreed." He snapped his fingers and Bernie emerged from the corner of the room. "Yes, sir?"

"Call our local office and tell them to arrange extra communications capacity for this room, then set up a conference call with all of our key people. And get me Azar Vida. I need to talk to her immediately to find out what the hell happened. And we're going to need to issue a statement to the press, let them know any rumors of my demise are greatly exaggerated, and that whoever's behind this theft will be swiftly brought to justice."

"Yes, sir. Anything else?"

"Get Chef Stephan at the hotel to arrange a meal for me."

Rainer frowned. "We have a perfectly fine kitchen here. I don't need the patients on this floor seeing someone getting preferential treatment."

"How many on this floor?"

"Excuse me?"

"How many on this floor need a meal?"

"I don't know the exact number. Thirty or forty."

He turned to Bernie. "Find out the exact number and if there are any specific dietary requirements. Have the chef prepare a meal for everyone, that way there's no preferential treatment."

"What about the rest of the hospital?" asked Rainer.

He gave her a look. "Don't push your luck."

Rainer laughed. "You're going to be a difficult one, aren't you?"

"At my age, I have the right to be." He pointed at Bernie then directed his finger toward the door. Bernie bowed slightly, then left, his thumbs already flying over the digital keyboard on his phone. The nurse left with Rainer as Holly entered, her permanent scowl darkening his mood further.

Michelle rushed over and sat on the side of his bed, taking his hand. "How are you feeling, Grandpa? Honestly. No lies that you tell doctors so they leave you alone."

He smiled and reached up, patting her tear-stained cheek. "I'm fine. Just a little tired. Pissed off. Worried. I don't care that twenty-two billion dollars was stolen from me. It wasn't mine anymore. I'm outraged that all those charities, all those organizations that were going to be able to help millions of people, have been robbed. We need to get that money back."

"Is it even possible?" asked Holly. "I mean, these were all electronic transfers. Can those even be reversed?"

"I don't know, my dear. I hope so, though if it can't be, then I don't know what I'll do."

Holly shook her head. "Such a waste."

He frowned at his youngest granddaughter, whose only accomplishment in life had been to give him a great-grandson who was turning out to be a far finer person than his mother. "Greed doesn't suit you, my dear."

Holly glared at him. "And showmanship doesn't suit you. You could have given away your money, but done it out of the public eye. Nobody would have known you were doing it, so no one would have known to steal it. But instead, no, you had to make a big splash to show off to the world that the great Mr. Meitner was doing something yet again, bigger and better than anyone else ever had. Your ego lost that money, and now instead of having a great legacy that your family could be proud of, you'll be the laughing-stock."

"Holly!" cried Michelle. "How could you say such a thing? That's uncalled for!"

Holly eyed her. "It's how I feel, and he's always said we should say how we're feeling."

"Well, you sound like an ungrateful selfish little bitch."

Holly gasped. "How dare you!"

Meitner's heart monitor beeped faster and he snapped. "The two of you, shut the hell up!"

Michelle's chin dropped to her chest. "Sorry, Grandpa."

"Your parents were rich. Yes, I gave your father his start, but he made his own fortune on top of that, and left both of you healthy inheritances that if managed wisely would last you a lifetime and then some. My money is none of your concern. I get to choose what happens to it. Not either of you, and definitely not some thief. Now, the two of you are either going to help find who's behind this, or you're going to leave. Which is it?"

Michelle leaned in. "I'll do whatever it takes to help you. You know that, Grandpa."

He turned to Holly, her scowl even more pronounced. "And you?"

She sighed heavily. "Fine. I'll try to help you. And if we find the money, maybe you'll come to your senses."

He jabbed a finger at the doorway. "Out! And I don't want to see you again until you're no longer consumed with greed."

Holly's jaw dropped as her eyes bulged. "You're seriously kicking me out?"

"You kicked yourself out. Now, go. I have twenty-two billion dollars to recover that could help millions of people who couldn't even fathom the lifestyle that you've lived. I don't know what made you into the twisted creature you are, but it certainly wasn't your parents. They were both generous and compassionate. Your sister is a wonderful woman, yet you're a bad seed. Now, get out of here, learn some humility, and rethink your priorities. Until you do, I don't want to see you again."

Holly's face was red with rage and shock, her eyes red, welling with tears. She rushed from the room and cried out in anguish as the door closed.

And it broke his heart.

He hadn't spoken a harsh word to either of his grandchildren in their entire lives. He closed his burning eyes and Michelle squeezed his hand. "I shouldn't have done that."

Michelle disagreed. "She needed to hear it. Something's overcome her in the past year or so. I'm not sure what is going on, but she's changed. She's become obsessed with money."

He squeezed her hand. "We'll deal with your sister later. You know I can't stay mad at her. Now, go see if you can find Bernie and give him a hand."

"Yes, Grandpa."

She left the room and he laid back on the pillows, closing his eyes and steadying his breathing, steeling for what was to come, disappointment threatening to overwhelm him. What was supposed to be the greatest day of his life was instead reminding him of the tragedy of his youth, where once again everything had been taken from him by those he thought he could trust.

CIA Headquarters, Operations Center 3

Langley, Virginia

CIA Analyst Supervisor Chris Leroux leaned back in his chair and stretched his arms high above his head. It was the end of his team's shift, a long, boring day finally over, though, in his line of work, boring was good. It meant all hell wasn't breaking loose somewhere. It meant people weren't dying on his watch.

Though that could change in a heartbeat.

His phone vibrated with a coded pattern, and as the clock ticked toward the top of the hour and his team prepared to hand over to the next shift, he logged into the secure app that his best friend, CIA Special Agent Dylan Kane, had installed on his phone for emergency communications. Kane was between assignments right now, decompressing in Thailand, and was due to return home tomorrow. Something must be going on, off the books, otherwise, if it were official, Kane would have used regular channels to contact him. He brought up the message and read it, then turned to his second-in-command, Sonya Tong, as she filled her handbag with her personal items.

"Sonya, can you bring up any feeds we have on Vienna? Is there something going on there?"

She stopped what she was doing, and he noted the entire room had paused their preparations to leave. His team was excellent. The best the CIA had to offer, in his opinion, and a bond had been formed over the years they had worked together, so if something concerned him, they were all concerned.

"Looks like there's a major incident in Vienna. At least a dozen explosions, plus one mass-casualty detonation. A car bomb. Looks like that Meitner charity event was disrupted."

Leroux grunted. "Huh, I had that taping. Any reports of our professor friends being involved?"

Tong gave him a look. "Are you serious?"

He shook his phone at her. "According to a source, they might be in pursuit of those involved."

Randy Child, their tech wunderkind, groaned as he spun in his chair. "Not again! I've got plans for tonight."

Nobody asked what they were, which resulted in several chuckles. Child flipped the bird and spun in his chair again, presenting it to the entire team.

"There's been a shooting. Three people are dead. Police are responding now."

The room fell silent and Leroux checked his phone. "Was it on Arndt Street?"

Tong's head slowly bobbed. "Yes, sir."

He tensed as he rose from his chair, snapping his fingers at Child. "Get me camera footage, now."

"On it." Any frivolity was gone from his voice as the youngest member of their team furiously worked his magic. Cameras showing various angles and positions down the long road revealed dozens of emergency vehicles racing through the frames.

"Second from the bottom left!" shouted someone from the back of the room. Leroux redirected his focus and cursed at the sight of a squad car stopped by the side of the road, a black SUV behind it riddled with bullet holes.

And three bodies lying on the pavement.

En Route to Shooting Scene

Vienna, Austria

Reading flinched, nearly having a heart attack when his phone vibrated furiously. He fished the device from his pocket and found over a dozen messages waiting for him. He quickly scanned through them, spotting one from Acton. He excitedly tapped on it, reading the update on their pursuit, then checked the time it was sent. And his shoulders sagged. It was a couple of minutes before the shooting had been reported. He typed a message.

Are you all right?

He waited for a ten-count, but no reply came. He flipped back and brought up the messages from Tommy, reading through them, relieved they were safe at the hotel. He sent a reply.

Stay at hotel unless directed otherwise. Spencer and I are fine. We'll update you shortly with status on Jim and Laura.

He found a message from his ex-wife and turned to Spencer. "We've got signals. Check your phone. Your mother is worried about you."

Spencer replied to his mother as Reading sent a text to Michelle Humphrey, his Interpol partner back in London, several texts received from her asking if he were involved.

Spencer and I are fine. Talk to the boss about getting me officially on the investigation. I'm already involved. Tommy and Mai are safe at the hotel, but Jim and Laura...

He hesitated on how to phrase the rest of the message, then decided optimism was the order of the day.

...are in pursuit of the suspects. I'm with local police en route to another crime scene.

He sent the message and received a reply seconds later.

Thank God you're all right! I was worried I'd have to break in a new partner. Contacting the boss now. Keep me posted.

Reading chuckled then frowned. His phone was working, the messages were going back and forth, yet still, there was no reply from his friend. He sent one to Laura's phone. She was probably driving, and if Acton had lost his device, they could be relying on hers.

Again, no reply.

Spencer held up his phone. "Mom says I'm not allowed to leave the country with you anymore."

"Bollocks to that."

Spencer grinned. "That's what *I* said."

"What did she say?"

Spencer shoved the phone in Reading's face, three dots pulsating. "She's been replying for the past minute at least."

Reading rolled his eyes. "That's never good."

"Tell me about it. I bet you if we put the windows down, we could hear her screaming all the way from London as she types."

Reading roared with laughter. His ex-wife's explosive temper was one of the things about her he did not miss, though in her defense, it mostly manifested when it came to her overprotective nature with their son. She had been livid when Spencer announced he was following in his father's footsteps and becoming law enforcement. It wasn't that she didn't respect the profession, it was that she was afraid something might happen to her son on the increasingly dangerous streets of London.

He didn't blame her. It was a dangerous job, but somebody had to do it. If the police were removed from the streets, chaos would ensue. There were countries in the world that did it, that had no police force, and instead relied on their military to provide security. Those were all fine dictatorships, and he often wondered if those who demanded the police be disbanded had a clue what they were talking about.

"We're here," announced Winter from the front passenger seat. Everyone fell silent and Reading's chest tightened as he caught a glimpse of the carnage ahead.

Vienna General Hospital

Vienna, Austria

Meitner sat up in his bed as Bernie brought him up to date. "A team from the local office is already on the way to set up the gear. A local police liaison is on their way, as is someone from the American Embassy. I've got several others of our ground team inbound, but nobody can reach Miss Vida."

Meitner eyed him. "What do you mean no one can reach her?"

Bernie shrugged. "I don't know what to say. Nobody's seen or heard from her since the evacuation was announced. There are still communications problems in the area. I had to call one of the satphones to reach our people on the ground. She could still be there working the problem, but if she's not with the others, she'd be incommunicado."

Meitner cursed. "Why wouldn't she have had a satphone issued?"

Bernie shrugged again. "I don't know. I would have thought she would have, but it's not on the list. There was one assigned to Mrs. Hatch before the car crash, but it looks like in the confusion after that, the assignment of a satellite phone was missed."

Meitner growled. "I knew we should have just promoted from within, but Michelle insisted Vida was excellent at what she did."

"It made sense at the time, sir. Her resumé was impeccable, and all indications were that she was doing a bang-up job. And by bringing her in, everybody remained in the positions they had been training for."

Meitner sighed heavily. "What would you do in this situation if you were her?"

"Sir?"

"How long have you worked for me?"

"I hesitate to say, sir, because it would date us both."

Meitner laughed. "Exactly. So, you've been around me long enough to see how I operate, so again I ask, if you were working for me and were in Vida's position, what would you do?"

"I'd be doing everything I could to contact you."

Meitner jabbed a finger at his trusted man. "Exactly! Anybody with her level of experience should be working the problem, and part of working the problem is getting in touch with the boss to let him know what's going on." He paused, his jaw slowly dropping as a thought occurred to him. "You said there were reports of a car bombing in front of the building?"

"Yes, sir."

"Could she be one of the victims?"

Bernie's eyes shot wide. "I suppose it's possible. She would have evacuated the building with everyone else, and it would certainly explain why we haven't heard from her."

Meitner's heart monitor started beating faster. "Contact that police liaison. Send her photo over. We need to know if she's one of the victims. In fact, get photos of our entire team over to them. I want to know if any of our people were killed in that blast."

"Right away, sir."

Bernie left and Michelle entered, a smile on her face. "I took over the food situation from Bernie. He's got more important things to do. You'll be pleased to know that everything's been taken care of. The hotel was only too happy to help out, and Chef Stephan said he will personally prepare all your meals and have them delivered to you here until such time as you're well enough to return to the hotel."

Meitner acknowledged the update with a slight nod of his head, but at the moment, he had no appetite, for something was gnawing at him. He turned to his granddaughter. "Tell me everything you know about Miss Vida."

Vienna, Austria

February 24, 1941

Daniel pressed into the corner, his back against the rear of a bakery. He had discovered it on his second night of homelessness, and was delighted at the warmth of the ovens on the opposite side of the wall. But with the good came the bad, and the lingering aromas from what was baked here taunted him.

He was starving.

He hadn't eaten since he had escaped from the Nazis five days ago. In the light of day, when the streets filled, he roamed freely, though had to force himself to stop from continually rubbing where the Star of David had once been for so long. It was only when he had seen a family with the armbands that he realized how much freedom not wearing it gave him. Nobody paid him any mind, though all eyes were on the family who scurried along, their heads down, their terror hidden from their own countrymen, their own neighbors.

He roamed the streets during the day and hid at night. He was cold and starving, but it was thirst that had overcome him before anything else had. He had taken to quenching it at a fountain near where Peter lived. The water didn't taste great, but it was better than nothing, and it had kept him going for a couple of days until he found a well in a courtyard surrounded by old residences. It had allowed him to meet his needs with deliciously fresh water, but did nothing for the hunger that ate away at him.

If he didn't find food soon, he would die, and his parents' sacrifice would have been for nothing.

Something scraped nearby. Metal on stone. His heart raced and he froze, peering into the near darkness at the narrow sliver of the world he now called home.

"Pssst!"

He searched for the sound's source but couldn't see anything.

"Down here."

He nearly soiled himself when he spotted a set of eyes peering out from a slightly askew manhole cover. It pushed aside and a girl appeared, just from the shoulders up.

She beckoned to him. "Come quickly! It's safer here!" she called in a harsh whisper.

He debated whether he should trust this stranger, but the debate only lasted for moments. She appeared to be around his age. Surely someone his age wouldn't betray him. He scrambled from his hiding place and over to the gaping maw in the road. As she retreated into the darkness, he peered over the edge.

"Come quickly."

He flipped around, lowering his legs inside. His feet searched for the rungs, finally finding one, and he scurried down into several inches of water. The girl rushed back up the ladder, pulling the manhole cover into place and sealing off what little light there was. She came back down and fingers found his arm then traced their way to his hand, gripping it tightly.

"Come with me. Just watch your step."

He nodded then realized she couldn't see him. "Yes."

They sloshed through the water, toward what, he didn't know, as he struggled to calm his hammering heart.

"My name is Petra. What's yours?"

"Daniel."

"Why are you on the street? Where are your parents?"

He squeezed his eyes shut. "They're dead."

"Sorry to hear that. So are mine. The Nazis shot them when we tried to escape. How did yours die?"

The ache in his chest was painful now, and he shook his head. "I don't want to talk about it."

She squeezed his hand a little tighter. "I understand. How long have you been on the street?"

"Almost a week, I think. You?"

"At least three months."

His eyes bulged. "Aren't you hungry?"

She giggled. "I'm always hungry. But there's food to be found if you're smart about it."

"Where?"

"Everywhere. People still need to eat. Watch, there's a step here going up."

His foot found it and he stumbled regardless.

"We're almost there."

A light flickered ahead, impossibly dim, but in the jet black of the past few minutes, it was welcoming. As they neared, it became brighter, and it was clear to him it was coming from under a closed door. He smiled broadly when the door was opened and they stepped into a small room, the walls made of stone, as were the ceiling and floor. It wasn't very inviting, but it was dry. A lone candle burned atop a collection of cobblestones in one corner of the room. Piles of newspaper were crumpled together in the far-left corner, a threadbare blanket tossed atop of it, and along the rear wall were dozens of items including forks, knives, spoons, and other things Petra had evidently collected over the months she thought might be useful.

"Are you hungry?"

His head bobbed rapidly. "More than I've ever been in my life."

She laughed then picked up a basket. Removing the top, she reached inside and pulled out half a loaf of bread. She tore off a large chunk and handed it to him. He snatched it, devouring it, every chew causing him to groan in ecstasy, swearing this was the best-tasting bread he had ever had. She reached back into the basket and pulled out a carrot. She snapped it in half and handed him the larger portion. He eyed it for a moment. It hadn't been washed. Petra laughed at him, apparently recognizing the reason for his hesitation.

"You'll starve to death before a little bit of dirt will kill you."

He took a small, tentative bite, and chewed. He shrugged. He was too hungry to care. Petra tore off a small piece of bread and ate it slowly. As she gnawed at her share of the carrot, he said nothing, terrified that at any moment somebody might interrupt their meal and demand the food back. He had to eat everything he could as quickly as he could manage.

When he finished, she handed him a wineskin and pulled the cork off. "Drink."

He held it up to his lips and tipped the bag up, cool delicious water pouring into his mouth. He drank his fill then handed it back to her. She took a swig then corked it, setting it back against the wall where several others lay.

He stared at her. "Where did you get all the food?"

"You have to know where to look. The easiest place to get the bread is at a tram stop. Women go to pick up their rations and then they put the bags down while they wait for the tram to arrive. All you have to do is sneak up, pull the bread out of their bag, then run. But you need to have an escape route. There's a tram that stops not far from here. I just make sure the grate in the alleyway is left open. I steal the bread, run down the street, duck into the alleyway, slide into the opening, then pull the grate back. If anyone's chasing me, they'll never find me. I'm too quick."

Daniel processed the story. "But doesn't that mean the person you stole from goes hungry?"

She shrugged. "These people didn't help my parents or my family. Why should I care about them?"

He stared at her for a moment. "Are you Jewish?"

She flinched. "So what if I am?"

He sighed in relief. "I'm Jewish too."

A smile spread and she lunged for him, hugging him hard. "Then you understand!" She let him go, and the moment they parted, he yearned for her embrace, craving human contact more than he had realized. "I'm so happy you're Jewish. Now I don't have to worry about you turning me into the Nazis."

His eyes shot wide. "Would someone actually do that?"

"You'd be shocked at what I've seen and heard. You can't trust anyone. Most of our countrymen hate us just because of our religion." She held up what remained of her carrot. "Most wouldn't hesitate to turn us over just for this."

He stared at her wide-eyed, then his eyes narrowed. "Where did you get the carrot?"

She grinned. "I'll show you tomorrow. There's a house nearby with a root cellar that you can access from outside. It's locked, but my father was a locksmith and taught me how to open anything that needed a key. The trick is to never take too much. Never more than two items. If you took everything you could carry, they would know the next time they went in and would stand watch. But by only taking one or two things, they never notice, or at least they haven't so far. Now that there are two of us, we'll have to be more careful." She pointed at the make-shift bed. "Let's get to sleep. Tomorrow is going to be a busy day."

"Why is that?" he asked as he rose and stepped over to the bed.

"I've found a place where I can get some clothes. Mine are falling apart, and if we're going to be seen on the streets, we need to fit in."

He patted his small suitcase that hadn't left his sight since he had escaped. "I have clothes. Maybe they'll fit."

She laughed. "I can't wear boy's clothes." She patted the bed, much like his father had, bringing a pang of remembrance that he fought off. He lay down, facing the wall, and closed his eyes, relishing in the warmth of her body as she snuggled closer. She wrapped her arms around him and he sighed, imagining it was his mother holding him one more time. He tucked his arms in, gripping the spoons hidden away in an inner pocket, and drifted off, thanking God for bringing him to Petra.

Shooting Scene

Vienna, Austria

Present Day

Reading forced himself to breathe as he threaded through the throng of first responders, Winter leading the way. There were three bodies covered in sheets and he tensed anew. He turned to Winter. "May I?"

Winter nodded and Reading kneeled beside the body located between the squad car and the SUV he presumed was that driven by his friends. He moved the sheet aside, what remained of a woman's face revealed. He turned his head away from the shocking sight, but not before he sighed in relief that it wasn't Laura. His stomach churned slightly with guilt as this was someone's daughter, perhaps wife, sister, or worse, mother. He covered her back up then closed his eyes for a moment as he said a silent prayer for the fallen hero.

He rose and stepped over to the next body then kneeled once again. He drew the sheet aside, finding a man with an impossibly square jaw.

156

He pulled the sheet down some more and examined the wounds. A double-tap to the chest, the grouping tight. This was just the type of shooting he would expect from his friends. He covered the man back up and stepped over to the third, confident now that this wouldn't be Acton or Laura, for the body's location in relation to the defensive position was all wrong. He flipped the sheet aside and was both relieved and surprised. He beckoned Spencer over.

"What's up?"

Reading pointed down at the man. "Does he look familiar to you?"

Spencer kneeled, his head shaking slowly, then he shot back to his feet. "That's the guard that was assigned to the necklace!"

"Exactly."

"So, he didn't abandon his post like a coward after all."

"No. I'm guessing he was never supposed to be assigned to the necklace. Meitner offering the privilege to Mai screwed up their plans slightly."

"You're convinced then that these people are involved?"

Reading gave his son a look. "You have doubts? Innocent people don't get in shootouts with police."

Spencer appeared crestfallen at the criticism. "Sorry, that was stupid."

"Yes, it was. You need to learn to trust your gut." He slapped his son's stomach with the back of his hand.

Winter stepped away from a gaggle of officers and joined them. "Were any of them your friends?"

Reading shook his head. "No." He pointed down at the last body. "But this one was assigned to guard a very expensive necklace that one of my friends was wearing. Not one of the ones that was missing, but a young lady, Mai Trinh, who's safely at our hotel."

"You really do have very rich friends, Agent."

Reading shook his head. "Nope. Not these ones. They're just starting out in life. When we were all meeting Mr. Meitner, he brought out the necklace and insisted she wear it, but because of the value, a guard was assigned. After the initial detonation, he disappeared. We had assumed he panicked, but it would appear he was part of what was going on all along. Since Tommy and Mai didn't mention recognizing one of the guards that were with Vida, I'm guessing he was the driver."

Winter indicated the shot-up SUV. "And this was what your friends were driving?"

"I believe so. It certainly looks like it, though I can't be certain, as the other vehicle might have been identical for all I know. Was there any blood inside?"

"No, nothing to indicate your friends were injured."

Reading exhaled in relief. He checked his phone again, and neither of them had replied to his message. "Then where the hell are they? They're not answering their phones."

"And they won't be. We found two phones tossed inside the SUV. I'm guessing they're theirs."

Reading cursed. "Well, they wouldn't do that voluntarily, and I can't see whoever they were pursuing letting them go after this, so they must have taken them hostage."

"But why not just kill them?" asked Spencer.

"They must want them for something."

"What?"

Reading slowly shook his head as he assessed the scene. "Things aren't going according to plan for them."

Spencer grunted. "I don't know about that. They seem to have gotten away with over twenty billion."

"It's one thing to steal the money, it's another thing to get away and enjoy it. If it weren't for Jim and Laura, no one would have known about Vida being involved. They would have made their escape and been long gone before anyone knew what was going on." He waved a hand at the scene. "This wasn't part of the plan." He turned to Winter. "You said your officer called in that she was breaking off a pursuit?"

"Yes, only moments after she began it."

Reading pointed at the SUV, parked behind the squad car. "The fact that they're behind your officer suggests she got between the two vehicles. You said she thought she was pulling over a speeder. Jim and Laura would know the truth, and probably somehow got her attention. That's when she called off the pursuit and pulled over."

Spencer's eyes narrowed. "But if she broke off the pursuit, why didn't they just keep going? They could have gotten away. Why come back and kill people?"

Reading regarded his son. "You're forgetting the most important thing about a police chase."

Spencer eyed him. "And what's that?"

"You can never outrun a radio."

Winter smiled slightly then frowned. "So, they came back to kill our officer so she couldn't radio in what your friends were going to tell her."

"Exactly. Only by killing her could they actually escape."

"But they had to know we'd respond and check the cameras."

"Yes, which means wherever they're going isn't far. They figured this would buy them enough time to get away."

"Then why take your friends?"

"Insurance. My guess is, if you catch up to them, they'll use them as hostages to try and make their escape."

"They have to know that won't work. We'll never let them leave."

Reading chewed his cheek. Winter was right. Criminals taking hostages and making demands never worked out. They would never escape in a car or a bus. Even if they demanded an airplane, they would never make the airport. Snipers would take them out. He paused at a thought. "They're heading for an airport."

"What?"

"They're heading for an airport. That's the only way they can get away."

"They could switch vehicles."

Reading shook his head. "They could, and quite possibly already have, but that's not the plan. The plan has to be to get out of the country, likely out of Europe, head to some non-extradition country, then lose themselves. Twenty billion buys new faces, new identities, new lives."

"Vienna International's not that far from here."

"No, they wouldn't be going through a major airport like that. They'll have a private plane waiting at a small airstrip somewhere nearby. The flight plan would have already been filed, my guess officially heading to some place like Greece. Somewhere in Southern Europe, still within the

EU's borders, and then they'll go off their flight plan, head to North Africa, and there'll be nothing we can do about it. It's not like we're going to blow them out of the sky."

Winter tilted his head to the side slightly. "For twenty billion, somebody might."

"Yet another reason to have hostages. We need to find the closest airstrip with a private jet that has a flight plan heading south, leaving in the next few minutes. That could be our only hope of saving Jim and Laura, and stopping Vida from getting away."

Winter spun on his heel as Reading's phone vibrated in a coded pattern in his pocket, indicating a message had come through Kane's secure app. He brought it up and smiled at the question from Chris Leroux.

How can we help?

CIA Headquarters, Operations Center 3

Langley, Virginia

Leroux chuckled as Reading stared up toward the sky then waved. It was a logical assumption they might have him on satellite, but in actuality, everything was hacked traffic cameras and security footage belonging to private businesses. The CIA kept a massive database of every single internet-connected camera they had found by continuously crawling IP addresses. When one was found, it was tested to see if basic security had been activated, and if it had, then standard default passwords were tried, along with the common lazy ones.

It was stunning how many cameras they had access to, through people either too lazy or too stupid to set up a robust password. If they had the IP address for the camera, anyone in the world could view their feed, whether the front door or a nursery. There were even websites set up where people who had discovered unsecured cameras would post the links, and voyeurs partaking in various levels of debauchery would sit back and watch the goings-on in private homes and businesses around the world.

It was disturbing.

But it was also useful.

The door to the state-of-the-art operations center hissed open and Leroux rose as his boss, National Clandestine Service Chief for the CIA, Leif Morrison, entered the room.

"What's this I hear about your team not giving up the room?"

Leroux laughed. "I wouldn't quite describe it like that, Chief." He pointed at the screen. "We caught a tip on the Vienna situation, and because of who's involved, I decided it was best to stick around. Everyone else volunteered to stay."

Morrison smirked. "On my dime, I'm sure."

The man was joking, of course, and Leroux could already tell he wasn't angry. He was here out of curiosity. Normally, Leroux would have brought him up to speed already, but only minutes had passed.

"So, what have we got?"

"You're aware of the money possibly stolen at that charity event in Vienna?"

"Yeah, the flash just came across my screen a few minutes ago. How the hell are you guys already on it?"

"If I showed you the guest list for that event, you wouldn't be asking that."

Morrison stared at him for a moment, then cursed. "Let me guess, our ridiculously wealthy professors were invited?"

"Yes, sir. And they apparently brought some friends." Leroux pointed at the display. "The man in center-frame of camera number four is Interpol Agent Hugh Reading."

Morrison folded his arms. "Okay, what's going on?"

"Apparently, the professors spotted somebody leaving the building that shouldn't be. They followed her and sent a message to Special Agent Kane to see if we could help. Kane passed the message on to us, and we just started pulling up whatever information we could find. There was an intercept of a shooting on the street that the professors were last reported on, so we brought up footage from traffic cameras showing three people down, including a police officer."

"The professors?"

"No, sir, they weren't among the dead. Agent Reading just arrived on the scene a few minutes ago. I've reached out to him. With your permission, I'd like my team to assist."

Morrison stepped closer to the displays, his hands now on his hips. "If the professors survived this, then they must have been taken by the hostiles, otherwise they would have contacted Agent Reading by now." He headed for the door. "Coordinate with Agent Reading, provide whatever assistance you can, but try not to step on too many European toes. Right now, we're going to use the excuse that over twenty billion was stolen from an American citizen, and at least one American citizen is missing. That should justify our involvement, at least temporarily. Keep me posted. I'm going to inform the Director."

"Yes, sir." Morrison left the room and Leroux turned to Tong. "Get me Agent Reading."

They were now official, and there was no need to use the secret app that only he and Tong were officially aware of in the room, though he had little doubt some of his brilliant team were aware there was some clandestine method of communication between him and his best friend. He watched as Reading answered his phone, and Leroux adjusted his headset as Tong gave a thumbs-up.

"Agent Reading, this is Chris Leroux."

"Good to hear your voice. I need your help."

"So I gathered."

"What do you know?"

"Very little. Initial reports are coming in about the bombings and the possible theft of over twenty billion, but these are purely headlines. We have nothing official. What can you tell us?"

"Quite a lot. Highlights first so we don't waste time. Pull everything you can on a woman named Azar Vida. She's the one who was running the show here, and we believe she's involved. It was her people that did this shooting."

Leroux snapped his fingers over his shoulder and Marc Therrien called from the rear of the room. "On it!"

"A black SUV left this area after the shooting. We believe they're heading for an airport, possibly to catch a private jet out of European jurisdiction, though that's just guesswork. Is there any way your people can pull footage and track that vehicle?"

Leroux pointed a finger over his shoulder at Randy Child.

"On it, boss," replied Child.

"Is there anything else you need?"

Reading grunted. "Yeah, a change of damn clothes."

Leroux laughed as Reading yanked the bow tie off. "Okay, Agent, why don't you fill us in on everything you know."

Reading walked over to a bench then sat down, and as the details of the evening were laid out, Leroux dropped into his chair, his head shaking at the implications. Over a dozen explosions. A car bomb that had killed fleeing guests. Power down, communications out. Everything designed to help those involved not only pull off the theft, but make their escape in the confusion. It was unbelievable, and at the moment, every indication was that the perpetrators were getting away with it.

Unknown Location

Acton forced himself to keep his breathing steady. His head pounded from where he had been hit from behind, but other than that, he felt fine. He had been awake for several minutes, but had kept up the pretense of still being out cold. He assumed they were in a vehicle, considering he was sitting upright on something soft, though they weren't moving. All he had heard was a man's voice say a few sentences in a one-sided conversation that must have taken place over a phone. It sounded Farsi to him, though he couldn't be certain. Their theory that it wasn't government might be wrong, though these men could simply be hired guns. The real questions that perplexed him were, why was he alive, and was Laura still?

He had to know.

People were sitting on either side of him. He had a sense that the one to his left was larger than the one to his right. He opened his right eye slightly and caught a glimpse of a bare set of legs he'd recognize anywhere. Laura was with him, and you don't bring dead bodies when you're in a hurry. He suppressed a sigh of relief that threatened to emerge. His hands were resting at his sides, unbound. That could be because they felt he wasn't a threat while unconscious, or that they had nothing to bind them with because this wasn't part of their plan. He had to let Laura know he was awake, so if an opportunity presented itself for escape, she wouldn't hesitate because she thought he was unconscious.

He pushed the knuckle of his forefinger into her leg three times, their secret code to each other, sometimes delivered through hugs, through squeezes of the hand, through taps on the brakes as one of them drove away.

I. Love. You.

She shifted slightly and his heart raced as she replied with three slight shrugs of her left shoulder. She was alive, she was awake, and she was aware he was all right.

Now, the question was why the hell had they been taken? These people had shown they would kill without mercy, and his heart ached for what had happened to the police officer. They had tried to save her life, but instead were responsible for her death. Yes, she had given up the pursuit thanks to them, but if they hadn't been chasing Vida, there would never have been a pursuit. That poor woman would have gone home to her family, enjoyed a long, happy, healthy life.

But now she was dead, a void left in a family, no thanks to them.

He wasn't sure why they always ran toward the trouble. He had certainly never been one to run away. Part of that came from being a professor that took his students to dangerous parts of the world. He was responsible for them, so when one of them got hurt or got themselves in trouble, he'd have to intervene and not show any fear.

Until the events in Peru, however, there had never been any serious danger in his civilian life. He had seen limited action as a National Guardsman in his youth, but over the past few years, trouble just seemed to find him.

Or them.

Laura was as bad as he was with always wanting to do the right thing. His theory was that it had something to do with her brother. She blamed herself for his death. Laura had never shared what had happened the day he died at one of her dig sites. Her desire to rush in to save someone in trouble could be because she thought she hadn't done enough to save her brother. He was certain it was nonsense, that there was nothing she could have done to save him, but it was a subject only ever referred to peripherally.

Whatever the reason, they both enabled each other. They really should learn to back off, and had even discussed pulling back from their international escapades and living a simple life as professors in Maryland.

But they always dismissed the idea.

Their lives were exciting, and as long as they were helping people, then why stop? People died every day, some from heart attacks because they sat on a couch all their lives, some hit by a bus as they rushed across the street to grab a coffee to keep them going a bit longer. If they died trying to save someone else, trying to do the right thing, then so be it. He just prayed that if Laura died, he'd die with her, because he couldn't imagine living life without her.

But today, a police officer was dead because of their meddling.

He cursed at himself. That was bullshit. A police officer was dead because bad people had stolen a lot of money and had killed her while making their escape. Yes, he and Laura had given chase creating the immediate circumstances, but if everyone went through life stopping themselves from doing the right thing because of what *might* happen, you might as well shut down every police force in the world.

Pursuing Vida had been the right thing to do. The blood of the police officer wasn't on his or Laura's hands, it was on Vida's and whomever she was working with or for. He would mourn the officer's death when he had time, but he wasn't accepting blame for what had happened. He would make certain any family she might be responsible for would be well provided for when this was all done.

Assuming we survive.

The man who had been talking said something, merely a few words, and a strange sound started. It was followed by several different beeping sounds and alarms, then something whined as an engine roared to life. It wasn't until the thumping started overhead that he realized where they were, and his heart hammered with the implications.

They were in a helicopter.

Nobody said anything as they lifted off, though Laura's body tensed beside him. Helicopters had limited range, and he wasn't sure why they were in one. He had to guess this was merely transportation to the next stage of the escape plan. He wasn't sure what their destination might be. His only fear now was what their captors might do to them once they arrived, for these weren't simply thieves.

These were proven coldblooded murderers.

Shooting Scene

Vienna, Austria

Reading ended his call with Leroux, thankful there were now experienced people assisting in the investigation, people accustomed to thinking of the big picture, and had the resources to track people internationally. He was certain that's what was going on here. Vida and the others would get themselves out of Europe as quickly as possible, and the local Viennese police weren't equipped to deal with something like that.

This would all have to be dealt with fast. They had to find out what plane they were on, where it was headed, then take them down on the ground with or without the cooperation of local authorities. Likely without, if they were headed for a non-extradition country. It could get ugly, and his friends' lives could be put at risk, though that was assuming they weren't already dead by the time the plane landed.

He sighed heavily. It was all supposition. For all he knew, those behind this were boarding a train and heading for France. With the money and resources that had to have been put behind this, they could be wearing disguises and traveling on new identities.

"What are you thinking?" asked Spencer, now sitting beside him on the bench.

Reading frowned. "I'm thinking there's nothing I can do to save my friends."

"You've already saved them if they can be."

Reading regarded his son. "What do you mean?"

"You got the CIA involved. If anybody can save them, it's them. We're just coppers. Our job is to solve the crimes, so I suggest that's what we do. Leave Jim and Laura to the CIA. Let's solve this crime here, so we know who did this and can bring them to justice and maybe even recover the money."

Reading smiled at his son and slapped him on the knee. "You're absolutely right. Enough wallowing in self-pity and blame." His phone vibrated and he checked the message. It was from his partner, Michelle.

You are now officially the Interpol liaison for this investigation.

He smiled and held up the phone for Spencer. "Now we can officially meddle." He rose and headed over to Winter, who was speaking with several of his colleagues.

Winter acknowledged him. "Agent Reading. You seemed to be having an intense conversation. Were your sources able to provide any useful information?"

Reading shook his head, deciding his "sources" should remain anonymous. "No, but they'll be keeping an eye out for anything." He wagged his phone. "I've just been named the official liaison for Interpol for this investigation."

"Excellent. I'd rather be dealing with someone I don't need to bring up to speed, and someone who hasn't been a bureaucrat his entire life."

Reading eyed him. "Excuse me?"

Winter chuckled. "While you were on the phone, your son told me you're an ex-Scotland Yard DCI."

"That's true."

"Then I'm working with a kindred spirit with access to more resources than I have, should this go international. Now, as a Detective Chief Inspector with at least a decade more experience than me, what would you do?"

"I'd be finding out if Meitner is still alive, then interviewing him. He's a man with a massive amount of resources who is extremely motivated. We need him on our side and working with us."

"Agreed. I've already found out where they took him. I've been assured he's alive and well, and is eager to discuss the situation with us, especially you. In fact, he's insisting on talking with you. Do you know why that is?"

Reading shrugged. "I doubt it's my charming demeanor."

Spencer snorted.

"If I had to hazard a guess, it would be because we've met. He knows I'm friends with Laura Palmer, whom he trusts, and he probably had me checked out before I even arrived in your country."

"So, he already knows he can trust you."

"That would be my guess."

"Then let's go and take advantage of that trust. We need information, and at the moment, we have next to nothing."

Unknown Location

Acton loved the smell of jet fuel. There was just something about it that brought a smile and quickened his pulse. Perhaps it was the fact that throughout his life, it meant he was going somewhere exciting, somewhere exotic, somewhere that held adventure. And an equal number of times, it meant heading home to all he knew and loved.

But today, it brought none of those sweet memories. Instead, it meant he had been right. They had been heading for an airport, and now, potentially, their final moments should their kidnappers feel they were no longer needed.

Something was slightly off, however. The helicopter had powered down and the doors had been opened, and though there was that smell of jet fuel, no planes were taking off. It meant one of two things. Either the power was out here as well, which he doubted, or they were at a small airport, which was far more likely. Effecting an escape from a major airport would be difficult for their captors. There was too much security.

A small private airport with a charter airplane? He had seen it before, and he had little doubt he'd see it again, should they survive the day.

"Let's go," ordered a gruff voice.

Acton continued to play possum. If he forced them to carry him, it could delay them an extra minute or two, and a minute or two, in this situation, could make all the difference if their friends were searching for them.

Something cold was pressed against his temple. "You don't think I know you're awake? Your breathing changed, you idiot. Get out now, or I do to you what I did to that cop."

Acton opened his eyes and shrugged. "It was worth a try."

The man stepped back and Acton glanced over at Laura, flashing her a smile as she climbed out the other side. He stepped out into the night, taking in the scene, confirming they were indeed at a small airport, a Dassault Falcon 7X idling nearby.

Vida strode silently toward the steps and climbed them, disappearing inside the jet as the men and the chopper pilot led him and Laura at gunpoint. His heart was hammering, and he struggled to control the adrenaline pumping into his system. The good news was that it appeared they weren't about to be executed and their captors felt having them alive was still useful, though once they were on that plane and in the air, they might never be seen again.

He just prayed Kane's people were on the case.

Vienna General Hospital

Vienna, Austria

Meitner sat in his hospital bed, a team from the local office having just arrived, communications gear and laptops being set up that would interface with a large mobile unit now parked outside. After a small argument with Dr. Rainer, it was agreed only two people would be in the room to facilitate things.

There was a knock at the door and Michelle entered, pushing a cart. "Hey, Grandpa, your food is here!"

Meitner perked up. He was starving, having refused anything offered by the hospital, knowing Chef Stephan was preparing him something exactly to his dietary requirements. Heavy creams and exotic flavors were no longer part of his life. He had lost the stomach for them years ago. Bland, nutritious, easy on the system were the order of the day.

Though nothing said it couldn't still be a work of art.

She pushed his tray table in position then loaded it with the dishes from the hotel. She removed the covers and was presented with a visual feast, the bright pinks of a seared salmon, the brilliant oranges of baby carrots, the golden browns of fingerling potatoes, and the brilliant greens of string beans bringing a smile.

"And the others?"

"Staff from the hotel are serving the first batch now. More is on the way."

"Excellent."

"Eat, Grandpa, I know you're hungry. Everyone else will be taken care of, but the founder of the feast shouldn't be kept waiting."

He chuckled. "You're right, of course." He attacked his plate, nothing on it requiring a knife, which was just the way he liked things these days, it wouldn't be long before someone would have to feed him, and once that day came, he wouldn't be long for this earth. Death didn't frighten him. He had seen enough of it in his life. He had outlasted his wife, outlasted his son, and in his youth, he had seen more death than anyone should in a lifetime. If everything had gone as planned tonight, he could have died tomorrow a content man, but now with his entire life's work stolen, he was certain he could never rest in peace until the matter was resolved.

He wasn't certain what to pray for. Justice, recovery of the money, or both. If he could have just one, it would be getting the money back. That $22 billion could do so much for so many. Was helping millions of people more important than bringing one, perhaps a few, to justice? He had to believe that helping people was more important, though if God would do him the favor of granting him both, he'd be forever grateful.

He chewed one of his carrots, pleased they were over-cooked as instructed. They could be mushed with a fork if he wanted, rather than served crunchy as they should normally be, but the flavor was all there. Simple, basic, delicious.

The door opened and Bernie entered with a huge smile. Meitner swallowed and took a drink of water. "What has you so happy?"

Bernie wagged his tablet. "Word is out all over social media about what happened."

"And that pleases you?"

"Yes, and I think it'll please you as well." He held out the tablet with the breaking news headline from the BBC.

World's Billionaires step up to do the right thing.

Meitner glanced at a list of names that had already pledged donations that more than replaced the amount stolen. He closed his eyes, feeling the burn for a moment as his heart monitor beeped a little faster.

It had worked.

A smile spread as he opened his eyes.

"See, I told you you'd be pleased."

Meitner stabbed a potato. "You were right." He chewed then swallowed. "Now, tell me what you found out about Miss Vida?"

"Everything your granddaughter told you matches up with the security check that was run against her when we hired her." Bernie scrolled through the file on his tablet. "She's been active on the convention scene for years. All of her letters of references checked out, no criminal record, no red flags. Keep in mind, this was a cursory check. There wasn't any time to really do a deep dive."

"Get the security team back on it. I want that deep dive done."

"At once, sir." Bernie tapped away on the display, sending a message.

One of the people setting up the equipment cleared his throat. "We're online, sir."

Meitner turned his attention to the two-man team. "Do we have a link established with the Control Center at the venue?"

"No, sir. Power is still out there, and even if it weren't, no connection is possible for security reasons. We only had one port open, and it was configured to only allow your bank to communicate with our internal network."

"Do we have any idea where the money actually went?"

"No, sir, and we won't be able to find out until we can get in there. The information should be on the computer that did the transfers."

Meitner cursed. "We need the memory stick. It had all the account numbers on it. I need to know if they used that list to do the transfers. If they did, then the account numbers were changed before I handed it over. If they didn't, then it was done after the fact."

Bernie shook his head. "I checked everything earlier today then handed it directly to you. There's no way those numbers were changed before you handed them over."

Meitner nodded. "You know I trust you one-hundred percent, but let's just reconfirm that the list you were verifying against was accurate and hadn't been switched out."

Bernie paled slightly. "I never thought to check."

"Nor should you have. None of us anticipated anything like this. We protected against attacks from the outside. None of us ever considered an inside job." He growled in frustration. "And we're still assuming that it is." He pointed at Bernie. "Get the list checked to make sure it's the right list. You should only need to confirm a few of the charities because nobody got their money except the first two, and they were the test runs to make sure the system was working. If even one of the other account numbers matches, we know you were working from the wrong list. But your number one priority is finding that memory stick. Talk to the authorities. See if we can get one of our people back in the room just to retrieve it. And get the workstation that was being used to coordinate the transfers while you're at it."

"Yes, sir." Bernie headed out of the room then reappeared a moment later. "Holly would like to see you, sir."

Meitner frowned. He didn't have the time or patience for another argument, but he had made a promise to himself years ago that family always came first. "Show her in." Bernie pulled open the door and Holly stepped inside as contrite as he had ever seen her. Her eyes were red, her cheeks were tear-stained, and her left hand clasped two fingers from her right.

And his heart broke at what he had done.

"I'm sorry, Grandpa."

His chest tightened and he held out his arms. She rushed forward and dropped onto him, hugging and sobbing as he held her.

"I'm so sorry. I've just been under so much stress. I've been scared to tell you."

He let her go and she stood back up. He patted the side of the bed and she perched on it. "Why don't you tell me what's going on? The truth."

She sniffed hard and squared her shoulders but couldn't make eye contact with him. "Almost all the money is gone."

His eyes shot wide and his jaw dropped, his heart monitor ramping up. But he held his tongue, controlling his anger. "How is that even possible?"

"My husband's an idiot."

He grunted. "I told you that the day you announced you were marrying him."

She sighed. "I know. In retrospect, I shouldn't have married him, but at the time, I was so lonely, I was desperate for someone to love me. Let's be honest, I'm not a very likable person, though in my defense, a lot of that is because I've been hurt so often." She gasped, biting a knuckle. "I'm not the prettiest girl out there."

Her shoulders shook and his chest ached. She was his granddaughter, and she would always be beautiful to him, though if he had to be honest with himself, she was right. She wasn't very pretty, but she wasn't ugly either. She was simply plain. Most people were. They were just average looking. Makeup and hair styles would make a difference, but Holly had long given up on that. If he recalled correctly, she had never really tried, perhaps a little too tomboyish in her youth. Michelle, however, was blessed with good looks, with or without a stylist, and she had embraced those good looks, using them to her advantage. And poor Holly had grown up with her vivacious, gorgeous sister to compare herself to. It must have been awful, but to marry who she did because she was afraid no one could ever love her was not only foolish, it was heartbreaking.

He reached out and took her hand. "You're far too hard on yourself, my dear. You are no ugly duckling."

She flashed him a weak smile. "You have to say that. You're my grandfather."

He chuckled and squeezed her hand. "Let's put a pin in that. You said the money is almost all gone, and your husband's an idiot. Did he do something?"

"He's made a string of bad investments. He sees some story online and habitually buys at the peak of the cycle. He's lost tens of millions on everything from cryptocurrency to shorting stocks, then I just recently discovered he's been going to Vegas to try to win it all back. I haven't checked our accounts in years because he handled all the finances, and I never paid it any mind. I assumed the bills were always being paid because nobody was chasing us out of our houses, no one was trying to repossess our cars. Tuition was always paid.

"But I found a casino chip in his pocket and we got in an argument and he confessed everything. I went and checked the accounts. There's almost nothing left. There might be a few million, but he's run up so much debt that there's barely enough money to even service it. He swears he has a way to get all the money back and more, but I don't believe him. He's always been an idiot, like you said. For all I know, he's going to take the last of what we have and buy lottery tickets."

Meitner's mind raced, struggling to listen to every word his grieving granddaughter was saying, for a horrible thought had occurred to him. He interrupted her. "Did he say what his plan was?"

Holly shook her head, fishing a tissue from her handbag. "No, we haven't really spoken for a couple of months. I've been staying at our house in San Bernardino, and he's been at the condo in Miami." She was about to erupt again with tears, but sucked in a deep breath and held it for a moment. "I think we're going to get a divorce." Her voice dropped to a whisper. "Then I'll be alone forever."

This was the first good news he had heard all evening, though he kept that to himself, instead patting her hand. "You have a wonderful son. You will never be alone."

"He's not a big fan of mine either."

"But he's your son, and trust me when I say, a son always loves his mother. All you need to do is put in the effort and repair the relationship, and you'll never be alone. And despite your best efforts, Michelle loves you too. You weren't always like this. Rid yourself of this toxic marriage you've been in for far too long, repair the relationship with your son and your sister, and you'll have a long, full, rich life. I promise you."

"I'll try, Grandpa, but what about the money?"

"Don't you worry about that. I'll have my lawyers deal with your husband and get things settled up. My concern at the moment, however, is what your husband thought he could do to replace a couple of hundred million dollars."

She shook her head. "The man's an idiot. He always thinks in terms of the next big payday, the next big score, the next big hot stock or fad, and he's almost always wrong."

"You don't see where I'm going with this?"

She stared at him.

"I mean, over twenty billion was stolen today. And it was an inside job. Is there any way he is involved?"

Her eyes bulged. "You don't think…"

"I don't know what to think."

She stared at him, then her eyes drifted away as she considered the possibility. "I wouldn't think so, though I got the distinct impression he's borrowed money from some questionable people."

"So then, it's possible."

Her shoulders slumped. "I don't know what to think anymore, Grandpa. Yes, I suppose it is possible, though if he were involved, I'd assume the theft would have failed."

He laughed weakly. "If he is involved, it's the first thing he's done that's ever been successful." He frowned. "I need your permission to have my people go through your finances. Everything."

"Done."

"Good. Now, go get Bernie. We need to get this going right away."

"Yes, Grandpa." She leaned in and gave him a hug and a kiss on the cheek. "You're the best."

He winked. "I know."

She left the room with a smile, and he sighed then frowned as he noticed the two young men standing behind the communications equipment in the corner, awkward expressions on their faces. "You, of course, heard none of that."

"Of course, sir."

Bernie entered. "Holly said you wanted to see me."

"Yes, I have something rather delicate I need you to take care of."

CIA Headquarters, Operations Center 3

Langley, Virginia

"I've got something." Child pointed toward the main displays as his other hand worked his keyboard. Camera footage appeared that rapidly fast-forwarded, tracking a black SUV. It disappeared inside a large building with a helipad on the top, a chopper square in the middle, its rotors still. The footage continued to race forward and a group of people appeared boarding the chopper.

"When did this happen?"

"Almost half an hour ago." Child opened up several more windows on the display showing close-ups of the group as the footage continued to race forward.

Tong squinted then took over control of the additional displays, initiating facial recognition. "The woman in the evening gown is definitely Professor Palmer," she said without waiting for the computer's confirmation.

Leroux agreed. "The one that's being carried over that guy's shoulder has to be Professor Acton."

"Dead or unconscious?"

Leroux shook his head. "I'm not seeing any movement, though that doesn't mean anything." He watched as the rotors spun up and the helicopter lifted off. His eyes narrowed. "How long did they sit there?"

"Three and a half minutes," replied Child.

Tong turned in her chair to face Leroux. "Why would they just sit there?"

"Because everything's timed to the minute, if not the second." He turned to Child. "Where did they go?"

Child skipped the footage ahead. "Vöslau Airfield. It's just south of the city, mostly used for private charters."

"Exactly as Reading suspected. Do we have footage?"

Child indicated the screen with a thrust of his chin. Leroux faced the displays and breathed a sigh of relief at the sight of everyone, including an alive and well Professor Acton, boarding a private jet.

"Well, at least we know he's alive," said Tong. "How long ago was that?"

"Five minutes."

Leroux stared at the image. "Is that plane in the air?"

Child nodded. "It took off almost immediately."

"Timed to the second. Flight plan?"

Child's fingers flew over the keyboard. "Athens."

"Well, we know that's not where they're probably actually headed. Let's get this info to Reading. Put together an executive summary for me.

I'll send it to the Chief and he can push it up the line to see how involved they want to get. If these people are holding twenty-plus billion dollars, they might want to get boots on the ground for when this thing lands."

"Yes, sir," replied Child.

Leroux turned to Tong. "See if we can get IDs on those faces. And find out what assets we have in the area that we could send into what I'm guessing is going to be North Africa."

"Yes, sir." Tong passed off the assignments to members of the team as Leroux stared at a map showing the flight data for the private jet while it banked south following its filed flight plan. For the moment.

"I've got something," called Therrien from the back.

"What?"

"One of our taps in the Caymans picked up a deposit into one of the accounts originating from Meitner's. A little under one million."

"Is it still there?"

"No, it was immediately split into what appear to be four random amounts, all sent to various banks in the Middle East and Asia. I'm still working to see if I can track them from there."

"Okay, keep working at it. But at least this settles one thing."

"What's that?" asked Child.

"This wasn't a technical glitch. The money is not sitting in the ether somewhere waiting for the glitch to be corrected. There's no doubt now that this money was actually stolen."

Over Austrian Airspace

Whoever was behind this had spared no expense. The private jet that Acton and Laura now found themselves captive in was luxurious, though there were no personal touches. This was simply a jet ordered with all the bells and whistles from the factory, no customization as one would expect if it were a private jet owned by someone involved. This was definitely a charter, which made sense. It would be too easy to track back. It was evident the plan all along had been to head from City Hall to the helicopter, then to the airport, uninterrupted.

This plane would take them someplace where the perpetrators would disappear and enjoy their billions, and judging from the demeanor of everyone on the aircraft, it would appear they all believed their plan was still working despite the interruption earlier. They had to know they would eventually be traced, but it would be too late by the time the authorities caught up to them. What they didn't know was that the CIA could already be tracking them, and if that were the case, they might be in for a surprise once they landed.

Vida, the woman he assumed was behind this part of the operation, sat a couple of rows back from them. He hadn't heard her say a word the entire time. One of the gunmen sat across from them, and the rest were in the back. When they had boarded, there had been four additional men, and almost nothing had been said. It was odd. If they thought they were about to successfully escape with $22 billion, shouldn't there at least be smiles?

But there was no jubilation here. Nothing. It could be because two of their men were dead, though that had to be expected in this line of work. No, there was something else going on here. It was as if this were just a job like any other, and not necessarily a well-paying one at that. It was as if these were employees on the clock, and when they reached their destination, they would punch their card and head home to their families.

He desperately wanted to know what was going on. He turned in his seat, his mouth opening to ask just that, when Laura's fingernails dug into the palm of his hand. She stared at him, shaking her head slightly. She was right. Curiosity killed, and right now, he was a cat in their trap. He could be misinterpreting everything. Their original plan likely had them thinking no one would be looking for them for quite some time. After all, they had gone to a lot of trouble to create confusion by taking down the power and communications, but with the shooting of the police officer, people were definitely now searching for them.

Though this could all be nerves. If they were professionals, they were likely thinking about what would happen when they hit the ground in a destination the authorities knew about. But this operation was extremely well-coordinated. They had to have a contingency for that. The only good thing about their situation was that they were still alive.

He chewed his cheek. Were they simply hostages, or were they being kept alive for a reason? Vida knew who they were. Meitner had introduced them. If she were in charge of the charity event, perhaps their files had come across her desk when they had been vetted. She might know exactly who they were and what they were worth, and depending on how good Meitner's people were, how well connected. As he thought about it, he realized the more they knew about who he and Laura were, the better chance they had of staying alive. For the moment, there was no indication they intended to kill them, so he was taking Laura's suggestion and keeping his mouth shut.

Rather than say anything that might change their minds.

En Route to Vienna General Hospital

Vienna, Austria

Reading skimmed the files that had just been sent to him by Leroux. They contained everything the CIA had found out about Vida, and the files were slim. Too slim. If someone were this accomplished, there should be far more information out there on them. As far as the CIA could tell, she was Turkish-born, attended university in California, and had obtained her citizenship shortly after. Her resumé, which appeared to have come from LinkedIn, showed steady employment for almost 20 years, much of it with companies he had never heard of, and then the last five years, she appeared to have switched from public relations to public events. The detailed resumé certainly suggested she was qualified for the job she was hired to do, with almost no notice.

But as was noted by the CIA analyst who had compiled the information, the LinkedIn profile had been created only a few weeks before. Now, that wasn't necessarily unheard of. People were joining the platform all the time at various points in their career. But he didn't believe in coincidences. There was no doubt Vida was involved, and this was yet more evidence that a grander conspiracy might be at play.

"We're here," said Winter from the front seat. Reading looked up from his phone to find them at the hospital. He surveyed the area and noticed a large RV parked nearby with men and women streaming in and out of it, its roof bristling with satellite dishes and antennae. It had to be Meitner's people.

"Uh oh."

Reading turned to his son. "What?"

Spencer pointed. "It looks like the press found out he's here."

Reading and Winter both turned, cursing at the same time, but in different languages. Winter glanced at his partner. "Let's get some people down here for crowd control."

"Yes, sir." Strobl stayed in the car to make the call as the rest of them entered the building. Within minutes, they were in Meitner's room, who, from all outward appearances, seemed well, and Reading knew enough about the numbers shown on the monitors to see that he wasn't in immediate danger.

After introductions were made, Meitner directed his attention toward Reading. "I'm surprised to see you're not with your friends."

Reading frowned. "Tommy and Mai are at the hotel and safe, with your necklace by the way, but Jim and Laura are missing."

"Missing?" The heart rate monitor ticked a little faster.

"They spotted Miss Vida leaving with several of the security team and thought that was suspicious, so they followed them. There was an incident involving the police. A police officer was killed and two of the security team are dead. It's my opinion Jim and Laura shot the hostiles. I just received word from some contacts of mine that have had time to analyze the camera footage. It appears they were captured at the shooting, then taken to a pre-positioned helicopter, which then took them to an airport south of the city where they boarded a private charter heading for Athens."

Meitner stared off in the distance as he processed this new information. "So, it is Vida," he finally said.

"It would appear so."

"I suspected as much. We need to intercept that aircraft when it lands."

Winter agreed. "We're already coordinating with the Greeks, though it's Agent Reading's opinion Athens isn't their ultimate destination."

Meitner regarded Reading for a moment. "You believe they're heading someplace else where they can disappear, like North Africa or the Middle East?"

Reading nodded. "Everything we've seen this evening has been planned down to the minute. Jim and Laura were never supposed to be part of the equation. If it weren't for them, Vida might not even be a suspect at the moment. They would have boarded that plane without incident, and we wouldn't have even thought to be looking for them. They'd land somewhere in a few hours, then transfer somewhere else as planned."

"But now they're going to have to change those plans," said Meitner.

"The shooting has changed things, yes."

"Then why take the professors?"

"We're assuming they took them to hide their escape, but now that they're in the plane, there's no real need to keep them alive unless they think they can use them as hostages should we catch up with them."

Meitner pursed his lips. "If they head somewhere like North Africa, there is no way we can catch them. This is so well-coordinated, they'll have bought off whoever they need to. They'll have planned for this contingency."

"Agreed," said Reading.

"Then what are we going to do?"

"My friends are quite well connected. I have little doubt plans are already underway that go far beyond anything we could do officially."

Winter eyed him. "What do you mean?"

Reading smirked slightly. "Let's just say that if I told you, I'd have to kill you."

Winter stared at him. "Excuse me?"

Spencer leaned in. "I think something was lost in the translation."

Reading chuckled. "I think so."

Winter's eyes widened. "Oh, I see."

Meitner frowned. "While I desire justice, my bigger concern is the money. We're trying to confirm what accounts the money was sent to. We're assuming the destination list was changed, but we don't know if it was changed before I handed the key over or after. We need to get access to the Control Center so we can get that key and check it."

Reading glanced at Winter. "Perhaps you can facilitate that, Inspector?"

"Absolutely." He turned to Strobl who wagged his phone and headed out into the corridor.

Spencer cleared his throat. "If you're looking for the memory stick, sir, Miss Vida has it."

Everyone in the room turned toward the young man.

"What do you mean?" asked Reading.

"I mean, when this whole thing happened and the money was disappearing, I saw her reach over and pull a memory stick from the workstation controlling everything. That had to be it."

Meitner leaned forward. "And that didn't stop the transfers?"

One of Meitner's people sitting in the corner rose. "It wouldn't, sir. That's not the way it was set up. The software was designed to pull all the information from the memory stick and copy it to the control computer. The memory stick wasn't needed after that."

Spencer eyed him. "Why would you do that?"

The man shrugged. "Why not? It reduces several points of possible failure."

Reading regarded the man. "Then that means the account list is on that computer, even if she took the memory stick?"

"Yes, sir, it should be."

Reading turned to Winter. "We need that machine."

Winter left the room and Meitner beckoned Reading closer. "These contacts of yours, these friends of the professors. I'm assuming there are three letters associated with them?"

Reading chuckled. "And then some."

"Do they think there's any hope of getting my money back?"

Reading frowned. "It's too early to say, though they were able to track one of the transfers, which confirms the money was indeed stolen. Trust me when I say, the best people in the world are working on it, but I wouldn't get my hopes up."

Meitner leaned back, his shoulders sagging. "Then I suppose justice is all I can hope for."

Kaduna, Nigeria

Command Sergeant Major Burt "Big Dog" Dawson peered through his binoculars. He wanted to be in the thick of today's operation, but they were merely there for support. Even the locals they were backing up didn't know who they were. They had been told his team was a special forces unit from their own country, which had, of course, necessitated keeping his men isolated the entirety of the time they had been in-country.

They were Delta Force, officially 1st Special Forces Operational Detachment—Delta, America's elite. A scalpel if needed, a sledgehammer when necessary, and today, they hoped to be neither.

Invisible.

Over 200 young girls had been kidnapped from their schools by Boko Haram. It was yet another atrocity committed by these insane Islamic fundamentalists. Why the world tolerated this garbage, he didn't know. Send in a few hundred specialized troops like him with orders to shoot anyone with a gun, and they could wipe out 90% of them in a matter of days, crippling their capacity to do significant harm.

But today was a rescue op. Someone had tipped off the local authorities about the girls' location, and the government had reached out to Washington for assistance. His team had been assigned, and if all went well, this would be over within minutes.

He activated his comm. "This is Zero-One. Sniper teams, report in, over."

"Team One in position," reported Sergeant Carl "Niner" Sung, the team's best sniper, paired with Sergeant Trip "Mickey" McDonald as his spotter.

"Team Two in position," rumbled Sergeant Leon "Atlas" James, partnered with Sergeant Will "Spock" Lightman.

"Team Three in position," replied Sergeant Gerry "Jimmy Olsen" Hudson, Sergeant Eugene "Jagger" Thomas playing spotter.

"Copy that," acknowledged Dawson. "Control, Zero-One, teams are in place. Signal the locals they're clear to proceed, over."

"Roger that, Zero-One. Stand by."

There was a pause as he continued to sweep the area for any surprises. They were targeting an abandoned school on the outskirts of a small town in northern Nigeria. To characterize this place as dirt poor would insult the dirt poor. He felt for these people. Not the terrorists, but the locals.

There but for the grace of God, go I.

He was blessed to have been born in the United States, but billions around the world were born into abject poverty. Back home, some of the ignorant blamed these people for their own plight, claiming they should get a better education, they should take advantage of the opportunities presented to them. Yet how do you take advantage of an education when your government's official policy was that girls couldn't go to school? Or where you lived in a place like this where groups like Boko Haram, where their name literally meant "Western education is forbidden," kidnapped girls for attending school? How could these people take advantage of an education when none was available? And what opportunities were there in this part of the world?

It wasn't as if Amazon was opening a distribution center a few miles down the road to employ the locals. The only opportunity most had was to continue to farm the land they had for generations, and if they got lucky, hope some mining or oil company would open up nearby seeking able-bodied people for the dangerous work. Yet the very people who would scream at their government to help these people were the same ones screaming to shut down every natural resource company in existence.

The disconnect was mind-numbing.

This was why he always found this type of mission satisfying. Assuming they were successful today, a good thing would be accomplished, and these poor girls would be returned home to their families, and the schools they had been kidnapped from.

"Zero-One, Control, locals are moving in, over."

"Copy that, Control. Bravo Team, locals are moving in. Eliminate any targets of opportunity at the first sign of any hostile activity."

A string of acknowledgments came through his earpiece as engines roared. He turned to his right and watched as half a dozen troop carriers sped down what could barely be called a road, violently jostling their passengers. He returned his attention to the village and cursed as several dozen men emptied from a mosque, each grabbing their weapon they had left outside, resting against the whitewashed walls while they prayed, the hypocrisy clearly lost on them.

Somebody barked orders, coordinating what would be the response. He appeared to know what he was doing, directing his men to exactly the same positions as Dawson would if he were in charge. He checked right and cursed. "Control, Zero-One, warn the locals they're about to enter a shooting gallery if they don't spread out now."

"Relaying. Stand by." He returned his attention to the defensive positions now setting up, listening for the sound of the engines to change.

But they didn't.

He cursed. This would be a massacre, and the undisciplined troops were liable to retreat, then the girls could be killed or moved. He withdrew his sidearm and fired it into the air. "Control, Zero-One. Hostilities have commenced. Engaging as per ROEs, over."

"Copy that, Zero-One."

He smiled slightly at his commanding officer's voice, Colonel Thomas Clancy. The tone suggested Clancy was fully aware of what he had just done, which meant his position must be covered by a drone. But none of that mattered right now. They had to act fast. "Bravo Team,

Zero-One. Engage targets of opportunity. If they've got a weapon, take them down."

Acknowledgments were quickly replaced by the thunderclap of sniper rifles set up in three different positions, giving them full coverage of the area. He peered through his binoculars as man after man dropped, half a dozen gone before their accomplices realized they were being engaged. More fell as the expert marksmen from his unit continued to work, the first truck rounding the final bend, four men standing in the back, their weapons held over the cab of their vehicle, pouring lead on the confused terrorists.

He spotted the man in charge racing toward a technical with a .50 cal in the back. "This is Zero-One, if anyone's got a bead on the guy in the red bandana heading for the technical, take him out."

"With pleasure," replied Niner, and a moment later red mist blasted from the man's back as he crumpled into a heap.

Dawson smiled. "Good shot, One-One."

"We aim to please."

Two more trucks of troops were now at the outskirts, men pouring out the back, spreading to the left and right, undisciplined fire raining down on the hostiles. He prayed stray bullets didn't hurt or kill any one of the girls he could hear screaming from inside the school. The enemy gunfire dwindled and one of the men threw down his AK-47, shoving his hands high over his head. Another followed, then another, and within moments, Boko Haram had surrendered.

"Bravo Team, hold your fire. Monitor for any surprises."

More acknowledgments came in as the locals swarmed the area. The terrorists were collected and lined up against the front of their mosque.

"Shit, are they about to do what I think they're about to do?" asked Niner.

"Cut the chatter," ordered Dawson. "Zero-One, Control. Should we intervene?"

"Zero-One, Control Actual. Negative, unless you can think of a way to do so without killing our partners on this mission."

Dawson rose, ready to sprint down to the village from his elevated position, when gunfire rang out, rendering moot anything he might say. He peered through his binoculars and cursed. The terrorists were dead, the whitewashed walls stained red. This had turned from a rescue op to a massacre, which was one reason his team's involvement was so secret. Ops like this with undisciplined troops could quickly turn ugly, and America couldn't be officially involved.

There had been many times when he wanted to execute his enemy, but it went against his training. Yes, sometimes the mission was to execute, though that was under direct orders, the targets often on the President's Termination List. They were legal orders.

But this was something different. Yes, these were terrorists, yes, they deserved to die, yet they should have been taken into custody and given a fair trial, then if the laws of the land permitted it, sentenced to death for what they had done.

This was cold-blooded revenge.

He didn't blame them. These were their children that had been kidnapped, but that was no excuse.

More transports rolled in and the doors of the school were opened. Half a dozen soldiers entered and, moments later, several adult women were hauled out and thrown to the ground. Dawson rose and sprinted toward the scene to stop yet another massacre, when the commander of the operation shouted something as he finally stepped from his jeep to properly take command of the situation. Words were spat at the women who cowered on the ground. He kicked one of them, then pointed. The women all scrambled to their feet and ran away, leaving Dawson relieved and taking cover.

A young girl emerged from the school, squinting into the light. The commander urged her forward and more followed. They were directed to the trucks and soldiers lifted them inside, and as each one was filled, it pulled away, each guarded by four troops.

"Activity on the rooftop. Engaging." Niner hadn't said which rooftop. A shot rang out, girls screamed, a soldier spun, and Dawson spotted the target drop from the roof of the mosque. Soldiers rushed forward, surrounding the man, several more shots put into him needlessly, Niner already having removed the vermin from God's earth. The evacuation continued with renewed vigor, and minutes later, the girls and the last of the troops pulled out of the area.

"Bravo Team, Zero-One. Rendezvous at evac point Alpha, over."

Acknowledgments were heard as he rose, heading for the chopper a couple of klicks away. He spotted Niner and Mickey to his right and made a beeline to join them. He heard someone behind him and he checked to see the massively muscled Atlas lumbering toward him. Dawson slowed up for the big man and Spock.

Atlas wiped the sweat off his brow as they all met up, the final team on the far side of the target area, a couple of minutes behind them. "I can't wait to get out of this godforsaken place. I'm sweating so much, even my balls have lost weight."

"Me too," agreed Niner.

Atlas gave him a sideways glance. "I'm sorry, dude, but those marbles you have can't be called balls."

Niner batted a hand at him. "See, I knew you were looking."

Spock cocked an eyebrow. "You guys should really talk to Vanessa and Angela about entering into some sort of polyamorous relationship."

Atlas and Niner both stared at him. "Huh?"

"What the hell is that?" rumbled Atlas.

Dawson grinned at Spock, having only recently discovered what it meant. It was a changing world, and he was of the opinion that he didn't care what people did, as long as everyone was consenting.

Spock shrugged. "Look it up when we get home, but think of your mathematics."

Niner rolled his eyes. "You're going to ruin good old sex with math?"

Atlas punched him on the shoulder. "We were talking about your balls. Who said anything about sex?"

Niner gave him a look. "*You* were talking about your balls *and* my balls. There's no *we* about it." His eyes shot wide. "Oh, I get it!"

"You get what?" rumbled Atlas.

"What polyamorous means." Niner winked at him. "I don't think you could handle me."

"Handle you?"

Everyone roared in laughter at Atlas' confusion. Niner reached over and cupped one of Atlas' ass cheeks, giving it a squeeze. "You know what I mean."

Niner was on the ground after a swat from Atlas' massive hand. "Sergeant Major, I'd like to file a formal complaint."

Dawson looked away. "I didn't see anything."

The others did the same.

Dawson extended a hand and Niner grabbed it. He hauled him to his feet. "So, how are things going with Angela? You haven't screwed it up yet?"

"They're going great. She could be the one."

Atlas eyed him. "What? The one that lasts beyond the first month?"

"Haha. We're actually getting along great. The fact she knows what I do makes things so much simpler. Every woman I've dated in the past—"

"Which would be none," interjected Spock.

A bird was flipped. "—had to start off with a lie and stay that way. I just never felt comfortable with it." Niner eyed Dawson. "And what about those wedding plans?"

Dawson was about to open his mouth to reply when his comm squawked in his ear. "Zero-One, Control Actual, come in, over."

"Control Actual, Zero-One, go ahead."

"Change of plans for your team. There's been an incident in Austria. We might need your involvement."

Dawson's eyes narrowed. "Austria? Why aren't the Europeans handling it?"

"The incident occurred in Austria, but the perpetrators could be heading for North Africa. They've taken hostages, including an American. Time is of the essence, Zero-One. They could be landing in as little as three hours."

"Copy that, Control. Count on us to not waste any time." He indicated to the others to pick up the pace, and he began a jog toward their evac point. "Do we know who the perpetrators are?"

"Negative, Zero-One, but the hostages are friends of yours."

Dawson slowed slightly. "Don't tell me it's who I think it is."

"It is."

"How in the hell did two archaeology professors manage to get themselves taken hostage in Austria, then flown to North Africa?"

"That, Zero-One, is something only a higher source can answer."

Vienna City Hall
Vienna, Austria

Wagner desperately had to pee. He hadn't had a chance since before the event had started. He certainly hadn't had a chance since the theft. He had been running around the outside of the building with the Interpol agent, and was now liaising with the police since Vida had left him in charge by disappearing.

And it was terrifying.

The police were escorting him and one other tech back into the building to retrieve the Transfer Station. The police had assured him the building had been swept and there was no danger. They were probably right, but this wasn't what he had signed up for. As an assistant project director, he was tasked to provide advice to senior management, and operate the Transfer Station during the event. Nowhere in his job description did it mention bombs or terrorists. Yet he had gone in willingly. If it weren't him, then someone else would take his place, and he wouldn't let one of his colleagues put their life at risk because of his cowardice.

He spotted a sign for the bathroom. "Sorry, guys. I have to hit the head. No choice." He pushed through the doors as one of the police officers protested. "No choice!" he shouted again over his shoulder. The tech appeared a moment later, and so did two of the officers, everyone draining a lizard. Sighs echoed.

I guess police officers have to go to the bathroom too.

With everyone finished and hands washed, they ran toward the Control Center to make up the time. Power was still out in the building, emergency lighting still operating, but their destination was on a generator. He swiped his pass and the door beeped. He pushed it aside and headed directly for the computer in question. He dropped in front of the keyboard and frowned at the dead terminal. He glanced around the room to see the others still on, then remembered Spencer had unplugged it.

The tech reached from behind the station to unplug everything and Wagner waved him off. "No, wait. Plug it back in."

"Wait? Are you kidding me? Let's get the hell out of here as fast as we can!"

"We will, but the moment that's un-hooked, we don't have access to the data until it's hooked back up somewhere else. We need that data now."

The tech cursed but plugged it back in. It took a few moments for the machine to reboot, then Wagner's fingers flew over the keyboard. He fished a memory stick from his pocket and plugged it in, then transferred the datafile downloaded from Meitner's memory stick earlier. He confirmed the data had transferred then shut the computer down and removed the storage device. "Okay, we're good."

The tech started yanking cables and Wagner lifted the computer from the desk and handed it to the much younger subordinate. He turned to the police. "We've got it."

"Good, then let's get out of here. Bomb techs have been known to miss things."

Wagner gulped and too many muscles relaxed.

And he thanked God he had gone to the bathroom when he did.

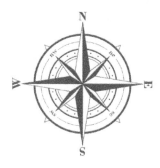

Unknown Location

41,000 feet

Acton's head throbbed from when he had been pistol-whipped. He could desperately use an ice pack, but he wasn't sure if he should ask for one, especially considering none were probably on board. An LED clock mounted at the front of the cabin indicated almost 45 minutes had gone by since they had taken off. If anything had been said by their captors, he hadn't heard it. Vida sat alone in the back, the half-dozen guards scattered through the cabin. One sat directly across from them, never taking his eyes off his charges, swapping out about every 15 minutes like clockwork.

Military precision.

It meant they were properly guarded. No tired eyes, no bored eyes, just 15 minutes of laser focus. They couldn't get away with anything, but it also meant he had an opportunity to closely examine each of them. They all appeared Middle Eastern, 35 to 45, in excellent shape, clean-shaven with Western-style haircuts. Their suits were mid-range, not cheap, but not bespoke, and their shoes were boots polished to a sheen.

The man currently guarding them eyed Laura's legs, and Acton glared at him, clenching his fists. They still weren't bound, leaving no doubt that hostages had never been part of the plan. But he wasn't about to punch the guy out for ogling his wife. It could result in something far worse than leering. This was the first person to stare, the first sign of any lack of discipline. If he were to try something, one would hope the others would stop him rather than join in.

Acton was convinced these were military, or former military. The question was, what country? With them all appearing Middle Eastern, that couldn't be a coincidence. And unfortunately, it meant an undisciplined military with soldiers who couldn't be trusted to do the right thing. Good men could do bad things when desperate, but stealing and rape were two completely different things. And even a good soldier turned bad would never commit such an atrocity or stand by while it was done.

But were these good soldiers?

Whether they were Iranian, Syrian, or some other military, he couldn't say, and while he wouldn't trust them as far as he could throw one of them, just because someone was from a certain country that was your enemy, didn't mean they were a bad person. It was why no German wanted to be on the Russian front. Get captured by an American, Brit, or Canadian, and you knew you would be appropriately treated. Get captured by a Russian, and you were allowed to be tortured then executed. In the final days of World War II, German civilians were desperate to be on the right side of the line, and that didn't mean the German side. Soviet troops were raping their way across eastern Germany with the blessing of their officers until Stalin finally put an end to it, though not before concerns were expressed by his civilized allies.

Right now, Acton had no idea what type of people he was dealing with. He didn't want to jump to conclusions, but he couldn't let his guard down.

The man reached into his breast pocket and pulled out a ringing satellite phone. The conversation was one-sided for the most part. The man's eyes bulged then his cheeks flushed as his jaw clenched. He ended the call and sprang to his feet, marching down the aisle to the back. Shouts erupted and Acton turned his head and peered between the seats. The entire security team was huddled together, and it was apparent they were all getting angry.

Yet Vida sat in her seat, emotionless, saying nothing.

Then the first finger was jabbed, the anger directed at her.

"What's going on?" whispered Laura.

"They're pissed about something, and it looks like they're directing their anger at Vida."

"How's your head?"

It still pounded, but he told her a little white lie. "It's fine. What do you think we should do?"

"Is there anything we *can* do? There are half a dozen guns against two sets of fists."

He pursed his lips. "All it would take is getting our hands on one gun, then we could shoot out a window."

Laura's eyes shot wide. "What the hell good would that do?"

"It would force them to land. Right now, we're still in Europe. Something tells me that's not our final destination."

"Depressurizing the aircraft could get us killed."

"And landing outside of Europe is probably going to get us killed too."

"And just how do you propose to get a gun?"

He jerked his head toward the growing argument. "They're angry now. Distracted. Discipline is failing, so their guard will be down. I suggest you show a little bit more thigh, then when our friend returns, I'll take him down, get his weapon, and shoot out one of the windows. That will force us to land and give the authorities a chance to save us."

"Or they could just execute us."

Acton shrugged. "At least we'll have died doing something."

She leaned in and gave him a kiss. "You're right. I'd rather go down fighting than executed the moment these people think they're safe."

"So, we're agreed then?"

Laura hiked up what remained of her dress. "Let's do this."

Vienna General Hospital

Vienna, Austria

Meitner stared at the display his team had set up, showing the flight status of Vida's private charter. Reading entered the room with his son, his eyebrows rising slightly.

"Is that what I think it is?"

"Yes."

"How did you find out the flight number?"

Meitner batted a hand. "It doesn't take a genius to find out the flight number of a plane leaving for Athens from the south of the city within the past hour. With that amount of search criteria, the result set is almost always one."

Reading grunted. "I suppose so. Any sign of deviation yet?"

"No, but I would suspect it would be last minute. Has there been any news?"

"Yes. Apparently, there's one cellphone tower working inside the dead zone which the powers that be thought was suspicious. Bomb techs were sent and they found an undetonated weapon. The Inspector and his partner are heading over there now. It might give us a clue as to who's behind this."

A phone rang in the corner and one of the techs answered it. "Sir, Mr. Wagner retrieved the data. He's uploading it now."

"Good. Get me Bernie."

Reading held up a hand. "I'll get him. He's just outside." He disappeared for a moment then returned with Meitner's longtime aide.

"Sir?"

"Wagner has the data. Do you have your official list?"

Wagner held up his tablet. "Yes, sir."

Meitner's heart rate monitor picked up slightly. This was the moment of truth. Had the betrayal happened before he handed over the memory stick thus widening the suspect pool dramatically, or had it happened after he handed it over, narrowing it to very few possibilities.

A paper rolled out of the printer and the tech handed it over to Bernie, who only took a split second to confirm what Meitner was hoping.

Bernie shook the page. "These are all wrong. Well, I assume they're all wrong. I've seen enough to know this isn't the list of approved account numbers."

Meitner slumped into his pillows, thanking God. So many suspects had just been eliminated, not the least of which was his granddaughter's husband. Though perhaps that was premature. Just because the accounts hadn't been changed before the handover, didn't mean any he suspected weren't still involved.

Reading regarded Bernie. "But that doesn't really tell us anything, does it?"

Bernie stared at him. "It tells us that the numbers were changed."

"Yes, but it doesn't tell us when. All we know for sure is that the numbers on the memory stick don't match what you thought were on the memory stick. It still could have been changed beforehand."

Bernie vehemently shook his head. "No, you're forgetting that I'm the one who put them on the stick. I verified the accounts and then handed it directly to Mr. Meitner."

"And it never left my possession," confirmed Meitner. "With the account numbers being different, we know it changed between the time I handed it over, and the time they were copied to the machine."

Reading smiled. "Then our suspect pool has narrowed down quite a bit. Who would have had it after you handed it over?"

"The young woman you saw should have taken it directly to Miss Vida, and she would have handed it to Wagner, who was the controller for the Transfer Station."

"She didn't have any security assigned to her, if I remember correctly."

Meitner sighed. "An oversight that I now regret. We assumed perimeter security was enough."

"It never is if there's someone on the inside working against you. We need to find her. She could be the key to all of this."

Meitner's eyes bulged. "Wait! We now have all the destination accounts, don't we?"

The tech nodded.

"Get the team on it. I want every one of those banks called to see if we can freeze those accounts."

"And forward it to me," said Reading. "My contacts might have a little more success."

Meitner snapped his fingers. "Do that first."

Reading's phone vibrated with the receipt of the account list and he tapped away at it for a moment. He held it up. "Done. Let's hope we get some back at least."

Bernie gasped and everyone turned toward him. "What is it?" asked Meitner.

Bernie stepped over and handed him the piece of paper. "Do you notice anything strange here?"

Meitner stared at a jumble of account numbers. "What am I supposed to be looking at?"

"Ignore the account numbers, sir. Well, don't entirely ignore them. Look at the amounts."

His eyes darted to the right of the page. Random numbers. He wasn't sure what his trusted man was referring to. Then his jaw dropped as he spotted the pattern. Half a dozen accounts, all getting one or two million dollars, and then an account would get over half a billion, the pattern sustained. He glanced over at the tech. "Is this the order they would have been done in?"

"Yes, sir."

Everything was set up to be dramatic. Meitner's chest tightened at just how dramatic it was. The first two transfers were legit, exactly as had been expected for the test run, but the rest all went into the wrong accounts for minuscule amounts, except every fifth or sixth transaction transferred an enormous amount all into the same account.

It would explain why the counter on the screen had continually dropped at the expected rate. The counter had been programmed to roll down consistently, not in big increments. His people had explained that audiences got more excited over a constantly decreasing number rather than one that would drop in spurts. It had disguised the half-billion-dollar withdrawals that should have been split over half a dozen charities.

Reading stood impatiently at the foot of the bed. "What is it? What have you two found?"

Meitner shook the page. "Almost all of the money went into a single account. Let your people know, just in case they miss it like I did. Forget all the other accounts. It's this one that's key." Reading's thumbs flew over his keyboard as Meitner turned to his people. "Find out what bank this is and get its president on the phone right now. Find out what jurisdiction it is, and get the president of that damn country on the phone right now. If there's any chance at stopping the money from being transferred further, we need to act fast."

CIA Headquarters, Operations Center 3

Langley, Virginia

"Where is the account located?" asked Leroux.

"Cayman Islands," replied Tong.

"Do we have a tap at that bank?"

"Limited. A security sweep two weeks ago removed most of our access, and we haven't been able to get back in for more than a few minutes. They appear to be actively monitoring."

Leroux regarded Tong as he scratched his chin. "Two weeks ago, huh?"

"Yes, sir."

"And that account, do we have any information on it?"

"Only some tombstone information. We can't access balances or anything anymore."

"Please tell me we've got a name."

"Oh, we've got a name. And you're not going to believe it."

Butterflies in his stomach shared in his excitement. "Who?"

"Jason Harper."

Leroux eyed her. "Who the hell is that? Why does it sound familiar?"

"It's the husband of one of Meitner's granddaughters, Holly Meitner. Both granddaughters kept the family name."

"So, this really was an inside job conducted by an idiot," interjected Child. "Who puts their real name on the account?"

Leroux's head slowly bobbed. Child was right. It was foolish, and it could only make sense if the person were utterly inept and had no idea what they were doing, or—

"Could someone be setting him up?" asked Tong, interrupting his thoughts.

"Definite possibility. When was that account opened?"

She checked her screen. "Two weeks ago."

Leroux chewed his cheek. "Again, two weeks. So, two weeks ago, an account is opened in Harper's name at a bank that conducts a security sweep at the same time, kicking us out of its servers, a LinkedIn profile is created for Vida, the primary on the project dies in a car accident, and Vida is hired within a couple of days of that. That's a lot of coincidences."

"Too many," agreed Tong.

"Okay, here's what we're going to do. Sonya, have someone pull the accident report for the car crash. Get our own forensics experts to go over the file, see if they spot anything unusual. And do a deep dive on Harper. We need to know everything there is to know about him. And find out if we have any specialists in the Caymans or near the Caymans, someone that could get inside and tell us what the hell's going on with that money."

Tong indicated one of the clocks on the wall showing their current time. "It's pretty late. The bank is going to be closed."

Leroux frowned. "We're going to need someone who can break in and bypass the alarms."

Tong worked her station and smiled. "We do have someone, but he's on vacation."

"Who?"

"Jack."

Leroux smiled. "Reach out. Let's hope he's not too far into a bottle."

Vienna, Austria

October 2, 1941

"Happy Birthday!"

Daniel spun around, his heart hammering at the unexpected greeting from Petra. Behind him, he gently pushed back into place the stone he had pried out only moments before. "Are you sure it's my birthday?" Of course he knew it was. He was thirteen today. He should be celebrating his bar mitzvah. He should be surrounded by his family and friends, receiving gifts, singing, dancing, eating.

But he had none of that.

"You know it's your birthday, silly." She jutted her chin toward the wall behind him. "What are you doing there?"

The blood drained from his face and he prayed she couldn't see it in the faint light cast by their lamp shining through the door of their hideaway. It was everything he could do to not rapidly shake his head, denying the one secret he had kept. "Nothing." He held up a stick with a rat on it that he had killed earlier for just this situation. "Just killing a rat."

Petra shivered and recoiled. "Oh, I hate those things! If we ever get out of here, I hope to never see another rat again."

He lifted the stick a little higher as he rose. "If we don't get more meat soon, we might have to figure out how to cook these."

Petra gagged and turned her head. "Just get it out of my sight."

He laughed and stepped down the corridor, tossing the stick with its victim into the slowly running water of the sewage and waste-water system.

"Come into the room. I've got something to show you."

"I'll be there in a second."

It had been months since he had met Petra, and a lot had happened. And a lot hadn't. She had taught him how to survive on the streets, how to get water, how to stay clean, how to feed himself, how to keep an eye out for items that might be of use. And their little collection had grown with all manner of tools, including the lamp that did so much more than the lone candles they had been using.

When he had first met her, he had assumed they were the same age, but he was mistaken. Her slight frame from barely surviving over months had misled him. They had celebrated her sixteenth birthday not a month ago. She was like his big sister and he loved it. They were making a home now, and thriving for the most part. Over the many months they had accomplished quite a bit. Their bed was now off the floor, and they still shared it rather than making a second. Each night, he'd climb in and place his back to her. She'd join him then wrap her arms around him, and he would close his eyes, imagining it was his mother.

It was the closest thing to normal he had in his life.

He eyed the stone that hid the only secret he had kept from her. The spoons. He kept them hidden on his person for the first few days, but had quickly realized there was no way to keep them from her for long. And when she had come back one day with a wallet she had stolen, she had been so excited about the new possibilities it represented, that his entire perspective changed.

He was living with a thief.

At the time, the very notion had horrified him, but the next day when she returned with real meat, he had embraced her new skill, and the two of them had practiced on each other for weeks. And now, the two of them were out pickpocketing whenever they weren't seeking something specific. Most days, they weren't successful, but they were successful enough.

Yet money didn't buy everything, especially when there was nothing to buy. Rationing was tight and the black-market prices kept going up. A healthy-sized piece of sausage now cost five times what it used to, and fewer people had full wallets.

It was getting tougher to survive, and those spoons he now understood were solid gold and worth a fortune, could change everything for them. He feared if Petra found them, she might insist they use them to make their lives easier, and he was having none of that. These belonged to his parents, they were all he had left of them beyond the contents of the small suitcase, so when she had been out on her own in those first few days, he had found a loose stone in the wall just around the corner from where they were hiding. He had managed to pry it out and hide the spoons without her ever knowing, and he checked on them regularly to make certain they were still there.

He hadn't been able to hide the package with his mother's message, however. It had been in the suitcase and she spotted it the first time he opened it to get out his pajamas. She had wanted to open the package, but he had refused. "Not until we're safe, then we'll open it together." She had been disappointed, but agreed, though each day he checked to make certain it remained untouched in the suitcase. He wasn't sure why. They had been through so much together that he trusted her, though perhaps deep down, he didn't. After all, this was survival. He had recognized long ago they were stronger together, though he feared the moment Petra felt they weren't, she might betray him, for she didn't really need him.

He had to accept the fact he couldn't truly trust anybody. His parents were dead. His friends and family were no longer part of his life. Everything and everyone that had kept him safe were gone. He had told the story to Petra, and her fifteen-year-old mind had comprehended what his twelve-year-old mind barely could. The powders were poisoned and they took them willingly. His mother had switched his powder for one that would just put him to sleep, to give him a chance for a life by escaping with his uncle.

An escape that had failed.

Yet what gnawed at him every time he was alone with his thoughts was the fact the truck had made it around the corner. Were Peter and his children still alive? His aunt was dead, and so was the stranger who had come to the apartment, but everyone else was inside that truck. The thought that Peter was out there somewhere with Hermann and Erica, perhaps safe in America, was comforting somehow. If they were alive, then it meant the memory of his family remained, and perhaps they might not be forgotten.

He entered their home, for that's what it was despite its true nature, a forgotten storage room built decades ago. He found Petra standing in the center of the room, a grin on her face.

"Happy Birthday!" she cried then stepped aside, revealing a box sitting on a table they had salvaged several months ago.

"What's that?"

"Open it."

He hurried over, his heart pounding in excitement at what might be inside. He dropped to his knees and unfolded the top, his eyes widening as he gasped. "A radio!" He glanced back over his shoulder at her. "Where did you find it?"

"I was scrounging a couple of streets over and it fell out of a window and hit the ground in front of me. I think it was an accident because I heard somebody swearing from above. When I realized what it was, I remembered the stories you told of fixing the radios and the other things with your father, so I collected all the pieces. Maybe you can get it to work. Maybe we can get some real news for once, instead of the lies printed in the newspapers."

His eyes glistened and he leaped to his feet, hugging her hard. "You're the best friend I ever had."

She squeezed him tight. "You're the best friend I ever had as well," she cried, her voice cracking. She stepped over to a small storage cabinet they had built from scraps, and opened the door. She pulled out a small package and placed it beside the box. "One last gift that I hope you'll share with me."

He couldn't imagine anything that could top the project that lay ahead contained within the box, but he eagerly opened the second package and nearly fainted.

It was a cupcake, complete with frosting.

"Where did you get it?" he whispered as he sat back on his haunches, simply staring at it.

"I managed to get a particularly fat wallet last week. I talked to the black-market guy that I've been dealing with, and he managed to get me it yesterday." She stepped over to the cabinet and pulled out a loaf of bread and a small piece of meat, holding both up triumphantly. "We won't go hungry tonight!"

He hopped back to his feet and stepped over to the shelves with all their collected tools. He picked up a knife and carefully cut the cupcake in half, then lifted his half to his mouth.

She wagged a finger at him. "Since when were you ever allowed to have dessert before dinner?"

He giggled and put the cupcake down. He took the loaf of bread and cut off several slices, then divided the piece of meat into four. They sat cross-legged at their little table, their lone candle, this one snatched from a nearby church, flickering inside the lamp, casting a gentle glow over their feast.

Petra chewed on one of her pieces of meat then swallowed. She jabbed a finger at his shoes. They had seen better days and were in tatters, the left held together with a string. "I might have found a place where we can get you some shoes."

Daniel paused chewing his bread. "Really?" he asked, his mouth full.

Petra admonished him with a wag of the finger. "Don't talk with your mouth full."

"Sorry," he said, his voice muffled as he placed a hand over his mouth. He finished chewing then swallowed. "Where?"

"Not too far from here. I saw some clothes out on a clothesline, and they looked like they were around your size. There was a boy playing in the yard. I saw him take his shoes off before he went inside. I'm going to go out tonight after dark and get them if they're still there."

"Isn't that dangerous?"

She shrugged. "You need shoes. You can't run in those. If you need to get away quick, they'll fall apart on you and they'll catch you."

"I'll go with you."

She shook her head, tilting it toward the shoes. "You'll do no such thing. You're liable to get us caught in those things. After we have our treat, you go to bed and I'll go out and see if I can get those shoes for you."

She was right. He could barely walk in them now, and they drew unwanted attention. Over the past months, they had managed to steal the clothes they needed from around the neighborhood, and Petra made it a point to make certain they stayed as clean as they could manage, though that was growing increasingly difficult as the weather turned. The easiest place to keep clean was in the river. They could jump in like any other child without drawing much attention. They would grab silt from the river's bottom and rub it over their bodies, cleaning themselves as best they could, then rinse out their clothing. Soap was never part of the equation, but it kept them from stinking. A pair of scissors Petra had found sitting out one day, their previous owner preparing to sharpen them, kept their hair fairly neat and trimmed. They weren't decent for Temple, but were kempt enough to be seen out on the street. So far, they were managing, and managing quite well in his mind.

He eyed the box. They had lasted this long, but how long would they have to survive? If he could repair the radio, they might listen to the broadcasts he and his parents once had. It might give them some idea of how the war was going, some sense of when they could rejoin society.

He finished his bread and meat, taking a drink from one of the wineskins, then waited impatiently for Petra to finish. He still devoured his food the moment it was in front of him, whereas she always took her time savoring every bite. Perhaps when he was her age, he might slow down as well. As he thought about it, he never ate that fast at home unless he was excited about something that he wanted to finish in his bedroom. The only thing he could think of that might be causing this new habit was his persistent fear that someone would come and interrupt the meal.

He eyed the door, the only thing protecting them from the outside, beyond the fact nobody apparently knew where they were hidden even existed. For now, the door served an essential purpose. It kept out the rats. Sometimes at night, he could hear them scurrying on the other side.

They terrified Petra. And when they were particularly loud, she would hold him tighter, and he would relish in the sensation. It made him feel like a man, and he had taken to sleeping between her and the door.

And today, as he eyed the frosting on his cupcake, he was officially a man, and it was his job to protect this family.

She swallowed the last piece of bread then gestured at the cupcake. "Go ahead." He grinned at her and snatched it off the table. He was about to shovel it into his mouth when he stopped and instead took a small bite as she would. He chewed it slowly and she smiled at him.

"See, a man for not even a day and you're already learning. Savor every chew because you don't know when your next one might come." She pointed at the cupcake in his hand. "Especially something like that. We may never get to enjoy something like this again."

He took another bite, the flavors exploding in his mouth, the frosting so sweet it hurt his teeth, yet he loved it and would take that pain all day, all night, just to experience the intense flavors entertaining his tongue. They sat in near silence as they both partook in the birthday treat, the only sounds their chewing, their licking of fingers, and the moans and groans of delight.

Finally finished, Daniel sat back and patted his stomach, protruding slightly. "I can't remember the last time I felt so full."

She giggled, patting her own bulging stomach. "Me neither. I only wish I had enough money to buy two."

He rolled his eyes. "I don't know if I could take that much. I'm ready to burst as it is."

She sighed heavily. "One day, you'll learn that just because you have it, doesn't mean you have to use it. Save the second cupcake for the next day, and you have a treat two days in a row."

He eyed her for a moment, then nodded as he realized how much he had to learn. His heart ached for a moment. His mother and father were supposed to teach him things like this. Petra was doing her best, but even she wasn't an adult. What lessons had her parents never had a chance to teach her? What things was she teaching him that were wrong? He was now an adept thief. He knew that was wrong, however, it was also the only way to survive. How could they, two Jewish children, possibly hope to without stealing?

There were fewer armbands on the street now. In fact, they were quite rare. Where had the Jews gone? Had they died, starving because they refused to steal or didn't have the skills that Petra had taught him? Or had the Nazis taken them? And if so, to where? He didn't have the answers to these questions, though he was certain he didn't want to find out firsthand.

He yawned, then leaned toward the box with the radio parts. Petra wagged a finger. "No, you go to bed. Do that in the morning. You need to get your rest. I'm going to go out now and see if I can get those shoes."

He rose and stepped over to his little suitcase, opening it. He stripped out of his clothes and put on his pajamas, then climbed into the bed. Petra gave him a peck on the cheek then opened the heavy door. It clicked shut and he lay there listening to her footfalls slowly fade. His eyes became heavy, and within moments, he was sound asleep.

Unaware he would never see her again.

Seven Mile Beach, Cayman Islands

Present Day

Jack—just Jack—stood on the beach, the waves rolling over his sandal-clad feet as he stared at the sunset, a Corona in one hand, a Cuban cigar in the other. It had been a dog's age since he'd been on vacation, or at least one he'd finished. He always made the mistake of picking a destination in the same part of the world he was assigned to. Too often it meant some emergency would come up and he'd be contacted, then yanked away to deal with some crisis.

So, this time, he had taken a tip from his handler.

"If you don't want me interrupting your vacation, then don't make it so easy."

He figured the Cayman Islands, nearly on the exact opposite side of the globe, was making it about as hard as he could. It would take at least 24 hours for him to get anywhere near his regular stomping grounds.

And so far, three days in, he hadn't heard a peep.

A couple of young local women were enjoying the sunset. One of them flashed him a smile and he acknowledged her with a nod, but that was it. It wasn't why he was here. He wanted to relax, talk only to those he wanted to talk to, and not get entangled with anyone from the opposite sex. He just wanted to be alone to enjoy the atmosphere, smell the ocean, enjoy the rhythmic pulse of the waves.

Detox.

And not worry about someone around every corner trying to kill him.

His CIA-customized TAG Heuer watch sent a gentle electrical pulse into his wrist and he muttered a curse. The moment someone put a hotel in space, he was booking a two-week vacation, because anywhere on this planet apparently wasn't far enough from his job. He pressed buttons around the outer edge of the watch face in a coded sequence, and a message scrolled across the crystal. It was an order to contact Langley. He recognized the identifier from several previous ops. Chris Leroux. Leroux had been Control on a couple of his missions and was good. Very good. He was newer in the game but already one of the best, if not the best, at what he did. Some people were naturals, and Leroux was one of them.

He stared at the bottle, its lime wedge floating at the halfway point. It was his first of the evening, so he couldn't use inebriation as an honest excuse to get out of whatever was planned for him. He sighed then dumped the bottle in the water, heading back to his hotel room, cursing himself for being so good at his job.

Maybe if I screwed up every once in a while, I wouldn't be in such demand.

Vienna General Hospital

Vienna, Austria

Reading stared at his phone, rereading the message from Leroux, not believing his eyes. Meitner picked up on his shock.

"What is it?"

"The account where all the money was transferred?"

"Yes."

"It was opened by your granddaughter's husband, Jason Harper, two weeks ago."

The heart rate monitor went into overdrive and Meitner's chest ached as he squeezed his eyes shut, rage consuming him at the betrayal. A hand gently held his forearm.

"Breathe slow and steady." It was Reading. Meitner relaxed the grip on his chest and bedsheets, then sucked a long breath before exhaling slowly, the monitor calming within moments. Reading patted his forearm. "There you go. Now, let's look at this in a positive light."

Meitner opened his eyes and regarded the Interpol agent. "There's a positive way to look at this?"

"Absolutely. One, if it is your grandson, then we can get the money back. Two, if it isn't your grandson, and someone is trying to frame him, then at least you know it's not your grandson." He flashed a grin.

Meitner grunted. "I think you're stretching it there. And let's not call him my grandson. He's my granddaughter's poor excuse for a husband."

Reading pursed his lips and Meitner could imagine what the man was thinking. There was no love lost between him and his granddaughter's choice in men. That could give Jason motive, and he had no doubt that's what the Interpol agent was thinking.

But he didn't know the entire truth.

"There's something you need to know."

Reading regarded him. "What's that?"

Meitner glanced at the two techs in the corner and snapped his fingers. Both fit noise-canceling headphones over their ears before giving thumbs-up. It was the only way there'd be any semblance of privacy here. He needed them in the room with him so that time wasn't being wasted with messages relayed by Bernie or someone else. "My granddaughter, Holly, confided in me earlier. She said that Jason has mismanaged their funds through bad investments and gambling, to the point where there's almost nothing left."

Reading's eyebrows climbed his forehead. "Just how much did he lose?"

"Hundreds of millions."

"Now, when you say almost nothing left, that means one thing to a billionaire, something completely different to a working stiff like me."

"I mean, they have several million left, which might sound like a lot to you, however, when you're carrying two estates with staff, plus apparently servicing a lot of high-interest debt he's run up, millions are used up very rapidly. If I don't bail them out, they're looking at bankruptcy."

"Interesting."

"It is, but there's more."

One eyebrow shot up. "And that is?"

"My granddaughter says that her husband claims he has a way to get the money back."

Reading folded his arms. "He has a way to turn several million dollars into several hundred million dollars?"

"That's his claim, but the man's an idiot."

Reading grunted. "Evidently."

"There's no way there's any legitimate investment that can increase their money a hundredfold in time to prevent financial collapse."

Reading scratched his chin. "Do you really think he could be behind this?"

"From the words I just spoke, yes, however after knowing the man for all these years, I just can't see it." Meitner sighed. "The man *is* an idiot, but he's more than that. He's reckless, and he treats my granddaughter like dirt. I've told her to divorce him for years, but she's too scared of being alone. She's finally come to her senses, however, none of that matters right now. What matters is whether he's behind this.

I would have said it was impossible until you discovered the bank account opened in his name with all my damn money in it." Meitner shook his head. "There's no way he came up with this by himself. Somebody must have approached him. But who?"

"You said he took on some high-interest debt. Maybe some of that came from questionable sources."

"Possibly, but does this look like the work of a gang to you, of the mob? We're in Austria, not Chicago. If he borrowed some money from loan sharks, they'd be local. It just doesn't make sense. Coordinated bombings, helicopters, private jets." He sighed. "Vida. She's the key. She has to be."

"And she was recommended by your other granddaughter, Michelle?"

"Yes."

"And does she have money issues?"

Meitner shook his head. "No. She and her husband have managed their money well."

"Was she aware of her sister's situation?"

Meitner paused, recognizing where Reading was going with this. "Not that I'm aware of, though her instinct wouldn't be to initiate a conspiracy to steal all my money."

"Michelle said she knew Vida through her charitable work?"

"Yes. Apparently, they've known each other for several years."

Reading sighed. "This case keeps getting more convoluted. The more we find out, the wider our suspect pool gets, and the more questions there are that demand answers."

Unknown Location

41,000 feet

"Maybe we should speak English. You've obviously betrayed your country. Your loyalties are with the Americans now."

Acton's eyebrows shot up as he exchanged a surprised look with Laura at the first words of English spoken since they had boarded the plane. The argument had raged for at least ten minutes, the men taking turns shouting at her, one even smacking her across the face several times, boiling Acton's blood.

"Where is the money? The General says only a fraction of what was supposed to be transferred arrived. We have couriers all around the world pulling out one and two million instead of ten or twenty. What the hell is going on? Tell me, you traitorous bitch, or I'm going to beat the living shit out of you until you do!"

"Then the General will never see his money."

Vida had finally broken her silence, and a hush fell over the group.

"So then, you do have the money."

"I have nothing else to say. Beat me if you want, but you'll get nothing. When the time is right, I'll speak to the General, and only the General."

A frustrated growl erupted and through the gap between the seats, Acton watched the man with the satellite phone dial a number as he headed back toward them. "This is it," he whispered to Laura.

She nodded, pulling her dress up another few inches for good measure. Acton turned his head and the man walked past as the call connected and a conversation began. The man came to a halt just in front of Laura, and his eyes took notice of what Acton considered the best damn set of sticks on seven continents. Laura looked up at him and gave him a slight smile. The man faced her.

Acton lunged to his feet, his fist darting out and connecting with the man's throat, crushing his windpipe. The phone clattered to the ground as his opponent collapsed to his knees, gasping for breath. Acton reached under the man's suit jacket, pulling his weapon from the shoulder holster. Shouts erupted from the rear of the plane but he didn't pay it any mind. He had one job to do, and one job only. He drew the weapon, a Glock, and dropped to a knee as Laura yanked her seat belt tight. He took a bead on the nearest window across the aisle when something moved to his left.

"James!" Laura's foot darted out and Acton raised the weapon so he didn't accidentally shoot her leg. Her foot made contact with the guard he thought he had disabled. The man grunted, falling backward, and Acton lowered the weapon to re-aim when his target was blocked, one of the guards from the rear reaching him. Acton fired twice and the man dropped in a heap. He took aim again when someone leaned over the seatback and pressed the barrel of a gun against his throbbing skull.

Acton debated for a split second whether to take the shot that would guarantee his death, and perhaps worse for Laura, then cursed. "Okay! Okay!" He raised both hands, releasing his hold on the weapon and squeezing the grip between his thumb and forefinger. One of the other guards snatched it from his hand then Laura's eyes bulged. He spun toward where she was looking, and cringed as the butt of a Glock rushed toward his head.

Freyung Street

Vienna, Austria

Winter stood well back from the scene as Strobl showed him photos of the undetonated device discovered near one of the intact communication hubs. The entire area surrounding City Hall had been successfully taken out except for this small oasis. Someone on the ball had thought to investigate, and the device was discovered a short while ago.

"What the hell am I looking at?"

Strobl shrugged. "No idea, but it's ugly. Sophisticated too."

Winter agreed. "This doesn't look like it was assembled in somebody's basement."

Strobl gestured toward the undetonated weapon. "He's going in."

Winter turned then headed to their left. The area had been evacuated, and an EOD specialist in full gear was walking calmly toward the device as everyone observing took cover. Winter remembered hearing somewhere that if the bomb techs were running, then you should be too.

Fortunately, no one was running. Yet. He headed for the cover of a nearby building and Strobl followed him toward the safer position when there was a shout. A brilliant flash erupted a split second before the specialist fell backward. Something fired from the device, slicing through the fence surrounding the communications hub, and a fireball engulfed the entire area as the fuel for the backup generator erupted, a horrific explosion belching out in all directions.

Winter grabbed Strobl by the arm as he plunged for the protection of the stone walls only paces away. Flame and debris surged toward them and he closed his eyes, inhaling deeply as he continued forward. A hot wind hit them, then a moment later, the sound changed as they reached the building. He opened his eyes and gasped for breath then spun toward Strobl. "Are you all right?"

The young man was shaking. "Yeah, I think so."

Winter checked over his partner then himself, and satisfied they were both intact, finally noticed how many were down.

And a desire for revenge, not justice, overwhelmed him.

Vienna General Hospital

Vienna, Austria

Reading rushed to the window as the building vibrated. He cursed at a fireball clawing at the sky in the distance, his thoughts immediately of Winter and Strobl.

"What is it?" asked Meitner.

"Another bomb, by the looks of it."

"So late?"

"It has to be the undetonated one Winter went to investigate." Reading grabbed his phone and quickly dialed a number. The call went unanswered before kicking into voicemail. "Inspector, this is Agent Reading. I just saw the explosion and I'm calling to make sure you're all right." His phone vibrated in his hand. He ended the call and smiled as he read the message. "It's from Strobl. He says he and Winter are all right, but there are officers down. Nobody hurt too bad. Looks like he's attached some photos." Reading brought them up, swiping his thumb through the half-dozen shots of the bomb before it went off. "It's photos of the device," he explained. He quickly forwarded them to Leroux.

"Thank God nobody died."

Reading agreed. "I imagine they set up a perimeter, though that was quite the fireball." He waved his phone. "And this device looks like a beast. I've never seen anything like it."

Meitner closed his eyes, placing a hand on his chest. "This is all my fault."

Reading regarded him, but not before checking the monitors for anything untoward. "How do you figure that?"

"Holly was right. I should have just donated the money. If I hadn't made such a spectacle out of it, then none of this would have happened."

"First, you can't be certain of that. If it is an inside job, then they might still have been able to steal the money. And secondly, blaming yourself for what criminals do is bollocks. If everyone went through life not doing things because they were afraid bad people would do bad things, the world would be a truly horrible place. You were doing a good thing and bad people took advantage. But you read the news reports. Billionaires and millionaires the world over are donating huge amounts of money. Your event generated the publicity you wanted, though not in the way you meant. Your act and the vicious betrayal you suffered has resulted in far more money being given than you had planned, not to mention your money isn't completely lost yet. We still might get it back." Reading tapped his phone. "I've been thinking. There's something that doesn't make sense."

"What's that?" asked Meitner, opening his eyes.

"Why the other accounts? Why have them? You were donating money to a couple of hundred charities and the revised list has a couple of hundred accounts. Ninety-nine percent of that money went into the one account, so why have the other couple of hundred accounts be changed as well? Why not just leave them as legit charity accounts and donate the one or two million dollars that went into each? Why have all these other accounts when your plan was to just put the vast majority into a single one?"

Meitner scratched his chin. "I don't know, but you're right. It doesn't make much sense now, does it? And why put it all into one account when you have hundreds of others available to you? A transaction that size raises all kinds of red flags, and if they want to withdraw it, there's not a bank in the world that has twenty-two billion sitting in their vault."

Reading perched on the windowsill. "You're right. I hadn't thought of that. How do they possibly think they're going to get the money out?"

"Transfer it to a couple hundred different accounts and then transfer it again to banks all around the world. You can pull out five or ten million here and there, and eventually get your money."

Spencer, standing in the corner with the techs, cleared his throat. "We were just thinking, maybe it's all in one account because no one's ever done this before."

"What do you mean?" asked Reading.

"I mean, no one has stolen this amount of money before."

"That we know of," interjected Reading.

Spencer shrugged. "You'd think we'd hear about something like that, but regardless, if you steal twenty-two billion, that's twenty-two-thousand million. The number of banks you need that don't ask questions would be enormous, and the number of people you would need to withdraw that money, even if you did it ten million at a time, would be huge. It would be in the thousands. There's no way anybody can pull that off. The only way you could do it would be to do it over time. And if this is just criminals, even if it's a terrorist group, they'd have to be a huge organization."

Meitner eyed him. "What are you saying?"

"I'm saying this has to be government, doesn't it? Only a government could pull off an operation like this and have personnel all around the world to make the withdrawals. They could send people out from their embassies. A terrorist group or a criminal organization like the Mafia simply couldn't pull something like this off."

Reading folded his arms and pursed his lips. "I agree that if the intention is to withdraw the money, then you would need a massive organization behind it, and it would have to be government or some mega-corporation. But—"

Meitner's heart rate monitor picked up slightly.

"What is it?" asked Reading.

"Just your mention of a mega-corporation. You're aware of what happened about six months ago when FQX Tech tried to buy us out?"

Reading shrugged. "I vaguely remember something about it."

"It was a hostile takeover bid. They needed our expertise to compete on a massive Department of Defense contract. I spoke out against it, and even though I had divested myself of most of my shares, I convinced enough of the major shareholders not to sell. The whole thing was scuttled, they lost the contract, and their share price took a nosedive. The CEO is a man named Getz. A real asshole, which is why I didn't want a man like that taking over my legacy. His company is big enough, with a presence all around the world, to pull something like this off if he wanted to."

Reading eyed him skeptically. "Do you really think he'd do something like this?"

Meitner sighed. "I don't know. I wouldn't think so. He's an asshole, but he's not a fool. If he got caught, he'd lose everything and go to prison. I only mentioned it because of your reference to a mega-corp."

Reading sent a message to Leroux with the theory. "I'll have my contacts check it out, but I think it's a long shot. Though to return to Spencer's point, he is right. No matter who's behind it, if they intend to withdraw the money, it's a massive undertaking. And to the earlier point, why put it all in one account? Like you said, it raises too many red flags."

"Maybe they don't intend to withdraw it," suggested Spencer. "Maybe they're just holding it in the one account for now."

Meitner's eyes narrowed. "Waiting for what? To make a ransom demand?"

Reading shook his head. "I doubt it. With twenty-two billion of your money, obviously they wouldn't ask for money. They'd be asking for something else that would have some sort of value to them, which couldn't possibly exceed twenty-two billion. If you were a government, then I could see there being the possibility of some sort of exchange. The money for someone in prison, but even then, there are not a lot of criminal or terrorist organizations in the world that would give up twenty-two billion they had managed to get their hands on, in exchange for their leader. Most would say eff him, let him rot, let's enjoy the money."

Meitner grunted. "I suppose you're right."

"Maybe the account is like a middleman."

Reading turned to Spencer. "What do you mean?"

Spencer shrugged. "Somebody needs a job done. They reach out to one of their contacts. He then hires somebody to do the job, they do it, get the money or the item. The middleman holds it until payment is received for the job. Once he's paid, he pays the people he hired, then hands the money or item over to whoever hired him."

Reading's head slowly bobbed. "So, what you're saying is that Vida and the others were hired to do a job, they're holding the money in the one account until they get paid, then they release it."

"Exactly."

"There's only one problem with that."

Spencer eyed him. "And what's that?"

"It's money."

"So?"

"So, let's say I'm going to pay you a hundred million to steal twenty-two billion. Why would you hold on to the twenty-two billion until I gave you one-hundred million? I'd just take the hundred million and give you twenty-one-point-nine billion instead."

Spencer's face slackened in embarrassment. "Oh yeah, I hadn't thought of that."

Reading wagged a finger. "But don't dismiss the idea completely. There might be something else that Vida and her people want from whoever hired them, assuming that's what happened in this case. They already have their money. If they control that account, there might be something else they're holding out for." He sighed and threw up his hands as there was one element he was completely forgetting. "We're making the assumption that the money is there."

Meitner frowned. "I can't believe they haven't been able to reach the president of the bank. Even the premier of the Cayman Islands can't reach anybody. It's ridiculous."

"It's a weekend, after hours, though I do find it curious that we can't reach *any*body."

"Could they be involved?" asked Spencer.

Reading nodded. "Possibly. They might be getting a cut of the money being sent through them in order to not ask any questions. Ten percent of twenty-two billion is enough for everyone at that bank to disappear and enjoy life with new identities anywhere in the world."

Spencer grunted. "When you live in paradise, where do you escape to?"

Reading chuckled. "A decision neither of us will ever have to make." He returned to the main discussion. "If we assume the money is still there, which really, if I think about it, is a long shot—"

Spencer interrupted him. "Maybe they're holding on to it until they make their escape?"

"That's definitely a possibility, though that would suggest that whoever is truly behind this is playing a part in their escape. By holding the money hostage, they're guaranteeing that those who hired them for the job will come through on their end."

Meitner sighed heavily. "So, yet again, more questions with no answers, and a suspect pool that keeps growing."

CIA Headquarters, Operations Center 3

Langley, Virginia

Leroux eyed the images of the explosive that Reading had sent them. "What the hell is that?" he muttered.

"It's an EFP," said Therrien from the back of the room. "Explosively Formed Penetrator. We were seeing a lot of these in Iraq. It's designed to funnel the explosive from a short distance. They'd set it beside the road then detonate it. It would fire its projectile, slice through any armor we'd put up against it, then blow the shit out of anything inside the vehicle."

Leroux watched several videos that Therrien had put up on the main displays demonstrating how it worked, and he cursed as his head shook. "That's brutal. And it doesn't look like something you assemble in a basement."

"No, this is Iranian. It's manufactured. It's not your typical IED that just anyone can throw together. It's too precise."

Leroux spun in his chair. "Iranian?"

"Yes. They were assembling them in Iran, then smuggling them across the Iraqi border to kill our troops."

"Wait a minute, are we saying these were made by the Iranian government?"

"That's what the intel says."

"Is there any way to know whether it came from Iran directly, or came through Iraq, just a remnant of what was going on there?"

Therrien shook his head. "There's no way to know for sure, but I can't believe that over a dozen of these things would have been left over. Those things would come across the border and those bastards would use them right away. I just can't see them holding on to so many for years."

"Agreed. The question now is, is this an Iranian Government operation, a rogue operation by Iranians, or someone supplied by them? Whoever it is, I think we can safely eliminate Jason Harper as being behind this. Sonya, get a team to track the footage of those bomb sites. This thing looks pretty heavy. There has to be footage of them being planted. With this being timed to the minute, I'm willing to bet they weren't in-country long. I wouldn't be surprised if they arrived in the city today and were put in place within minutes of being detonated. They wouldn't want to risk any of the devices being discovered."

"On it," replied Tong.

Leroux sent a message to Morrison, updating him on the possible Iranian connection as the door hissed. Half a dozen additional staff entered to assist the growing operation. Leroux turned in his seat.

"Randy, why don't you take charge of tracing those bombs? Use the supplementary assets."

"You got it, boss."

"Sir, the plane the professors are on has just deviated from its flight plan," said Tong.

Leroux spun in his chair to face the main displays as Tong brought up a map showing the approved flight plan in blue, a red line indicating the actual flight path deviating south of Athens. "Okay, people, this is it. The Hellenic Air Force should respond within several minutes, but that will result in nothing since the Greeks aren't about to shoot it down if it stays at altitude. My guess is they're going to take the shortest route to international airspace then head for their destination. Where is Delta?"

Tong zoomed the map out to include North and Central Africa, a red dot shown. "They're about an hour and a half away from being in position, if we're assuming North Africa's the destination."

"And how long until the target reaches the North African coast?"

"Roughly the same. Depends on where they're heading. Egypt is closer than Morocco."

"So, this is going to be close. Contact Bragg. Let them know we don't have a destination yet. We need to know how much fuel that plane has in case it needs to circle for a while."

Tong gestured toward the screen. "Sir, the Greeks are scrambling fighters now."

"Put it on speaker. And pray they know there are hostages on board."

Unknown Location

41,000 feet

There would be no more escape attempts. Laura's upper body was lashed to her seat with a blanket. James was beside her, similarly restrained, still unconscious, and though he said he was fine before the second hit, she knew him well enough to know he was lying for her benefit. They had been through a lot over the past few years. Shot, stabbed, scraped, bruised, and the only thing neither of them had never recovered from completely was the loss of her ability to have children.

But blows to the head could have cumulative damage, and God knows they had both been cracked in the skull too many times to count. Was this one time too many? He had been out cold for at least half an hour, and her pleas to untie him, let him lie down, for an ice pack, for anything that might help, had been met with a gun pressed to her forehead, along with the warning that if she didn't shut up, she'd never have to worry about him again.

It had silenced her, though not their captors. The argument in the rear of the plane continued, occasionally punctuated with another smack as frustrations grew and Vida continued her stony silence.

An announcement came over the PA system, something said in what she was convinced was Farsi. Whatever it was silenced the angry men and had them all rushing for window seats. The clock at the front of the cabin indicated they had been flying for almost two hours, and the stars told her they had been heading generally south. It suggested they should be over Greek territory, which made sense. In order to not attract attention, this plane would have had a flight plan probably filed days ago. If she and James hadn't intervened, no one would likely know that Vida and her team were on this plane, so they would have done everything by the book until they had to leave European airspace.

It was just another indication of how well planned this was. This was military or government level precision. And if they were speaking Farsi, it meant the Iranians were behind this. But why? It didn't make any sense. If the Iranian government managed to get away with it, they would have $22 billion. A country like that would burn through it in no time. It would make no material difference to their day-to-day lives. Yet if they were found out, any sympathy they might have around the world would be lost to anybody but the most diehard of zealots. Stealing from the poor? It was indefensible.

She paused at a thought. Could it be the charities? Could it be a specific charity that they didn't want to get any money because they worked against the Iranian government? It was a possibility, though still, preventing some charity from getting $100 million that was working against the fundamentalist regime couldn't possibly be worth the risk. No, only a fool would think stealing from hundreds of charities in an effort to block only one would be a wise move.

Yet Iran had proven time and again they were fools. Blind devotion to any cause or belief too often resulted in idiocy, especially in the heat of the moment. Yet the facts staring her in the face, no matter how much her logical mind dismissed the idea that anybody could be so stupid, were that $22 billion had been stolen, bombs had detonated in a coordinated attack that had brought down power and communications infrastructure, helicopters and planes had been employed in the escape, a general had been referenced, everyone was speaking Farsi, and a reference to a betrayal of Vida's country, all pointed to a government, and likely the Iranian government.

She tensed at the thought. The Iranians never hesitated to torture or kill, and had a particular hatred for Western women. She glanced at James, still unconscious, the blood trickling from his forehead now stopped. She returned her attention to the window and whatever it was outside that had everyone excited, then gasped as a fighter jet blasted past them, the Hellenic blue and white of the Greek flag emblazoned on the tail.

Her heart hammered at what might be about to happen then she drew a deep breath, calming herself as she dismissed her fears. Their altitude was displayed underneath the clock. There was no way they were a threat to anybody at this altitude. She could think of only two reasons why the Greeks would be responding like this. One was that they were aware of who was on this plane, and the second was that the plane had deviated from its flight plan. She couldn't imagine the Greeks shooting them down unless the aircraft were to reduce altitude and potentially become a risk to buildings below.

But if the plane, clearly over Greece, had no intention of landing, then just what was their final destination?

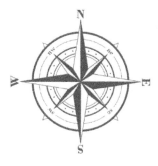

Outside BBG International
George Town, Cayman Islands

Jack—just Jack—peered at the laptop screen, flipping through four different drone feeds, examining the bank building from various angles. It wasn't a substantial edifice as you'd expect back stateside, though the briefing notes indicated the amount of money that went through this institution daily was stunning. Dirty money was being laundered here by shady governments, corporations, and criminal organizations, yet proving it was challenging.

Due to privacy laws and banking laws, corrupt governments and corrupt officials of honest governments, getting the information needed to stop the dirty money from moving around the world was difficult, which was one reason the CIA had an active program to hack these institutions. It was a constant battle of thrusts and parries with, unfortunately, the most corrupt of banks having the most robust security.

And the bank Langley had tasked him to get inside had detected their digital intrusion two weeks ago and purged it, and all Langley had managed to accomplish since then was a tap that could access nothing but the most basic data about the account in question. He could be going to all this effort for nothing. The bank account could be empty, and it should be if you weren't a complete idiot. Parking $22 billion in an account was insanity, but the brains in Virginia were convinced something was going on where this somehow made sense.

He had been activated, briefed, and equipped within half an hour. The CIA had weapons and supply caches in every country globally, and every major city in those countries. Quite often, those were inside embassies or consulates, other times safe houses or stashed with local contacts. There had been a knock at his hotel room door soon after leaving the beach, and a local had delivered two duffel bags containing everything needed for the op.

He activated his comm. "Control, this is Rawhide. I've got two security guards on patrol outside. Confirm that, over."

"Confirmed, Rawhide. We're showing the same, over."

"Any luck accessing their security feeds?"

"Negative. It appears to be all self-contained."

Jack tapped an icon on the screen and all the camera positions Langley had spotted were highlighted with their cones of coverage displayed. "Control, confirm that there's a blind spot on the number two side."

"Confirmed, Rawhide. It's a sliver, but if you suck it in, you should be able to make it. They had a bit of a windstorm last week that must have shifted one of the positions slightly."

"Copy that. I'm heading in now." Jack closed up the laptop and climbed out of the SUV he had rented for his stay. He strode across the street with purpose, a duffel bag slung over his shoulder. He crossed in front of the bank, ignoring it, and turned the corner to the left side of the building. He spotted where the gap should be, then cleared his throat, signaling Langley he needed guidance.

"Ten more paces," said the voice in his ear, monitoring everything from one of the mini-drones hovering overhead he had deployed. "Guards are at the three-four corner. Turn right in five, four, three, two, one. Turn right."

Jack pivoted on his heel, 90 degrees, then walked across the grass, directly toward the wall of the bank.

"Adjust left ten degrees."

He steadied his heart that threatened to race out of control. Once he was within a few feet of the wall, he'd be safe, the cameras positioned to catch people approaching, not already there.

"You're clear."

He breathed a sigh of relief then hugged the wall as he prepared for the next phase of his plan. "Location on the guards?"

"Guards are on the number three side, approaching the two-three corner."

He tapped the frame of his glasses then slid his finger down the side as feeds from the various drones flashed by. He headed for the corner in question as the approaching guards appeared on the inside of the lens. He gently lowered the duffel bag to the ground and retrieved two stun guns, then pressed his back against the wall. The two men reached the corner then rounded it. Jack stepped forward, emerging from the shadows, and pressed a weapon against each of their chests, the crackling of electricity pleasant if you weren't on the receiving end. Both men yelped in shock then collapsed to the ground, still shaking. He pulled them into the shadows, then bound and gagged the portlier of the two before removing the shirt and hat from the other one closer to his size. Tucking the shirt into his black pants that resembled the standard guard's uniform, he then fit the hat over his head and removed the building pass from the man's belt.

"Control, status?"

"You're still clear, and it appears nobody is aware you're there."

"Copy that." He grabbed the duffel bag and rushed along the side of the building toward the front. The next part would have to be done quickly. Langley had a detailed layout of the building, last updated a year ago. Though that helped, he had no idea how many guards were inside. If this had been a planned op rather than a last-minute emergency, they would have been monitoring all day for the shift change. Unfortunately, he was going in cold. It could be one guard, it could be ten, though he doubted it.

He strode to the front door, slid the pass through the reader, the click and buzz indicating he had access. He hauled open the door then crossed the ornate lobby, no expense spared at making questionable clientele comfortable. A guard stationed at the security desk looked up and his eyes bulged. Jack drew a weapon from his belt and fired. A tranquilizer dart embedded itself in the man's chest. He slumped in his chair and Jack swung over the desk then checked the internal camera feeds shown on several monitors.

"Control, Rawhide. I'm in. One guard down, non-lethal. Internal camera feeds show two other guards in the hallways, only one in the way. Heading to the server room now." Jack snapped transmitters onto the back of each of the monitor cables, giving Langley access to the internal security feeds. He made for a side door and swiped his pass, then headed down a corridor leading to a set of stairs to the basement.

"Rawhide, Control. You've got a guard five meters down the corridor you're about to enter, facing away from you."

He continued down the stairs as he drew his stun gun. "Copy that." He swiped the pass, the click and buzz causing him to cringe.

"He knows you're there."

"Copy that." He pushed the door open a sliver, holding it with the toe of his left shoe. "Is he coming my way?"

"Affirmative. Five meters, four, three, two."

Jack shoved the door open and surged through, jamming his stun gun against the chest of the surprised man. He dropped in a puddle of his own urine and Jack stepped back before it got on his shoes.

"Anyone else in the vicinity, Control?"

"Negative, Rawhide. You're clear."

With the floor covered in urine, there was little point in dragging the body out of sight. If another guard saw the mess, they would raise the alarm regardless. He zip-tied the man then jogged down the corridor.

"Next door on your right."

"Copy that."

He swiped his pass and shoved the door aside, entering a room with an impressive array of hardware. He headed for the rack-mounted console and took a seat. Unzipping his duffel bag, he hauled out several pieces of equipment and connected Langley to the system.

"Control, Rawhide, confirm status, over."

"We're in. Stand by."

Jack sat quietly, closing his eyes and relaxing his entire body. He could leave now if they were assured the access wouldn't be interrupted by some sort of communications failure. However, if something did go wrong with the connection, all of this would have been for naught if he were to leave too soon. He just hoped Langley didn't take too long.

A male voice cut in, the entire operation to this point run by a woman. This one he recognized as the big man himself, Leroux.

"Rawhide, Control Actual. Abort immediately! I say again, abort immediately! Leave the hardware in place. Just get your ass out of there now!"

CIA Headquarters, Operations Center 3

Langley, Virginia

"Who the hell are they?"

"No idea," replied Child as they watched four men exit an SUV that had just screeched to a halt moments before.

Leroux leaned closer. "Did we trip a silent alarm?"

"There's no indication of that."

"Aborting as ordered," came Jack's voice over the comm. "What's going on?"

Leroux pointed at Tong, who took back over as Control.

"Four unsubs just arrived in a single vehicle. They're heading for the main entrance now."

"You are aware, Control, that there is no rear exit to this building?"

"We are aware, Rawhide."

"Control, I need to know who these people are. Are they just security doing their job, or are they hostiles?"

"We're determining that now, Rawhide. Suggest you seek cover."

"Roger that."

Leroux cursed as the four men pulled weapons, one of them shooting out the glass of the front doors, confirming this definitely wasn't a security team responding to an alarm. He snapped his fingers at Tong, who was way ahead of him.

"Rawhide, Control. New arrivals are confirmed hostile, all armed. One has shot out the front entrance glass and they're making entry now. Lethal force is authorized should you deem it necessary."

"Copy that, Control. Is my task to escape, or to prevent them from gaining access?"

"Stand by, Rawhide." Tong turned to Leroux and shrugged.

"Do we have anything on them?" he asked as he turned toward Child.

Child's eyes bulged at what was on his screen. "Holy shit, boss. That SUV is registered to the Iranian consulate."

Leroux cursed. This all but confirmed it was Iranians behind this. Why, didn't matter. That was a debate for when this was over. Yet if they were there, it had to be to gain access to the account. Something was going on that they didn't understand. If they hoped to retrieve the money and gain leverage that might help free the professors, they had to steal the money themselves.

He turned to one of his specialists. "Marc, what's the status on that money?"

Therrien shook his head. "I confirmed it, sir. Over twenty-two billion are in the account, but I can't touch it."

"What do you mean?"

"I mean, there's some sort of block on the account. I can't transfer it out."

"What kind of block are you talking about?"

"I don't know. If I had another five or ten minutes, I might be able to tell you, but right now, there's nothing I can do but give you the balance and the transaction history."

"Anything there?"

"Negative. Just a string of large deposits, all a couple of hours ago as we expected. Nothing before."

"Sir, what should I have Rawhide do?" prompted Tong.

Leroux's mind raced. If his team couldn't access the money, the question was whether the Iranians could. What didn't make sense was, if this were the Iranians' account, why wouldn't they just initiate a regular transfer from outside the building? Something was definitely going on here, but nothing made sense. Had the Iranians been double-crossed? Had the money they had meant to steal been stolen by someone else, a traitor on the inside? Was Vida that traitor? Had she transferred all the money to this different account? And if she had, how did the Iranians find out? The only people who should know the account number would be Vida, anyone she had told, Reading, Meitner, and his people.

But none of that mattered. For now, what mattered was Jack's life.

He shook his head. "Something's not right, here. His mission is to get out safely. Forget the data. I have a feeling the Iranians aren't going to be able to do any more than we can."

Tong relayed the instructions, and as Leroux watched, the four new arrivals began a room-to-room search, clearly unaware of where the server room was located. An unfortunate development. It meant Jack couldn't simply take cover in another room without the risk of being discovered.

He sighed.

This entire op was turning into a Charlie-Foxtrot.

BBG International

George Town, Cayman Islands

Jack sprinted up the stairs to the main floor. He couldn't risk being trapped in the basement—there were too few doors. But the ground floor offered possibilities.

"You're clear, but only for about five seconds."

Jack rushed for the door, shoved it open and stepped through into the hall, the pneumatic door closer slowly doing its job behind him. He darted across the hall and swiped his pass, stepping inside an executive office. He closed the door behind him with a click, then surveyed the room.

"Two hostiles coming your way, kicking open each door."

"Copy that," whispered Jack as he desperately sought a place to hide. The desk was glass. There were no couches, and the several chairs were too low to provide any cover.

"They're approaching your room now. Five seconds."

He muttered another curse, then ducked behind the door, praying the room merited nothing but the most cursory of glances. There was a loud bang and the door flew open as the frame splintered. He raised a hand to protect his face as the door slammed into him. He grabbed the handle with his free hand and held it in place, preventing it from swinging back and revealing his position.

"Not it."

"Wait," said a second voice, both speaking Farsi, a language Jack understood enough to eavesdrop on but would never try to pass himself off as a native speaker. "Maybe we can access it through this computer. The door says this is a VP's office."

"Let's give it a try and let the others keep searching."

Jack cursed to himself and peered out from behind the door. One of the men was now sitting at the desk, plugging in a USB key undoubtedly designed to hack the system. The man stared at the screen while the other remained out of sight, blocked by the door. There was a slight tug on the handle. Jack let go, carefully drawing his weapon and screwing in the suppressor as the door moved several inches away from him.

"I'm in," said the man at the desk.

The door stopped moving and the man stepped toward the desk as Jack gently pulled the door closer to him. Something was said that Jack didn't recognize, though through the tone, he expected it was a colorful curse.

"Twenty-two billion dollars just sitting there, like the General said."

"You have the account number?"

"Yes."

272

"Then transfer the money."

Jack's trigger finger ran along the guard. The money billion could be about to disappear permanently, yet his mission had been aborted. His job was to get out alive, though no one had said anything about getting out with no one knowing. Gear was still plugged into a station in the server room, and someone would eventually know there had been a breach.

And he was cleared to use lethal force to make his escape.

To hell with it.

He cleared his throat as he pushed the door aside, extending his weapon.

"Pardon me, gentlemen, but I can't let you do that."

The man at the desk quickly resumed typing as the other reached for his gun. Jack put two in the seated man's chest, then one in the other's shoulder. The man collapsed to a knee, but with his good arm, drew a knife with the smooth motion of a practiced thrower. Jack cursed and delivered a double-tap to the man's chest. He had hoped to interrogate him, but that was now out of the question. He stepped behind the desk and confirmed the money was still in the account.

"Rawhide, Control, report your status, over."

Jack liberated the wallets of the two downed targets then stepped over to the door. "Two targets eliminated. They didn't get a chance to transfer the money. Report on the other two."

"They're in the basement. They've found the server room."

Jack frowned. "Can you stop them?"

"Negative. They're using their own hack. It's overwritten ours."

Jack eyed the computer. "Do you have an account number I can transfer the money to?"

"Explain."

"I'm logged in, no doubt with the same hack they're using. If they've got access, then I've got access. I just need an account number."

"Good thinking, Rawhide. Stand by."

Jack closed over the door then returned to the desk, dumping the corpse from the chair then taking a seat. He read the display. It was already set up for the transfer, an account number partially entered. He deleted it, then keyed in the number fed to him by Langley. He confirmed it, his heart racing as he was about to steal back $22 billion from under the noses of the Iranians. He hit Enter and an error message appeared, the same one he had seen downstairs.

Transfer unsuccessful.

"It's a no-go, Control. These guys have no more access than we did."

"Copy that, Rawhide. I recommend you make your exit now."

"Roger that."

He yanked the USB stick that the Iranians had brought, then headed out the door and down the corridor. He stepped through the broken glass of the front entrance and calmly headed for his vehicle, parked just out of sight of any cameras, and as he climbed inside, he was left wondering why those behind the theft couldn't access their own account. It made no sense.

Unless they weren't behind this at all.

He chewed his cheek as he pulled away, another possibility occurring to him. Perhaps they were double-crossed. The Iranians clearly didn't have proper access to the building. It was obviously a rush job, and a double-cross would fit with all the money being in a single account. The fact they knew about the account indeed suggested they were in on the original theft. However, if they were double-crossed and the money had been transferred to an account they didn't have control of, then the elephant in the room could be the key to everything.

How had they found out about the account?

CIA Headquarters, Operations Center 3

Langley, Virginia

Tong pointed at the screen showing the two surviving Iranians carrying their comrades out in fireman holds. They dumped the bodies in the back seat then peeled away from the curb, leaving behind a mess of questions.

"Can you reactivate our equipment?" asked Leroux.

Therrien shook his head. "No. It looks like they took it with them."

Leroux sighed. "Fine. Spike it."

"Yes, sir." Therrien tapped at his keyboard then stared at his monitor for a moment as a signal was transmitted instructing the devices to fry their circuitry. He gave a thumbs-up. Leroux acknowledged the confirmation, his attention returning to the private jet that had just left Greek airspace, the F-16s breaking off their pursuit.

Leroux watched as the plane adjusted its heading. "Project its course."

Tong worked her station and a cone appeared, the tip at the aircraft's current location, then widening ahead. The cone continued to swing toward the west, past Egypt, then finally settled as the pilot completed the course change.

And Leroux frowned.

"Libya," muttered Child unnecessarily. "Of course it's Libya."

Libya was the least stable country in North Africa, with many revolutionary factions backed by Iran. And if there were one country where they were least likely to get meaningful cooperation against Iran, it was Libya, since those factions had won. This was obviously always their destination, and with this operation so well planned, he had little doubt any palms that needed to be greased had been.

He continued to stare at the cone aimed directly at the North African nation. "ETA to the coast?"

"Ninety minutes at their current speed."

"Okay, inform Delta. I'll let the Chief know so he can find out if Washington still wants to go ahead with this. Anything from facial recognition yet?"

"No," replied Tong. "Everybody's coming back clean, though that doesn't mean they are. I'm checking international arrivals now."

"Assume they're traveling on fake passports."

Tong nodded. "Way ahead of you, boss."

He chuckled, turning his chair to face Child. "What's the status on tracking that truck you found that transported the weapon to the last detonation site?"

"Still tracking it back," replied Child. "It looks like the one vehicle was used to position at least half the weapons so far, so it's going to take time."

Leroux frowned. "We have to speed this up. This had to come in by airplane. If they tried to bring the explosives in by train, they'd have no way to change their plans if something went wrong. They could bring it in by vehicle, but they'd run the risk of being caught at one of the external borders to the Schengen Agreement."

"Boat?" suggested Tong, knowing it wasn't a real possibility.

"Boat is possible, but still risky. Austria is landlocked, so it would be quite the drive to reach there."

"Then it has to be by plane, like we thought."

"Exactly, and it has to be a plane they would have complete control over, so we're not talking something that flew in from Spain or Italy. This would be something that came from a place where bribes would be welcome, and with everything planned to the minute, I'm willing to bet it landed no earlier than a few hours from the first detonation."

"What about the same airport they left from? Hell, it could've been the same plane," suggested Child.

Leroux shook his head. "No, that's about an hour's drive. Too many things could go wrong. Flat tire, broken taillight that invites a traffic stop. No, they'd land smack dab in the city to reduce the risks of something going wrong." He turned to Tong. "I assume the Vienna International Airport is the only one that would fit the bill?"

"If we're assuming they want to do an offload like crated cargo, then yes, that would be the place. It certainly wouldn't look out of the ordinary. But they have customs, don't they? Wouldn't the cargo be inspected?"

Leroux smiled slightly. "Not if it were labeled as diplomatic cargo." He smacked his hands together. "Okay, let's get on this. Randy, you keep tracking back that truck. Sonya, I want to know what planes landed within that window with diplomatic cargo."

"From Iran?"

He shook his head. "No, from any country. We have to assume the Iranians, if that's who's behind this, would have done everything they could to hide their involvement." He headed for the door. "I'm going to brief the Chief. Call me if you find anything."

"Yes, sir," said Tong.

He pushed through the hissing door and headed for the elevators, his pulse racing with excitement. Things were drawing to a close, though he still didn't know how they would turn out. And one thing gnawed at him, something Jack had also picked up on after his failed op. How had they known about the account? He chewed his cheek and pulled out his phone, sending a message to the best person for the job, and the only person they had on the ground where the leak had to have occurred.

Vienna, Austria

October 25, 1941

Daniel both hated her and loved her terribly. He had woken the next morning to find Petra not in bed with him. He had immediately grown concerned, though without knowing if he had been asleep for half an hour or for hours, he couldn't be certain if she were overdue. He had sat up in bed for hours waiting for her, his imagination running wild with what might have happened. By the time he finally stepped out that door, he was certain she had been captured or was dead, and he wasn't sure what to do. All he could think was to go out and search for her.

But when he opened the door, he had his answer.

The pair of shoes were sitting in front of it, atop some neatly folded clothes, with a note. He reached down and picked up the piece of paper.

My Dearest Daniel,

I'm so sorry, but I can't take it anymore. There was only enough for one, otherwise you know I would have taken you with me.

Please forgive me.

Petra

His eyes narrowed as he read the note. What did it mean? His heart leaped into his throat as a thought occurred to him. He rushed down the passageway and dropped to his knees, crying out at the sight of the rock that hid his spoons pried away and lying on the floor. He stuck his hand in the opening, confirming what he already knew.

They were gone.

She had stolen them like the thief she was.

He returned to the only home he had known for so long, tears flowing, his entire body shaking with the betrayal, then reread the note.

There was only enough for one.

He thought back to the night at Peter's home, to the conversation he had overheard between his uncle and his mother. There hadn't been enough money to save him and his parents, only himself. The spoons had been handed over for payment. The man whose name he had forgotten had said they were more than enough, but like anything, escape to America must now cost more.

Petra had obviously found the spoons. He had become careless over the months they were together, and she must have spotted him at his hiding place and investigated. She then would have made the arrangements, probably through her black-market contact, then taken her opportunity to escape this horror. The timing had left him wondering. She had left on his birthday, leaving him with a fresh pair of shoes and clothes, and as a man in the eyes of God. And a man should be able to take care of himself. And thanks to the skills she had taught him over their time together, he had survived.

But he was alone, desperately alone.

And it was soul-crushing.

It had been weeks since her betrayal. The first few days had been spent lying in the bed they had once shared, crying, feeling sorry for himself and wishing his mother hadn't changed the powder. Once he had worked his way through the last of their food and water, thirst and hunger forced him back onto the streets, and he quickly discovered he had mastered the skills she had taught him.

After a few weeks of subsisting on bread and the odd vegetable, he had picked enough pockets to purchase some meat and cheese from their black-market contact. It had been nerve-racking the first time, for Petra was the one who usually dealt with him, and he was likely the man who had arranged her escape. He had handed over the money, and a small package wrapped in newspaper was pushed toward him. He unwrapped it to make certain he wasn't cheated, then folded it back up. He was about to leave, but he had to know.

He stared at his feet. "Did she get away?"

The usually gruff man, who he only knew as the Shopkeeper, leaned down, placing his elbows on the counter. "You don't know why she did it, do you?"

His chest tightened, his stomach in knots. "Because she's a lying thief?"

"Oh, she was definitely a thief and probably a lying one like you said. But that's not why she did it."

He glanced up at the man, tears filling his eyes. "What do you mean?"

"They caught her a few weeks before she left."

Daniel's jaw dropped, his eyes shooting wide. "She didn't tell me that!" He thought for a moment, puzzled. "Why did they let her go?"

"They didn't. She escaped, but not before the two soldiers who caught her did something to her."

Daniel's eyes narrowed. "What did they do?"

The Shopkeeper shook his head and straightened. "Something a boy your age doesn't need to know. But trust me when I say, she was right to do what she did. She had to escape. The streets are no place for a pretty girl like her. She wanted to tell you, but decided she would rather spend her last days with you happy. She left on your birthday, didn't she?"

He nodded.

"She had planned that day for weeks, and she was so excited when she found that broken radio on the street. Did you get it working?"

Daniel shook his head. "I haven't tried."

"Do you think you can?"

He shrugged. "I don't know. Maybe."

The Shopkeeper scratched his chin. "I'll tell you what. If you can get it working, you eat for free."

Daniel's eyes shot wide. "What do you mean?"

"I mean, there are a lot of people with broken radios. If you think you can fix them, then I'll give them to you, and for every one you bring to me that can pick up the Allied broadcasts, I'll give you a week's worth of rations."

Daniel's eyeballs bulged then he took a page from Petra's book. "Two weeks."

The Shopkeeper laughed. "You're just like her. She taught you well. All right, kid, two weeks. But first, you need to bring me that radio she found, in good working order."

"What if I need parts?"

"You come to me with what you need, and maybe you can get a working part from one of the broken ones."

Daniel had agreed to the deal and returned to his sanctuary, finally pulling out the box containing his birthday present. He had been working on it for days, and had just figured out, he hoped, what was wrong. He twisted the knob and the radio hummed to life. He leaped to his feet, jumping up and down, his fists raised in the air, shouting in triumph. He slapped both hands over his mouth, remembering the rule Petra had taught him.

Never make noise.

He turned off the radio and pressed an ear to the door, listening for a few moments. He heard nothing and sat back in front of the radio. He turned it on and twisted the dial, picking up nothing but static. He frowned. Perhaps he hadn't fixed it after all. He adjusted the antenna to better pick up a signal when he tossed his head back and rolled his eyes.

He was underground.

His father had explained that the radio was picking up waves in the air, and being so deep underground, surrounded by stone, he doubted those waves could reach him. There was only one way he was testing this, and that was on the street.

Which was risky.

Very risky.

But two weeks' rations, without having to go topside and steal? That was worth it.

He turned off the radio then dressed for outside, leaving his hiding place for the first time at night since he had been alone. It was terrifying, and perhaps stupid. In fact, it was definitely stupid. He should wait until morning, but if someone spotted him in the light of day with a radio, it might draw unwanted attention.

And besides, he had to know.

He pushed the grate up and peered out, finding the alley empty. He shoved it aside, wincing at the metal scraping on the stone, then poked his head out, listening once again. He could try the radio here, but if he were seen, they would know where he was hiding. He couldn't take that chance. He climbed out and onto the cobblestone, scurrying to the far end of the alley, listening for any soldiers on patrol. Hearing none, he sat in a doorway then clicked on the radio.

It hummed to life, and he quickly dialed in the station he remembered his parents would listen to every night.

And nearly cried out at the sound of the BBC. He closed his eyes and could almost sense the warmth of his mother and father sitting on either side of him on the couch in his father's office. He opened his eyes then stared up at the heavens. And gulped when he spotted someone in a window, leaning out. He scrambled to his feet and grabbed the radio.

"No, wait!"

He froze.

"Let us hear it. Just for a little while."

He slowly turned back and stared up at the building. At least half a dozen people were in their windows. No lights, just faces. He turned back toward them then did something foolish. He cranked the volume knob up and held the radio high over his head. As he stood there, more came to the windows, eagerly listening, and a warmth spread through his body as if he were being hugged by his mother.

Or by Petra.

And for the first time since she had left, he didn't feel so alone.

Vienna General Hospital

Vienna, Austria

Present Day

Spencer's eyes rolled into the back of his head. "My God, this is so good. I think everything I've eaten to this point in my life has been pure shit."

Reading stood in the hallway with his son, sampling hors d'oeuvres from trays brought in by the staff from Meitner's hotel. He had been treated to enough five-star restaurants by his friends that he certainly had food as good in the past, though he could honestly claim never better. He was about to agree with his son when his phone vibrated with a message. He read it and his eyes bulged.

"What is it?" asked Spencer.

Reading smiled at his son. "Their first unforced error." He headed for Meitner's room and pushed open the door, Spencer on his heels. "Mr. Meitner, we need to talk."

"About?"

Reading shook his head. "You, me, and Spencer. Nobody else."

Meitner dismissed the room with a wave of his hand. "Everybody out. And disable any microphones. I don't want anybody listening in on a headset."

Headphones were unhooked and the room emptied. Reading poked his head outside the door to make certain no one was eavesdropping, then turned to his son. "Keep an eye out." Spencer positioned himself so he could see through the narrow strip of glass as Reading turned to Meitner. "We need to discuss something frankly and honestly."

The heart monitor picked up a couple of beats. "I thought we had been."

"Yes, but something's come to light in the past few minutes, and we need to entertain every possibility as to who's involved. Nobody's excluded, including friends, family, and staff. *Everybody* is a viable suspect. Agreed?"

Meitner nodded. "Of course. What's this new bit of information?"

"I'm going to reveal something to you that you can't repeat to anyone."

"I'll take it to my grave," replied the nonagenarian with a slight smile.

Reading chuckled. "My contacts just physically accessed the bank where the money was transferred to and confirmed it's still in the account. However, there was a block that prevented them from transferring it out. While their operative was there, four men they believe are from the Iranian consulate showed up to transfer the money as well."

"The Iranians? Why would the Iranians want to steal the money?"

"I don't know, but that's not what's important here."

Meitner's eyebrows rose. "It isn't?"

"It's how did they get the account number?"

Meitner shrugged. "Well, if they're the ones stealing the money, then of course they'd have it."

Reading shook his head. "No, they weren't able to transfer the money either. Whoever put the block on it didn't want them to have access. And besides, if they controlled the account, they would simply have transferred the money electronically from outside. According to my contacts, this team of four showed up in what appeared to be a rush job. They hadn't planned on going to the bank."

Meitner scratched his chin. "What do you think that means?"

"We think that means the Iranians are involved, but someone on their team betrayed them, and instead of transferring the money into the agreed-upon accounts, they transferred the bulk of it into their own."

Meitner pursed his lips. "That does seem to fit the facts as we know them, but have we actually learned anything beyond that the Iranians are involved?"

"We've learned that one critical question needs to be answered."

Meitner perked up. "Oh?"

"If the Iranians are involved, and someone on their team stole the money out from under them, how did the Iranians get the account number?"

Meitner regarded him for a moment then gasped. "Oh my God, you're right! There's no way they could know it. But if it wasn't the Iranians, then who was it, and why did they put the account in Jason's name? I still don't understand that."

Reading shook his head. "I'm not sure either. It could be to sow confusion. Remember, this is someone on the inside. Almost nobody knew about that account number." He jabbed a finger at the floor. "It has to be somebody who's been in this room."

Meitner stared at him for a moment. "Maybe they found their betrayer and tortured them for the account number."

"If they did, they would have made them transfer the money, or at least give them instructions on how to remove the block. What happened in the Cayman Islands suggests that all they had was the account number. I believe that this goes beyond what we thought. I believe the Iranians were indeed behind this in some form, that someone betrayed them, and *that* someone wasn't working alone. They had someone deeper inside than we realized."

"But who?"

Reading pulled out a chair from behind one of the workstations and took a seat, exhausted from the long evening. "We need to review, without prejudice, who has been exposed to that account number."

Meitner inhaled deeply then held out a hand as he rhymed off several names, extending a finger for each. "The two techs, Bernie, yourself, myself, your son, Inspector Winter—"

Reading shook his head. "No. He had left before we got that piece of information."

"The police liaison, embassy liaison."

Again, Reading shook his head to both. "They were only here briefly to tell us they would provide anything that we needed, then left."

"Hospital staff?"

"They might have overheard something, but they never would have seen the account number. Your granddaughters?"

Meitner's eyes bulged at the suggestion, his heart rate picking up 10 points. "You don't think…"

"Without prejudice, sir. We are merely listing everyone that could have possibly had access, not who might have done it."

Meitner relaxed slightly then waved his hand. "You're right, of course. Yes, they've been in and out of here so often, they could have seen or heard anything." He chewed his cheek for a moment. "Perhaps one of the techs passed on the information to someone else."

"That's possible, however, they would have to be involved, or by some miracle have passed it on accidentally to someone who actually was. It is a possibility we shouldn't dismiss yet, however. Can you think of anyone else?"

Meitner shook his head. "No."

"Good. Neither can I, which makes it a very short list. We can, of course, eliminate you, me, and my son."

"And my granddaughters."

Reading shook his head. "No, I'm afraid we can't. You have one granddaughter who's almost broke, and another granddaughter who recommended our prime suspect, Miss Vida."

Meitner frowned. "I hate that we can't eliminate my own family."

"As do I, sir. Now, as to the techs, do you know who they are? Have you ever met them before?"

Meitner shook his head. "No. They're simply two locals sent over at my request, part of a team in the mobile unit out front."

"That's quite the unit."

Meitner smiled. "It is, isn't it? There's so much tech packed into that thing, you could run a small war from just one of them."

Reading mulled that comment for a moment. "Do you sell them to the military?"

"Yes. US, Aussies, NATO only. It's too advanced for anyone else to get their hands on. Obviously, the military version has armor and various other capabilities that a civilian unit wouldn't need."

Reading scratched behind his ear. "I have, of course, heard of Meitner Telecom, but beyond telecommunications, I don't really know much about the company. Do you do a lot of business with the American military?"

"They're our biggest customer. We supply communications equipment, guidance systems, satellites. I could sit here all day and rhyme off what we provide."

Reading's head slowly bobbed. "So, you wouldn't be too popular with the Iranian government now, would you?"

Meitner's eyes shot wide as he propped up on his elbows. "Could this entire thing be revenge? Certainly, equipment provided by us has been used in the Middle East. Every weapon system in existence has been."

"It could be why the Iranians are involved," agreed Reading. "But let's forget that for now. We need to narrow down the suspect pool. We were discussing your people."

"The techs in the room are local, as are the people downstairs."

"And were any of them involved in the Control Center?"

"Local personnel were used to help set it up, but it was all manned by people we brought in, who had trained for the event back home."

"I think we can safely say that the chances of one of your local personnel being the inside person are very slim."

"I would agree with that," said Meitner.

"Then unfortunately, that leaves only three people. Your granddaughters, and Bernie."

"There's no way it's Bernie. He's been with me for almost forty years. He's like a son to me. He even lives at the residence."

"Again, Mr. Meitner, everyone's a suspect until we can exclude them. Let's revisit your granddaughters. Holly, you said, is nearly broke, with a husband who's an idiot, that has claimed he has a way of getting all the money back. She would be the prime suspect because of the name on the account. However, I think we can agree even her husband isn't that big an idiot."

Meitner rolled his eyes. "I wouldn't be too quick to jump to that conclusion, however, yes, I'm sure he's not."

"Which means someone tried to frame him, however, did it so obviously, it doesn't make sense. Could your granddaughter be behind this, and she hates her husband so much, she tried to frame him?"

Meitner frowned. "I suppose it's possible. And she has been opposed to my donating the money from the beginning, though I think that's because she was so desperate, she felt an inheritance from me was the only thing that could save her."

"And was it?"

"Of course not. I've made provisions for both my granddaughters and my great-grandchildren in the will. They'll be taken care of so that they'll never struggle. It is, however, merely a safety net, as I had believed they all had hundreds of millions of their own from their parents. When Holly confessed what was going on, I promised her I would take care of her, and assuming I live long enough to see my lawyer tomorrow, she will be." He sighed. "It crushes me to say that Michelle is the more likely suspect, since she's the one who recommended Vida, and we're positive she's involved."

"I would agree. She's absolutely a prime suspect. My contacts have checked out Vida, and she's kept a fairly low profile over the years. No social media accounts, a recently created LinkedIn profile, and that's about it. We haven't been able to verify her references yet because of the hour, and by the time we do tomorrow, it will be too late."

"You think it's a fake identity?"

"If it weren't for the fact that your granddaughter has known her for several years, I would say that all indications are. However, if you were to look me up, you would find no social media either. And depending on the time of day, would have a hard time checking my references. Not embracing today's insanity might make one a dinosaur in some people's eyes, but not necessarily a thief. I think we need to talk to Michelle."

Meitner agreed. "I think so. I'll let you do the questioning, however. I fear I'll be too soft on her."

"Thank you, sir."

Reading gestured at Spencer and he left the room, returning a few moments later with Michelle. She smiled pleasantly. If there were a guilty bone in her body, she wasn't revealing it to them.

"You wanted to see me, Grandpa?"

"Agent Reading has some questions for you."

A hint of color left her cheeks as Reading rose from his chair. He smiled at her.

"No need to worry, ma'am. We just need to know some more about Miss Vida. What can you tell us about her?"

Michelle shrugged. "What do you want to know?"

"How did you meet her?"

"At a fundraising event a few years back. I can't remember which event it was, but she was one of the organizers. I thought she had done a fantastic job, so I asked her to help on an event I was working on."

"Are you friends?"

Her head tilted slightly to the side. "We're friendly, but we never call each other up and gab, though when we're working on a project, we get along quite well. There's a bit of an age gap there. And then, of course, there are the cultural differences. She's Turkish." She raised a finger, stopping herself. "Actually, she was born in Turkey, but her parents were Iranian diplomats, I believe." She paused, her eyes narrowing as she thought. "No, wait. Sorry, I'm trying to remember. It was convoluted. Her mother was Turkish, married to an Iranian diplomat, so she had Turkish citizenship before she became American. Raised very strict until she came to America and threw off those shackles, though she never went quite as wild as the typical Western liberated woman."

Reading was barely listening anymore, as he, Spencer, and Meitner all exchanged excited looks. "You said her father's Iranian?"

"Yes. Why? Is that important?"

"It could be." Reading faced her squarely. "Now, I need you to be completely honest with me."

"Of course."

"You have actually met this woman before?"

Her eyes widened in surprise. "Of course! On many occasions."

"In person. Shook her hand?"

"Yes, absolutely. What are you getting at?"

"And the woman tonight that was running the show is the same woman you've met?"

"Yes, absolutely. I went to the Control Center to wish her well."

"There's no doubt that it was Azar, no doubt whatsoever? There wasn't anything unfamiliar about her, as if she might be in disguise, a mask, anything? You're absolutely certain?"

"I believe I just said that."

"So then, a woman that you've known for years, who's helped you with various charity events, does something like this, that's completely out of character?"

"Completely, which is why I simply can't believe she's involved, though from everything I've been told she absolutely is. It has to be against her will. I just can't see her doing something like this voluntarily."

"And when the person originally hired to do the job died in the car accident, did Miss Vida reach out to you, or did you reach out to her?"

"I reached out to her. In fact, when I heard about the death, I thought we should cancel the event, but Grandpa was insistent it move ahead, and then the debate was whether to promote someone internally or bring in someone from the outside. I immediately thought of her and suggested her name."

Meitner agreed. "I recall the conversation. She proposed Vida. I asked a few questions, but I trust my granddaughter's judgment when it comes to these things, so I said that if she wanted the job, it was hers, as long as she passed the security checks and was willing."

Reading chewed his cheek for a moment. "Who else was in the room?"

Meitner squinted. "Myself, Michelle, Bernie, Wagner. I believe that's it."

Reading scratched his chin as he regarded Michelle. "You're sure you suggested Miss Vida unprompted? No one else in the room suggested her first?"

Michelle shook her head. "No, it was my idea."

Meitner's mouth opened then he raised a finger. "No, it wasn't." The excitement in his voice suggested a revelation, and everyone turned to face the old man as his heart monitor raced. Michelle stepped over to his bedside and took his hand.

"Calm yourself, Grandpa."

Meitner closed his eyes, breathing deeply through his nose then exhaling loudly, repeating the process several times as half a dozen points were shaved off his heart rate. He nodded then opened his eyes. "One of the curses of being hooked up to this damn machine." He winked at

Spencer. "Good thing a pretty nurse hasn't come into the room in a while."

Spencer snorted and Meitner patted his granddaughter's hand.

Reading prompted the man. "You were saying it wasn't her idea."

Meitner shook his head. "No, it wasn't. If you recall, my dear, we were discussing who we could bring in."

"Yes, I remember, and I said Azar could do the job."

"Yes, that's what you said, but you're forgetting what was said just before that."

Her eyes narrowed. "What are you talking about?"

"Bernie said, 'What about the woman who ran the Sunshine Children's Charity event?'"

Michelle's eyes shot wide and her jaw dropped. "Oh my God, that's right! I totally forgot! Bernie said that, and then that's when I recommended Azar." She paused. "Wait a minute, you're not suggesting…" She didn't finish the sentence, but everyone knew exactly what this new fact could mean.

If there were a person ideally placed inside, Bernie was the candidate. If he had suggested Vida for the job, then he was involved from the beginning. He had access to everything. Accounts, the memory key, every aspect of Meitner's life. The fact that Holly's husband's name had been used to open the account suggested something personal. It all made sense, except for one thing. Vida had the connections to Iran, not Bernie.

Or did he?

Reading turned to Meitner. "Is there anything in Bernie's past that would suggest a connection to Iran?"

Meitner shook his head. "No, absolutely not. And with our military contracts, DoD and every other agency in the world has crawled in and out of all our asses for decades. If there were anything to be found, they would have found it."

"Then it still doesn't make sense. Everything's backward." Reading growled in frustration. "There's something we're missing. If he has no Iranian connections, then he can't be the primary in this. It just doesn't make sense. We know the Iranians are involved. There's absolutely no doubt about that. Men from their consulate in the Caymans hit that bank to try to get the money. An American citizen can't just reach out and call up the Iranian government and say, 'Hey, want to steal twenty-five billion dollars?' And we can't even be sure that it isn't a rogue element within the Iranian government doing this, because it just doesn't make sense what they're doing. The fallout from this could be harsh."

"Then how do you explain it?" asked Meitner. "If he's the one that planted the seed to have Vida chosen for the job, then doesn't that mean he has to be involved?"

"Oh, I think he's involved, though we have no evidence to prove that yet. It's possible he could have innocently suggested Vida, but we can't forget one thing."

"What's that?"

"The car accident. My contacts are reviewing the evidence to see if they can spot anything that suggests it wasn't an accident, but we have to assume that it wasn't. Your employee was murdered to create the space for the Iranians to move Vida in."

Michelle gasped. "I can't believe Azar would murder or even be involved in such a thing!"

"Yet here we are. Over a dozen bombs have detonated, people are dead, a police officer dead, and my friends have been kidnapped, so we know she's capable of being involved."

"I still can't believe it's willingly."

"And I'm willing to concede that there's a possibility she isn't. We need to know who the mole is on the inside that's feeding them information. Has Bernie ever given any indication he wasn't happy with you?"

Meitner shook his head. "Absolutely none. He's been a loyal employee for as long as I can remember. I consider him my friend and confidant. He knows more about me than probably anyone."

Reading folded his arms. "Then we need proof before we accuse him of being the inside man on the biggest theft in history. He could be completely innocent in this."

Spencer cleared his throat and Reading turned toward his son.

"Yes?"

"He hasn't left the hospital, has he, since we arrived?"

Meitner shook his head. "No. He's been either in the room or in the hallway."

"And he didn't plan on being here, so he would know nothing about this hospital."

"What's your point?" asked Reading.

"My point is, we know that somebody provided the account number. We didn't know the account number until a short while ago, so whoever sent that communication had to have used an electronic device, and if it were him, he probably still has it on him."

Michelle raised a finger. "Aren't we forgetting something? I mean, if he is in on it, then wouldn't he know the account number already?"

Meitner patted his granddaughter's hand. "I'm afraid you missed a few conversations, my dear. While we believe the Iranians are behind this, it's our belief they've been betrayed by one of their own people."

"But, if he is in on this, and the Iranians hit the bank like you said, then he sent the account number to them, which means he's in league with *them*, not whoever betrayed them."

Reading agreed, and encouraged her to continue with her train of thought. "Go on."

"Well, like I've said, Azar is such a nice person, such a good person that I've known for years, and this seems so out of character for her, that I'm willing to bet she's the one who betrayed the Iranians."

"Keep going."

"Well, let's say the Iranians wanted to steal the money for some reason. Maybe it's revenge for one of Grandpa's military deals. They find out about the charity event—it wasn't exactly a secret, nor was the fact the money was actually going to be transferred in a big public event. They realized this was their opportunity for revenge, whether it's an official government thing or some rogue operation. The event's been publicized for at least a couple of months, so that gives them plenty of time to put together a plan. They realize they need someone on the inside, so they start checking us all out, looking for any leverage they can get over any of us. With so much of our lives on social media now, I'm sure there are photos of me with Azar at some of our events."

"But we found almost no social media footprint for her," interjected Meitner.

"Yes, she hated social media, but they wouldn't be checking her out, they would be checking our family and employees out. And we're all over social media and in the press, every gossip rag, every Page Six. They find my connection to Azar. With her father being an Iranian diplomat, she would be in their files. I'm quite certain both her parents are alive, so that's their leverage over her."

Reading was impressed. The woman was right. It all made sense. Vida could have been forced into it, her parents used as leverage against her. The question was, why would Bernie have brought her up? If he were innocent and not the mole, then who was? Could there be someone else entirely outside of their bubble? Could Vida herself have provided the account number? He dismissed the idea again. If she had provided the number, she would have provided instructions on bypassing the block on the account, or simply transferred the money from on board the airplane.

He regarded Spencer, debating his idea of checking Bernie's electronic devices. They would need a warrant, and there was no time for anything like that. He turned to Meitner. "I think my son's right. If the inside person has been in this room, then very few people could be involved. They would have had to send the information electronically, which means they most likely have the device still on them. If Bernie is our man, then you should demand he hand over his devices for inspection."

"But what if he refuses?" asked Michelle.

"Then we know he's the one. If he's got nothing to hide, he should volunteer to hand them over so we can eliminate him as a suspect and move on."

Meitner shook his head. "I just can't believe it's him."

"From everything you've told us about him, neither can I. Perhaps he's being coerced as well, but we need to know."

Meitner agreed. "Get him."

Bernie savored the caviar and crème fraîche tartlets, every chew a delight. Chef Stephan was a genius in the kitchen, an artist in the true sense, the contrast of the black and white of the primary ingredients shaped into a yin and yang symbol rather than simply divided into halves. He wasn't sure what he would miss most. The food, the five-star accommodations, the limousines, the private jets.

The never wanting for anything.

It was a lifestyle few could imagine, and even fewer would ever experience, yet it had been his life for decades. He was paid a salary, a generous one compared to most, though it could never provide the lifestyle he had grown accustomed to. This was the lifestyle tens of billions of dollars of wealth provided. A mid six-figure salary could never hope to come close.

When Meitner died, his life as he knew it was over. He was already in his mid-60s. No one would hire him, certainly not another billionaire that could provide him with this lifestyle. He had no doubt he'd be given a job at the company, if he wanted it, perhaps an aide to one of the executives. But it wouldn't be like this. Nothing could be like this.

He had hoped that Meitner would provide for him in his will, something very generous after all they had been through. But Meitner had made it clear he was leaving all of his money to the poor and destitute of the world. Even his own family was getting little to nothing because they already had their own substantial wealth. He, on the other hand, only had what he had managed to save over the years. It was a tidy sum, but it would be blown on the purchase of a home that would fit the lifestyle he had grown accustomed to, and a car he wouldn't be ashamed to be seen in. The furnishings alone would chew through so much of his savings, he would have little left.

His lifestyle needed millions a year.

There was an old saying he had heard, something along the lines of. "It's better to have never been rich, than to have been rich then poor." The vast majority of people had no idea what they were missing. They couldn't fathom the lifestyles of the truly rich. He had grown up in a home that could barely be called middle class. There had always been struggles, though food was always on the table. His parents had both worked hard to make sure he and his sister had everything they needed, including an education.

He had loved public communications, and when hired at the tender age of 24 by Meitner's company, it had been the greatest day of his life. He had quickly worked his way up to being one of the assistants to the big man himself, and Meitner had taken a shine to him after he had suggested to get out ahead of a potential public relations problem rather than trying to bury it. Meitner had liked the idea, told them to move forward with it, and the transparent approach had saved them from what could have been a nightmare.

There's no dirt if you don't have to dig.

Meitner had begun asking his opinion more frequently, and eventually became his mentor. In less than five years at the company, he was offered the position of Meitner's aide. He had leaped at the opportunity, though at the time, didn't realize the price he would pay for taking the job. It meant living on Meitner's estate, it meant traveling with him wherever he went.

It meant no time for a personal life.

He never married, had never really had a girlfriend, never had the joy of holding his own child, of kissing his own grandchild. He had no one. His chest tightened.

I'm so alone!

But his loneliness was nothing compared to what it soon would be. Meitner didn't have many years left, and could die tomorrow. And once that happened, the one constant in his life for 40 years would be gone, the family he had come to know would push him away as the employee he was, and he'd be forced to start over. He would be all alone, starting life anew when most men were retiring to enjoy the fruits of their labor.

It was something he dreaded, and if honest with himself, his fear of it had at times had him contemplating suicide. Yet that wasn't him. That was the coward's way out. He would somehow figure out a way to survive. He could make new friends, build a new life.

Yet he could never make the money he needed.

It was impossible.

Or so he had thought.

Everything changed three weeks ago. He was heading for his car after receiving a massage, a special massage, something he did once a week to relieve his stress and give him a modicum of the human contact missing in his life. Two men had approached him.

"You look like a relaxed man, my friend."

Bernie had unlocked the car doors with his fob, already uncomfortable with their demeanor. He ignored them and continued toward the door when one blocked his path.

"Bernie, we need to talk."

Bernie froze.

How do they know my name?

A tablet was held in front of him, a video playing of what had happened mere minutes ago. He nearly fainted.

"Now, this sort of behavior doesn't bother us, however, what would Mr. Meitner think if he were to receive an email with the link to this video on the Internet? How long do you think you'd be employed?"

Bernie reached out and grabbed the car, steadying himself as he struggled to remember to breathe. "How? How did you get that?"

"We've been watching you. If you want something like this to be kept secret, you shouldn't go to the same place on the same day at the same time every week."

"What do you want? I can pay you."

The man chuckled. "You misunderstand, my friend, *we* want to pay *you.*"

Bernie's eyebrows shot up. "What do you mean?"

"Your employer has a large charity event coming up soon."

"Yes. What of it?"

"The people who've hired us, wish to embarrass your employer. In order to do so, we require someone on the inside."

Bernie's eyes bulged. "You don't mean me, do you?"

The man laughed. "No, of course not. We have our own person. All you need to do is make sure they get hired."

"But how? The team's already been set. They've been training for weeks. There's no way to get somebody in there, especially for *me* to get someone in there."

The man smiled. "You leave that to us. We'll create the opportunity, then you just need to come through. Once our person is on the inside and the job is done, you'll be paid."

Bernie shook his head. "I can't do that. Not to Mr. Meitner. He's been too good to me."

"Mr. Meitner isn't going to be around much longer, which means you may well be out of a job. Something tells me you're going to miss living the lifestyle you now enjoy." The man waved the tablet with the video still playing. "And don't forget, we release this, you'll lose that lifestyle far sooner than you could have imagined, and your reputation will be destroyed. All we're asking is that you make sure our person gets hired when the time comes, so that we can embarrass your employer."

"What do you mean by embarrass?"

The man shrugged. "Nothing you need to concern yourself with, however, you'll be paid handsomely should things go well. But if they don't, then you won't get paid, so it's in your best interest to make sure if any hiccups happen along the way, you smooth them out."

"Why me? Why are you blackmailing me?"

"Because you're the one we found with a secret to hide, and with the access we need. And like I said, you'll be paid handsomely."

Bernie firmly shook his head. "No, no amount of money can make me betray him. He's been too good to me. He'll understand. He'll forgive me."

"Not even for one-hundred million dollars?"

Bernie's eyes bulged. "What?"

"One-hundred million, and all you need to do is make sure our person gets hired. You're not hurting anyone, you're not stabbing or shooting anyone, you're just making sure someone gets hired, and that person will take care of the rest."

Bernie's mind raced. It could solve all the problems worrying him recently. He didn't need billions to live the lifestyle of a billionaire. A hundred million would give him a nearly equivalent lifestyle. Even if he lasted another 30 years, it would be over three million a year he could live off, not counting the interest. It would be more than enough to have an incredible home, staff, cars, chef-prepared meals, fine wine, and luxury travel around the world.

"I see we've piqued your interest."

Bernie closed his eyes, his shoulders slumping.

You're a horrible person.

But it was simply too much money to not consider.

"Do we have an understanding?"

Bernie sighed, then reluctantly nodded. "Yes."

"Good. You'll be contacted soon. And now that we have an understanding, you need to understand this. Those who break their word to us die horrible deaths."

They had left and he had climbed into his car, sitting there for the better part of half an hour, shaking, debating what he should do. His trips to the massage parlor were his secret shame for years. In the early days, he had been more careful about it, but after getting away with it for so long, he had become complacent. The man was right. He should have been mixing up the dates and times and locations, but he had been a fool, and now was paying the price.

He could go to Meitner and tell him everything. He was certain Meitner would forgive him, especially for sacrificing his reputation to save him. But were these men serious? Would they kill him? Meitner had security. Could these people get through it? And how long would he have to be protected? And if he needed protection, he couldn't do his job. His very presence would be a threat to Meitner.

He would lose everything regardless.

And besides, all they planned to do was embarrass Meitner, and he knew the man well enough to know he couldn't care less about something like that. Meitner was well known in the business world, but he had pulled back long ago. These people clearly misunderstood the purpose of the charity event. It wasn't for Meitner to go out in a blaze of glory. It was to raise money for the charities, to inspire others like him to leave their fortunes to the poor of the world. It had nothing to do with ego. If they embarrassed him, then so what? Meitner would push past whatever social gaffe they forced, donate the money regardless, and inspire others to do the same.

And $100 million?

The thought of it brought a smile. His future would be secure, with no one truly hurt.

Or so he had thought at the time.

He realized he was in over his head when told about the car accident. Within less than an hour, he had received a call with his instructions. He had to make certain Azar Vida was the replacement, and make certain any red flags on the vetting process were buried. He had been shocked at the name. He had met the woman before, and couldn't believe she was in on it. Though because he knew her, and knew she was a friend of Michelle's, it had set his mind at ease, though only slightly.

There was no way the car crash had been an accident. The timing was too convenient. They had obviously arranged it, making it appear to be an accident, which meant these people were murderers. But he was in too deep. If he went to Meitner now, he could be charged by the police for involvement in her murder as an accessory.

The next day, the meeting had been held. He, of course, was there, and he suggested her, not by name, but by reference, and Michelle had immediately picked up on it. He had volunteered to take care of the security checks, as he often did with things that didn't involve the corporation, but because it was a rush job, a deep dive couldn't be done. Regardless, no red flags were raised. By the time Vida had been hired, he had actually done nothing but utter a single sentence that had prompted Michelle to advocate on behalf of her friend, a fully qualified candidate.

It eased his guilty conscience somewhat, though a woman was still dead, and he could have prevented it by coming forward. But then he'd be dead too, and they might still have found a way inside, for surely he wasn't the sole person they could blackmail with skeletons in their closet.

He had thought his job was over, his $100 million payday secure, until tonight, when things went horribly wrong. They had certainly embarrassed Meitner in some ways, but this was more than that. It was a theft. And now so many people were dead. And it wasn't over yet. He could have prevented it, yet he was in too deep now. They had given him a number with instructions to reach out to with any information he felt they needed to know, and he had done so when he found out about the account number.

It was too late. The crime had been committed. The money was gone. All he could do now was get his share and try to get through this without anyone knowing his involvement. Everyone was focusing on Vida. She would take the fall, not him. He just had to keep it together to get through this night, and if Reading's contacts were as good as he said, it could all be over by morning. If they got the money back, if they captured or killed those behind this, he would lose his payday, but he wasn't so concerned about that anymore. Right now, he just wanted to get through this without going to jail. Any money he might get would simply be gravy.

The door to Meitner's hospital room opened. Reading and his son emerged, both scanning the area, their eyes coming to rest on him. The color drained from his face at their expressions. They knew. But how?

How had they figured it out? He had done everything right. No one could possibly know.

They strode toward him. Reading flashed his Interpol identification, making it official, and causing the police officers stationed in the area to perk up.

"Sir, I'm going to have to ask you to give me all your electronic devices."

Bernie closed his eyes, his shoulders slumping. He could refuse, but there was no point. All that would do was delay the inevitable. He had been caught, and the best thing he could do now, as he had suggested 40 years ago, was to get out in front of this and make the best of a bad situation.

He opened his eyes and stared at Reading. "I'll answer any questions you have, but it has to be in front of Mr. Meitner. I at least owe him that."

Over the Mediterranean Sea

Vida sat in her seat, her face throbbing from the blows. They hadn't touched her in over half an hour, and the window of opportunity to harm her further was rapidly narrowing. They were approaching the Libyan coast, and she would soon be in front of the general behind this. She didn't care what happened to her. She wasn't doing this because she wanted to. She wasn't doing this because of any threats to her safety.

She was doing this to save her family.

Several weeks ago, two men had approached her after her hot yoga class. She had immediately tensed when Farsi was spoken. It was the language of her homeland, and she had barely heard it since remaining behind in the United States after finishing her degree.

Her parents hadn't been happy. She had been sent to America to get an education so she could return home and improve her country, but what they hadn't realized was that her father's career as a diplomat had exposed her to the world throughout her youth, and she hated Iran. Not her people, but the regime.

If it were a democracy where everyone had equal rights, she would have returned in a heartbeat, but it wasn't, and it appeared it never would be unless something drastic happened. She had seen her parents several times over the years, never, of course, in Iran, but if they were posted to some foreign embassy or consulate, she would always make a point to fly out and see them. It was at one of these reunions that her mother confessed to her with a whispered message that she thanked God every day her daughter lived in America and not Iran.

It was then she realized all the screaming and shouting over the phone had been for the benefit of the ears listening in on the conversations. It had rid her of the guilt and allowed her to live her life, and eventually thrive in it. The desire to give back had her switching her career to charitable causes, which was how she had met Michelle Meitner. It had changed her life, the connections the woman brought with her ensuring steady employment, not only through various causes that the Meitners backed, but those their friends did as well.

She had Michelle to thank for the lifestyle she now lived, but she also had Michelle to thank for her current predicament. She had been "invited" into the back seat of an SUV with blacked-out windows. She hadn't protested, she hadn't fought, she hadn't argued. There was no point. If she didn't cooperate, her family back in Iran could be at risk.

The doors had slammed shut, with one man in the driver's seat, the other beside her in the back.

"You haven't been home in a long time, Miss Vida."

She had to choose her words carefully. Her concern wasn't for herself, it was for those she had no way to protect. She didn't respond, as it wasn't a question, it was a statement.

"We need you to do a job for your homeland."

She tensed, her mouth filling with bile. She swallowed, but still said nothing.

"You have a friend, Michelle Meitner."

A wave of weakness swept through her. "What have you done to her?"

The man smiled slightly. "So, you do speak. Nothing. We haven't touched her nor will we. However, we found you through her, which was truly fortunate with your father now back in Tehran and not some dangerous foreign country."

The blood drained from her cheeks. "What have you done to my family?"

"Nothing, and again, nor will we, as long as we have your complete cooperation."

She closed her eyes and drew a long, deep breath before exhaling. She opened her eyes. "What is it you want from me?"

"I assume you've heard of your friend's grandfather's charity event."

There was no harm in answering that, everyone in her business had. She nodded.

"Well, they're going to require someone to take over running it."

Her eyebrows rose. "Why? They already have someone. She's very good."

315

"She, unfortunately, won't be available on the night in question, and they'll be looking for a last-minute replacement. That's going to be you."

Her eyes shot wide. "Me? And what do you mean, she won't be available?"

"You need not concern yourself with the details. All you need to worry about is your family back home. You will cooperate with us fully. If you don't, they will suffer painfully slow deaths."

The conversation had continued for a short while longer, most of it a droning fog as her mind was blocked with horrifying images of her parents pleading to her for answers, for why she hadn't just done what they asked. There were more meetings after that, and a week later, she had received a call from Michelle telling her of the car accident and her desperate need for someone to come in. She had vomited after the call. Someone was dead. That knowledge made everything so real. If they were willing to kill an innocent woman to get her inside, then they wouldn't hesitate to do the same to her family. She had no choice but to cooperate.

Yet she knew how these people operated. She knew she couldn't trust them, so she had come up with a plan. A quick Google search gave the name of a bank with questionable business practices, and a phone call had been made. A representative arrived at her home later that day, and she explained, using only vague details, what she would require and when. A 10% fee was agreed upon, and she had an account set up that she put in Jason Harper's name to redirect any suspicion toward Holly's side of the family, rather than Michelle's. It could buy her more time should what she was doing be discovered.

Security was a concern. In her search, she had read an article about the CIA tapping banks such as this, and the representative assured her that a full security sweep of the system would be performed immediately. A block was set up on the account so no transfers could be made out of it without a password she had chosen, and for 24 hours from the evening in question, all the bank staff would be at a private retreat and unavailable to the authorities.

A 10% share of tens of billions bought a lot of cooperation.

With the deal made, she had then turned her attention to how to get the account in play. Wagner had explained all the technical details, and that part proved relatively easy. When handed the memory key, all she had to do was palm it to one of the security personnel she had "recommended" for the job after several called in sick with food poisoning. He then went into a back room and plugged it into a machine with software that would replace Meitner's destination accounts with their own. What her employers hadn't realized was that she had pulled a switch on the switch. The rest had little to do with her, and everything else went off without a hitch until they had been pursued by Meitner's guests.

She felt for them. They were innocent in all of this, though why the fools had pursued them, she had no idea. But their lives weren't her responsibility, they were their own. All that mattered now was using the leverage she had over the general in charge. The beating she had taken certainly suggested the money transfer had been successful, and that the deal she had made with the bank honored.

She had the $22 billion. She didn't want it, and she had no intention of keeping it. It would all be returned to Meitner as soon as this was all over, if she could manage it, but until her family was safely outside of Iran and she had heard their voices, that money was staying in that account.

One new piece of information she had garnered through the undisciplined ravings of those around her, was that this was not an official Iranian government operation, though they were Iranian soldiers. An unnamed general was behind this. What his motives might be, she had no idea, and they didn't concern her.

The plane began to descend, and one of the men spat in her face.

"You'll be answering to the General soon."

She sneered at him. "And so will you."

Abandoned Airstrip

West of Benghazi, Libya

Dawson surveyed the area. It was an abandoned airstrip outside of Benghazi. The runway was serviceable, and he had no doubt various illegal flights came in and out of here on a regular basis, but there were no manned facilities. In fact, there wasn't a soul here. If the plane were landing here, like Langley said, there was no one to meet the passengers. From what he had gathered from the briefing, this was an operation timed to the minute, and whoever those on the plane were meeting, would likely arrive at the same time.

He activated his comm. "Control, Zero-One. No sign of activity, over."

"Copy that, Zero-One. We have two vehicles approaching your position now from the east, and the plane is on approach. ETA sixty seconds."

"Copy that, Control." Dawson adjusted his binoculars. A cloud of dust obscured the stars to the east, no doubt the vehicles to which Langley had referred.

Niner pointed ahead. "There!"

Dawson lowered the binoculars and peered into the night sky, spotting the approaching plane. He activated his comm. "Bravo Team, Zero-One, this is it. Everyone holds their fire until we see the professors and Azar Vida. We can't risk engaging with them still on the plane."

The plane landed and the tires chirped then the engines roared. He stretched his fingers, easing the tension on his M4. The aircraft came to a stop and the engines were cut. The two vehicles Langley had reported raced down the runway then turned hard around the plane's nose as a door opened on the fuselage and the stairs lowered. Dawson peered through the scope on his M4, his eyes narrowing as what appeared to be the pilot and copilot stepped onto the tarmac, carrying a body. They loaded it into the back of one of the vehicles, then climbed into the other.

"Control, do we have an ID on that body?"

"Negative, Zero-One, however, it's not one of the professors or Vida, over."

"Copy that, Control." Dawson watched as the two vehicles pulled away and the airplane was left abandoned. "What the hell is going on here?"

Niner rolled to his side and looked at him. "Is everyone else still on board?"

Dawson shook his head. "Why would they be? It makes no sense. Control, Zero-One, are there any other vehicles approaching, over?"

"Negative, Zero-One, we have no movement in the area."

"Do you have any better eyes than we do? Is there any movement inside that plane?"

"Negative, Zero-One, we've got nothing."

Dawson cursed. "Teams Two and Three, hold your positions, we're moving in." He rose with Niner and Jimmy and sprinted down the runway toward the aircraft. They reached the nose undetected. Dawson listened, and hearing nothing, pulled out a flashbang, popped the pin, then tossed it inside the open door. It detonated and the customary cries of shock he would expect didn't materialize.

He rushed up the steps with Niner and Jimmy on his heels. The cabin lighting was still on, operated by battery power, and he surged down the aisle of the private jet as Jimmy and Niner turned in the opposite direction to check the cockpit. A quick search confirmed the plane was empty. A panel was pulled from the floor and he poked his head inside the cargo hold, finding it too was empty.

He shook his head. "Control, Zero-One, there's nobody here. I repeat, there's nobody here. The plane is empty, over."

"Stand by, Zero-One."

Niner pointed at the floor near the front of the plane. "Looks like blood."

Jimmy took a knee and eyed it closer. "Well, they did carry a body out of here. Would they have shot one of their own?"

Dawson shrugged. "Anything's possible, though if the professors were on this plane, it wouldn't surprise me if they somehow had a hand in it."

"What do we do now?"

"We wait for evac and hope that Langley can figure out where the hell our targets disappeared to between Vienna and here, when they've been at forty-thousand feet the entire damn time."

CIA Headquarters, Operations Center 3

Langley, Virginia

Leroux turned to his team. "Okay. Theories?"

Child spun in his chair, staring at the ceiling. "Well, we know they got on in Vienna, and there were no stops until now, so either they were abducted by aliens, or they jumped out of the damn plane."

Leroux was willing to entertain any thoughts at the moment, though jumping from the airplane made the most sense. He rose from his chair and stepped toward the displays. "Show me their flight path."

Tong brought it up, a red line tracking the flight. He pointed at the beginning of the route. "There's no way they'd jump out over Europe. It would defeat the entire purpose of trying to escape."

Tong folded her arms as she leaned back. "They wouldn't bail over the Mediterranean. Not at night."

Child dropped his elbows onto his desk. "Don't forget too that they were at cruising altitude almost the entire flight. To jump from that altitude, they would have had to have HALO gear and be very experienced. And why risk it? They landed the plane in Libya with no problem. They had people rendezvous with the aircrew. It doesn't make sense. Why wouldn't they have just landed with the plane?"

"Because they knew we might be there," said Tong. "Remember, the Iranians hit the bank in the Caymans, two of their men were taken out, they found CIA equipment plugged in, they knew we knew. So, they had to change their plans."

"Or it was never their plan to land with the plane."

"Either way, they changed their plans because they knew we were on to them, or it was never their intent because they knew we *could* be on to them."

Leroux wagged a finger in the air as he puzzled it out. "You're right. This was always the plan. They were always going to deviate when they reached Athens, which means they would automatically be brought to our attention. Then there would be almost an hour-and-a-half for all the agencies to figure out these must be the people involved in what had happened in Vienna. So, regardless of whether the professors screwed up their plans, they were never landing. The pilots probably had instructions that if they were caught, to simply claim they were forced to do whatever it was they did, and to tell the truth about the others bailing."

Child tapped at his keyboard then gestured toward the displays. "I'm sending the drone north along their flight path. If they jumped, then it's between the airstrip and the coast, and that's not far."

The aerial view whipped by, the eerie green glow from the night vision mode racing past. Then a collective gasp erupted from the room.

Leroux smiled. "Now, would you look at that?"

Libyan Airspace

Ten minutes earlier

Acton stared at the digital read-out of the altimeter as it rapidly dropped. His head pounded and he was a little queasy. He had been out for some time, according to the clock, but he was alive, though if they were about to land, he wasn't sure for how long.

Laura smiled at him, though he could see the concern in her eyes. "How are you feeling?"

"Peachy."

No guard was sitting across from them anymore, the blankets used to strap them to their seats enough to prevent any more foolishness, though something else was going on. He turned to peer through the seats again, and immediately regretted it as a searing flash of pain split his skull. He closed his eyes and took a deep breath before making another attempt, slower this time.

Everyone was gathered in the back. The argument had subsided, and they were focused on something else now. Something was being handed out, and one of the men turned, heading down the aisle toward them, carrying two black bags. Acton faced forward and the man dropped the bags in front of them.

Parachutes?

"Do you know how to use these?"

They both nodded.

"Good, then I won't waste my time explaining things." He drew a knife from behind his back. "Now, I'm going to untie you. Any foolishness, and I slit your throats. Understood?"

Again, they both nodded.

The man kneeled in front of Laura and, still gripping the knife, worked the large knot in the blanket. Acton was convinced they had tied them in the front so the man who originally tied it could stare at Laura's bounty.

The fact this man's eyes were glued to his wife's chest had him thinking he was right. He struggled with the large knot and finally put the knife on the floor so he could work with both hands. Laura leaned in and rolled her shoulders forward slightly, enhancing the show. Acton wondered what she was up to, for she had to be up to something, when he noticed her left foot turn outward, slowly pushing the knife toward him. He adjusted his position as she leaned forward some more. He placed his foot over the blade and slowly drew it back, under his seat, as the man's eyes were almost buried in her chest.

Then the knot was free.

"Thank you," said Laura as she pulled the blanket out from around her then stood. The man shuffled over to Acton's seat and went to work on the knot when Laura dropped the blanket on the floor. "Oops. So clumsy of me." She bent completely over to pick it up, her behind on full display as the torn dress left nothing to the imagination.

The work on the knot slowed and Acton cleared his throat. The man's head whipped from its position glued to Laura's ass, and he flushed when he realized he had been caught. The knot was quickly loosened then the man stepped back as Acton removed the blanket, tossing it to the floor, covering his feet and the knife.

"We jump in two minutes. Make sure you're ready." The man beat a hasty retreat to join his friends, and Acton smiled slightly as he spotted a brow wipe.

"That was quite the show."

Laura shrugged. "I'm allowed to use my feminine wiles now and again. I find it especially works on sexually repressed cultures."

Acton grinned. "It certainly worked on this sexually repressed vulture."

She gave him a look then handed him his parachute. "Put this on before you hurt yourself."

He shrugged into the harness then snapped the straps in place, tightening them. He kneeled and picked up the knife from under the seat, sliding it under his shirt, using the crisscrossed straps to hold it tight against his torso. He would have to be careful to not bend too much, otherwise he might slice himself badly.

Laura checked his chute and he hers. He stepped closer, lowering his voice. "You realize this is our best opportunity."

"Yes."

"So, we're doing this?"

"Absolutely."

"Let's go!" shouted the ogler from the back.

Acton followed Laura down the aisle. A floor panel had been removed, several of the men already in the hold below. Vida climbed down, wind whipping at her clothing, and Laura followed, then Acton, and finally Laura's fan. A hatch was open at the rear of the plane, clear of the engines, and one of the Iranians was already in position. The pilot's voice came over the PA system, saying something in Farsi, and the first man jumped, quickly followed by several more.

Vida positioned herself and hesitated for a moment before diving clear. The rest save their escort followed, and Laura shuffled forward, jumping without hesitation as Acton and his pounding head followed suit. He remembered his training and arched, quickly gaining control of his body. He spotted Laura to his right, just below him. He tucked his arms in and dove to her level before steadying himself once again.

"You good?"

She turned her head and gave him the thumbs-up. He returned it then stared at the ground below. The only light was from the stars and a half-moon, and they revealed little. There were no signs of civilization below them whatsoever, yet they had to have a designated landing zone. The pilot had signaled when to jump, but he had seen no evidence that anyone was using a GPS to guide them in. They had been at nearly 5000 feet when they dove, and time would be running out quickly before they could make their break.

But he couldn't until he knew where to break away from.

Suddenly a light appeared below them, bright and white, shining like a Hollywood premiere. Shouts from below reached him as their captors spotted it as well.

And he smiled.

Now they had a destination.

And a place to avoid.

He looked over at Laura who gave him another thumbs-up, indicating she was ready. "Break right!"

She tucked her arm against her body and abruptly changed directions. He followed, heading 90 degrees away from their target, then straightened out. He glanced down and behind, spotting chutes opening, leaving the others committed. "Open your chute!"

Laura pulled on the ripcord and her chute deployed, fluttering above her as her speed was killed. He blasted past her, checking for a good deployment, then pulled his own. He was yanked by the straps as the thin fabric filled with air, the sensation one of almost being stopped in midair. But he was still falling toward the ground, albeit slower now. He checked for four good corners, then grabbed his toggles, testing them with a left then a right turn.

He gained his bearings, and made certain they were heading away from the others. All they had to do was land safely, then head in the opposite direction. This operation had been well timed, and he was certain they had no window built into their plan to search for missing, unplanned-for hostages. They had to hope their captors would give up on them and simply take their billions and leave.

It had to work.

Laura's chute flapped above him and he turned his still pounding head gently to see if he could spot her.

And he didn't.

Instead, he found her ogler, a couple of hundred feet above and behind him.

With a weapon pointed directly at him.

Abandoned Airstrip

West of Benghazi, Libya

As always, Dawson was the last boot off the ground. The Sea Hawk lifted into the air, delivering them toward where Langley believed their targets might be. Fortunately, their operation was timed to the minute as well, and the Sea Hawk had already been inbound to pick them up, so little time had been lost. A drone had detected a couple of dozen heat signatures about 10 klicks north of their position, along the aircraft's flight path. The only explanation was that the Iranians had bailed. And it made sense. They had to know there was a possibility they would be met with hostile force upon landing.

He stepped to the front of the cabin and poked his head between the seats. "Set us down about two klicks shy of the target area. And try to keep the noise down, okay?"

The pilot eyed him. "Keep the noise down? You Army boys are a little special, aren't you?"

Dawson flashed a grin. "Just keep us tight to the deck. They'll hear us coming, but they don't need to know where we touch down."

"Roger that, Sergeant Major."

"What's our ETA?"

"Five minutes."

"Okay." Dawson took a seat with the others. "Five minutes, people. Weapons check."

Everyone inspected their equipment and the conversation turned to the mission. "So, just to refresh for those who were napping, we've got six vehicles including two technicals with rear-mounted fifty cals, and twenty to twenty-five on the ground."

"Have we confirmed it's the Iranians yet?" asked Spock.

Niner leaped to his feet and started thrusting his hips forward as he smacked either side of an imaginary ass in front of him. "Yeah, I'm gonna show those Iranians who's boss."

Atlas reached up and grabbed him by the back of the collar, hauling him into his seat. "You're a pig."

Niner gave him a look. "You're the one who taught me that."

Atlas shook his head. "Yeah, but when you do it, it looks like a mouse trying to hump an elephant."

Everyone, including the flight crew, pissed themselves laughing and Niner delivered double birds to them all. Dawson let things continue for a moment before raising his hand and silencing the team. "Nobody fires until I give the order. For all we know, it could be a group of Bedouins camping for the night."

Spock's eyebrow shot up. "With two Toyota pickup trucks equipped with the heavy machine gun option from the factory?"

Dawson shrugged. "Hey, it's Libya, not Vermont."

"One minute!" shouted the pilot.

Dawson drew a breath and held it, steadying the adrenaline. "This is it, ladies."

East of Landing Zone

West of Benghazi, Libya

Acton cursed. His perfect plan had failed. He wasn't thinking straight. The pain in his head was growing worse and he couldn't focus. He had forgotten entirely about the Iranian behind them. He would have seen what they were doing and given pursuit, and since the man possessed the lone gun in the equation, they had little hope of coming out on top.

He was bringing a knife to a gunfight.

Literally.

He stared down at the ground. It was barren, with nothing to hide behind, no advantage to be gained anywhere. Their only hope would be if he could get out of his chute fast enough to engage the enemy while the man was preoccupied with his landing. He looked down at the straps and their fasteners, reviewing every step he would have to take so nothing would delay him, when he heard a surprised cry from above. He twisted his head, regretting it, but smiled, nonetheless.

Laura had repositioned herself overtop their captor. Her chute was flared, taking the wind out of it, and she had dropped into the Iranian's, collapsing it as well. She raised her toggles, the air returning to her chute as their opponent rapidly descended to the ground. Acton flared his chute as he reached the desert floor. He tossed his toggles, rapidly releasing the clasps, then shrugged out of the harness before the chute was caught by the wind of the desert night.

He pulled the knife from under his shirt and raced toward the Iranian who had smacked into the ground moments before. The man lay in the sand, gripping his knee, his face twisted in agony, but he spotted Acton coming. He grabbed his weapon sitting in the sand and Acton whipped his knife, the blade piercing the man's chest, opposite his heart. He cried out in agony, dropping the gun. Acton reached him and skidded to the ground, diving for the abandoned weapon. A fist connected with his jaw, ringing his bell as he reached for the gun. He grabbed it, as did his opponent, and they struggled as the throbbing in his head intensified.

He heard a thud and a grunt, and he looked up to see Laura standing above them, her foot returning to the ground after having delivered a blow to the man's head. Acton grabbed the gun and rolled to his knees as the man yanked the knife out of his chest and swung it toward Laura. Acton squeezed the trigger twice and the man's body went limp, the blade collapsing to the desert floor, followed by their opponent.

Laura dropped to her knees beside him. "Thank God that's over."

But he feared their troubles weren't, for the gunshots had revealed their position.

Landing Zone

West of Benghazi, Libya

Vida had been skydiving only once before in her life. Two weeks ago. The Iranians had sent her to a local dive club, and she thanked God they had. Diving in the daylight was one thing, doing it at night, never having done it before, would have been something entirely different. She had reached the ground unscathed, remembering her lesson, and hadn't noticed the professors were missing until she was already out of her chute and walking toward the array of vehicles parked in the desert, their lights revealing the barren landscape.

"Where's Bahadur? And where are the prisoners he was in charge of?" asked one of the men.

Another shrugged. "They must have broken off from us and then he followed them."

Curses erupted and a man in a business suit stepped into the lights. His demeanor suggested this was the general referred to, the man who had dragged her into this, the man responsible for all the deaths, the man who held her parents.

"What's going on?" he demanded.

"The two hostages are missing, as is one of our men."

The General dismissed the concerns with a wave of his hand. "We don't need them." He walked over to her. "You must be Azar Vida."

"I am."

"You betrayed me."

She shook her head. "I did no such thing. I merely protected my family."

The General regarded her for a moment, his head slowly bobbing. "I can respect that. Family is everything, isn't it?"

"Yes, it is."

"We'd do anything for our families."

"Yes."

"Are you willing to die for yours? I know I am for mine."

She tensed. She was ready, though she would prefer not to. She ignored the question. "I have your money. All I want is my family safe as we discussed, and you can have it."

The General shook his head. "This isn't about the money."

Her eyes narrowed. "If it isn't about the money, then what's it about?"

"It's about destroying Meitner."

"I don't understand."

"Meitner and his company are responsible for untold numbers of deaths. Our Muslim brothers and sisters have been slaughtered for decades with weapon systems his company developed. My son…" He paused, his lip trembling for a moment. "My son was one of those killed by men like Meitner, and now I have destroyed his legacy. I never dreamed I'd get the chance to seek my revenge, but when I heard what he had planned, I knew I had to take action to avenge the death of my son. And now, thanks to you, I've done that. I don't want the money. As long as Meitner doesn't have it, then I don't care. It will be used to fund Jihad worldwide, and bring the Zionist Meitner and the imperial American pigs to their knees." He flicked a finger and several guns were aimed at her. "Now, let's discuss your parents."

She gulped and clenched her fists as her heart raced wildly. "You promised me they'd be released when I did the job for you."

"I did, however, you betrayed me."

"No, I merely guaranteed your word, and if you were going to keep it, then they'd already be out of Iran and standing in front of the American Embassy in Istanbul. Now, I need confirmation that they are there."

"And I need the password to the account."

"You'll have it as soon as I know you kept your end of the bargain."

He stared at her, his eyes burning into her. She had to steel her resolve despite her body's desperate desire to betray her. If she could maintain control, then this could all be over soon. "Very well." He pulled a phone from his jacket pocket and dialed a number. "Are you in position?" She couldn't hear the reply. "Put the mother on." He handed her the phone and she pressed it to her ear.

"Mother?"

"Azar, is that you?"

She nearly collapsed in relief. "Yes, it is, mother. Are you and father safe?"

"I'm not sure."

She tensed. "Where are you?"

"We're standing across the street from the American Embassy in Istanbul, but there are two men with us and they have guns."

"Okay, just wait and you'll be safe soon. As soon as they let you go, walk across the street to the American Embassy and tell them you want to apply for a visa to visit. You just need to get inside and then I'll contact you."

The General grabbed the phone out of her hand. "That's enough. Now it's time for you to fulfill your end of the bargain."

Two gunshots rang out and everyone spun toward the sound.

"What the hell was that?

One of the men peered into the dark. "Maybe it's Bahadur. Maybe he shot the hostages."

The General shook his head. "Not that. Not the gunshots. What's that other sound?"

Vida cocked an ear, as did everyone else, and if her heart could beat any faster, it did. A helicopter was approaching.

The General grabbed her by the arm. "Let's get the hell out of here!"

South of Landing Zone

West of Benghazi, Libya

Dawson jumped from the Sea Hawk, clearing the rotors, then took a knee as the chopper lifted off and banked away to hold position should they need support. He indicated for the team to advance and everyone sprinted toward the Iranian position. They reached the top of a ridge as two gunshots rang out. He raised a fist and everyone dropped, Niner beside him.

"Are we lost?"

Dawson eyed him. "What?"

Niner pointed to the right. "Those shots came from over there. I thought the hostiles were directly ahead."

"They're supposed to be." Dawson activated his comm. "Control, Zero-One, we just heard gunshots to our three-o'clock. Confirm we were dropped in the right location, over."

"Stand by, Zero-One." There was a pause as Langley figured out what was going on. "Confirmed the hostiles are directly ahead of your position, less than one klick, but we've got three targets two klicks to your right, directly east. It's the professors. I repeat, it's the professors. It appears one hostile is down and the professors are now alone. The Iranians are heading for their vehicles. It looks like they know you're here, over."

"Copy that." Dawson rose and sprinted ahead with the others. "With the professors on the ground, are we confirming that these are the hostiles, and we have permission to engage?"

"Affirmative, Zero-One. You're clear to engage. Remember, we want Azar Vida alive if possible."

"Copy that, Control, Zero-One, out." With hand motions, he directed his men to spread out. Vehicle engines roared to life just ahead and headlights sliced through the darkness. He turned to Niner. "As soon as you have a shot, take out the technicals."

"Roger that."

Dawson came over the crest of a dune and the hostiles were revealed below. He dropped to a knee and raised his M4 as the others did the same. "Bravo Team, Zero-One, we need Vida alive. Everyone else is open season." He took the bead on the first man in his arc and squeezed the trigger, dropping him in a heap. Niner's weapon belched lead into the engine block of the first technical, steam hissing out of it a moment later.

As Bravo Team opened fire, the Iranians were caught flat-footed, a dozen down before they knew it. The remaining hostiles took cover, returning fire blindly. Dawson lay prone on the ground and spotted Vida, gripped by a man in a business suit, hauling her toward what was no doubt an armored car, that once inside, they'd have a hell of a time stopping without killing her. "I've got eyes on Vida heading to the Mercedes sedan. One-one, remove her captor."

"Removing," replied Niner. The clap of a round from Niner's SWS thundered, and a fist-sized hole appeared, spoiling a perfectly good suit. The body crumpled to the ground and Vida stood there in stunned silence.

"Get down, you idiot," muttered Dawson as he took out another hostile. The gunfire dwindled, then a roar of rage erupted as one of the remaining hostiles emerged from behind a vehicle, firing blindly in the night as he screamed, "Allahu Akbar!" Two more joined him, and Dawson's team fulfilled the Iranians' wishes, sending them to whatever hell they were destined for.

And then there was silence.

East of Landing Zone

West of Benghazi, Libya

The roar of engines grew louder as vehicles approached their position. Acton lay against a sand dune, Laura beside him. He gripped the gun in his hand and she held the knife. He had to assume Iranians were arriving in numbers, but there had been one hell of a lot of gunfire a few minutes ago. Had it been a dispute between those on the ground and those in the plane, or had some other party ambushed them?

"What do you want to do?" he asked Laura.

She shrugged. "We killed four of them. Something tells me they're not going to let us live."

He grunted. "You're probably right. So, we go down in a blaze of glory?"

She smiled. "Sounds good to me."

He leaned forward and gave her a kiss, what might be their last one, and as it grew in passion, so did the pounding in his head. He jerked back as a blinding white light seared through him. Someone cried out in agony, and as he collapsed onto the desert sand, he realized it was him.

"James!"

Dawson raised a fist and the two commandeered vehicles came to a halt. He stepped out and surveyed the area. According to Langley, the professors should be on the other side of the sand dune in front of them. "Professor Acton! Professor Palmer! Friendlies approaching!"

"BD, is that you?" cried Laura.

Something was wrong. He could hear it in her voice. "Affirmative!"

"Over here! Help me! Please, God, help me!"

Dawson sprinted up the sand, along with the others, and spotted Laura leaning over a downed Acton. He tumbled down the side and rolled to his knees. "What happened? Has he been shot?"

She shook her head. "No. He just collapsed. I think it's his head. He's been hit a couple of times today, pistol-whipped."

Dawson indicated for Niner to get to work. The experienced medic rushed over and Laura moved out of the way, her shoulders shaking as she sobbed. Atlas wrapped an arm around her, and she collapsed against his chest as she stared at Niner, checking her husband's vitals. Dawson activated his comm as Niner shook his head. "Control, Zero-One, we need emergency evac now. Target Alpha is down with possible head trauma."

"Copy that, Zero-One. Chopper is inbound now."

The rotors of the Sea Hawk pounded in the distance, and Dawson watched helplessly with the others as a friend, and a comrade, battled for his life.

US Naval Hospital

Naples, Italy

One Week Later

"He's awake!"

Acton wasn't sure who had shouted, and he wasn't entirely sure that he was awake. Everything was a fog. He struggled to remember what had happened, but was drawing a blank. He instead focused on where he was. He could hear a beeping sound, and something that must be fans.

Someone gripped his hand.

He forced his eyes open but quickly closed them. They were far too sensitive. He opened them again, just a sliver, then blinked several times. Everything was a blur. Somebody moved beside him and the form took shape. His vision slowly cleared and he smiled. "Hey, babe." He swallowed, his mouth as arid as the desert he last remembered. The thought excited him, his memory coming back. Then it all came rushing at him, overwhelming him, sending his heart racing and the beeping nearby into overdrive. He squeezed his eyes shut, bracing for the pain to come.

"It's okay. You're safe."

"Water," he said, and something pressed against his lips. He leaned forward, taking the straw into his mouth. He took several drags on the water, swishing it around, then swallowing, the cool liquid bringing him strength. He let go of the straw and looked about. He was in a hospital room. Tommy and Mai stood against the far wall, and Laura was at his bedside. The door swung open, and the large frame of Reading peered in. A smile spread on his friend's face.

"I thought I heard good news."

Acton managed a weak wave then looked at Laura. "What the hell's going on? What happened?"

"You passed out," said Laura. "You had a concussion. The pressure build-up in your head was too much. Thank God BD and the others showed up when they did."

His eyes shot wide. "They were there?"

Laura patted his hand. "Yes, I guess you passed out before they arrived. They were in the vehicles we heard approaching."

He thought back. It made sense. He should have recognized the weapons used from the sound of them, but his head hadn't been cooperating. "What happened?"

"They evac-ed us by helicopter to a Navy ship off the coast of Libya."

"And they drilled a hole in your head!" said Reading, enjoying that fact a little too much.

Acton's eyes shot wide again, and he raised his hand to feel for what was no longer a proverbial extra hole that he didn't need, but a literal one.

Laura grabbed his hand. "Don't go reaching about like a fool!"

He chuckled then winced at the anticipated pain that never came.

"How's your head feeling?"

"Good. Back to normal, I guess. As normal as it ever was."

Laura closed her eyes and kissed his hand. "Thank God. I was so worried about you."

He looked about. "We're not on a ship. Where are we?"

"They evac-ed you to Italy. You've been out for almost a week."

"A week?"

"Yes. They had you in an induced coma until the pressure came back to normal. They stopped the drugs last night, and then they just let you wake up naturally."

Reading stepped forward. "There's someone out there who wants to see you. When he heard you were going to be wakened today, he flew in especially for the occasion. Are you feeling up to it?"

Acton nodded, and again was relieved there was no pain.

Reading walked over to the door and opened it, beckoning someone. A moment later, Meitner was pushed in by a woman, followed by another. Acton's eyes narrowed, wondering where Bernie was.

"I'm relieved to see you're alive and well, young man."

Acton grunted. "I don't know about the young part, and I'm not too sure about the well, but I am alive."

Meitner laughed. "Anyone under the age of eighty is young to me. I just wanted to thank you and Dr. Palmer for helping retrieve my money."

Acton pushed up on his elbows and Laura tsked him as she grabbed the remote control and raised the head of the bed. He lay back down against it. "The money, you got it back?"

"Yes, we did. Agent Reading's contacts arrived in time. They rescued Miss Vida, and she provided the codes to retrieve the money. It's all been transferred to the charities."

"And this time it wasn't on prime-time television," said one of the women.

Meitner gestured at them. "I don't believe you met my granddaughters, Holly and Michelle."

Both women bowed their heads slightly at Acton, who returned the gesture. "A pleasure. So, who was behind it?"

"Several people for different reasons," said Meitner. "An Iranian general who blamed me for his son's death and is now dead himself, a trusted aide who feared an impoverished future who is now in a jail cell, and a blackmailed young woman who has been reunited with her parents. I'll let your wife explain it to you later. I don't want to take up too much of your time. I simply wanted to express my thanks, and"—he turned in his chair toward Mai—"to ask the young lady if she's forgotten something."

Mai's eyes bulged and she opened her handbag, pulling out a carefully wrapped package. She gave it to Meitner with trembling hands, and he passed it to Holly, who unwrapped it and smiled as she showed her grandfather the priceless necklace.

Mai exhaled loudly. "You have no idea how stressed out I've been with that thing still in my possession."

Meitner chuckled. "Yes, I suppose it would be."

Laura smiled at the man. "Michelle tells me there's a story behind that necklace."

Meitner's head slowly bobbed and his eyes glistened. "Yes, there is. Quite the story."

New York City, New York

April 26, 1952

The war was over. The good guys had won. When the Russians had arrived, there had been terror in the streets, for the Austrians had embraced Hitler, had embraced the Nazis. They weren't being liberated, they were being conquered. He had just turned seventeen when the gunfire stopped. He waited several days before heading outside. He was mostly ignored, and life didn't really change that much, except that the Nazis were replaced with Russians. He quickly learned to avoid them, as they treated everybody like the enemy, and he didn't blame them. He remembered the day the Nazis arrived. The parade, the celebration, the smiles, the cheers. The Austrians wanted the Nazis there because they supported what they stood for, and as he had witnessed with his own eyes and paid so dearly a price for through the death of his parents, he had quickly realized that Austria was no place for him.

It was never his home. It was only where his family lived.

How could a home be surrounded by those who would hate you just because of your religion? How could a home be a place where you live in constant fear that your neighbors might turn you in just because of how you worshipped? How could a place be a home, when an entire nation had embraced the very embodiment of hatred toward all that was different?

As things had calmed and newspapers once again printed the truth, he was horrified to discover what the Nazis had truly done to his people. When he read about the concentration camps, the ovens, the gas chambers, the mass graves, the millions dead, he had wept.

His parents had known.

They had known what they were facing, and he finally understood why they had taken their own lives. Committing the ultimate sin was preferable to dying at the hands of the Nazis. And he understood why his mother had chosen a different path for him. She trusted Peter, and had wanted her son to have a chance at a real life, in America, away from the hatred of his homeland. The plan had failed, yet he had survived, thanks to Petra. What she had taught him in their time together had got him through, and when he was old enough to understand what the Shopkeeper meant, he had forgiven her and added her to his nightly prayers.

His hatred for her and what she had done was long gone.

And with the war over, and no desire to remain in a country that had openly hated his kind, and now merely hid their loathing of the few that remained behind, he was determined to fulfill his mother's dream and make it to America.

Eventually, Vienna was split into four zones, and he made certain he was in the American zone before that happened. He registered at a Red Cross station and eventually immigrated to New York City. And when he sat in the rooming house that first night, his suitcase open beside him, he finally retrieved the carefully wrapped package with the note from his mother.

For Daniel, when he is safe.

He untied the string, setting it beside him, then carefully unfolded the heavy paper, gasping at what he found inside. It was a necklace filled with diamonds and jewels. Tears rolled down his face as he remembered his mother wearing it, but only on special occasions. Very special occasions.

He lifted it up, then noticed another paper underneath with a photograph of his mother and father sitting on either side of him when he was impossibly young and innocent. Tears flowed as he stared at the photo, and it took him several minutes to calm himself enough to read the letter. He set the necklace aside and unfolded the message.

Dear Daniel,

If you are reading this, then I hope you are safe in America with Uncle Peter. Please forgive us for leaving you alone. There was no other choice. Your uncle will explain.

Use this necklace to secure your new future. It has been in the family for generations, and I once considered it priceless. You and your memories are all that are left of us now. You are what is priceless. Use what I once thought was important to take care of yourself and to start your own family.

I pray you will never forget us, but should your memories fade, ask your uncle about us.

Live your life well, my beloved son, and remember to help those who need it like we did, for when neighbor turns upon neighbor, we are all truly lost.

Never forget, your father and I always loved you, and pray you find within your heart to forgive us for what we have done.

Love,

Eema

He had stared at the photo for hours that night, sobbing uncontrollably. Eventually, he had fallen asleep, and the next day swore he would make his parents proud. He found a synagogue, found the rabbi, and once trust had been built, told the man everything, including about the necklace. Arrangements were made and it was auctioned off for what the rabbi thought was an incredible sum. Daniel made a generous donation to the temple, then fulfilled his dream.

And as he stood outside that dream, he stared up at the sign that stretched across the front of the building. The logo he had designed, larger than ever after the recent expansion, brought a tear to his eye—a small boy defiantly holding a radio over his head, sharing with his small world the truth of the day. And when asked what it meant, he would lovingly share the memory of him and his father, tinkering away on the weekends, and how that shared love, that shared time together, had led to the business he now owned.

Meitner Radio and Small Appliance Repair.

THE END

ACKNOWLEDGMENTS

This book started off as a joy to write. I love World War II history, and exploring the Austrian aspect was new for me. As the character of Daniel developed, and I threw more and more tragedy at him, he became an inspiration for his resilience.

A resilience I found myself in need of.

As I was writing this book, I heard from my wife, trapped in the Philippines since the pandemic began, that she was extremely ill. She was terrified to go to the hospital because of Covid, but she finally couldn't take it anymore. She was admitted, spent two nights, and was diagnosed with food poisoning and sent home.

She began to feel better, then two days later had trouble breathing. She was rushed to the hospital, put in isolation, and tested for Covid. It came back as positive. She was on a ventilator for two days, nearly unconscious, before making a rapid recovery. She was finally transferred by ambulance to a mandatory quarantine facility.

While there, we both feared for her safety. People were roaming the halls, screaming and crying, pounding on doors, slowly going insane. She persevered, her biggest complaint the food, and was discharged shortly before these acknowledgments were written.

For a few days, I wasn't sure if I was losing my wife, and being stuck on the opposite side of the world, I was helpless to do anything. All I could do was send money to pay for her care, and pray for her recovery.

And during all this, I had a deadline.

Once she had recovered, I threw myself back into this novel, and got it done, meeting said deadline, though I put Meitner in a hospital room instead of a boardroom to puzzle out what had happened.

As usual, there are people to thank. My dad for all the research, my daughter for some Gen Z social media terminology, Isabelle Laprise-Enright for some baking info, Brandon Galitz for some terminology info, Emma Taylor for some British slang, Brent Richards for some weapons info, Ian Kennedy for some ordnance info, Chris Holder for some tech info, and Michael Broughton for some knife throwing info, and, as always, my wife, my late mother who will always be an angel on my shoulder as I write, as well as my friends for their continued support, and my fantastic proofreading team!

To those who have not already done so, please visit my website at www.jrobertkennedy.com, then sign up for the Insider's Club to be notified of new book releases. Your email address will never be shared or sold.

Thank you once again for reading.

Made in United States
North Haven, CT
20 July 2023